THE
UNWRITTEN CHRONICLES
OF
ROBERT E. LEE

Also by the author:

The Rio Loja Ringmaster
American Baroque

THE
UNWRITTEN
CHRONICLES

OF

Robert E. Lee

LAMAR HERRIN

ST. MARTIN'S PRESS
NEW YORK

Design by Susan Hood

Library of Congress Cataloging-in-Publication Data

Herrin, Lamar.
    The unwritten chronicles of Robert E. Lee / Lamar Herrin.
        p.   cm.
    "A Thomas Dunne book."
    ISBN 0-312-03448-2
    1. Lee, Robert E. (Robert Edward), 1807–1870 Fiction. 2. United States—History—Civil War, 1861–1865—Fiction.   I. Title.
PS3558.E754U5   1989
813'.54—dc20   89-34431
                                                                CIP

First Edition
10   9   8   7   6   5   4   3   2   1

For Ruth Shelnutt Herrin, my mother,
and Sally Herrin English, my sister,
there in their South

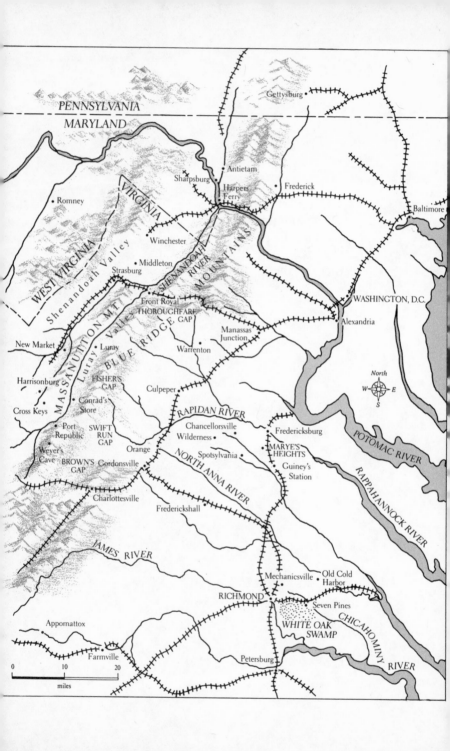

All history is nothing but myth ... each moment fades each moment into the realm of the imaginary, and hardly are you dead before you are off, with the speed of light, to join the centaurs and the angels ...

Paul Valéry

Part One

FEEDING THE BEAUTY

Why, with his face wrapped up in a wet towel and the barbershop chair cranked back so that only the soles of his shoes are showing, should the men of the town seek him out? That is one of my earliest memories of my father. I am watching him get his curly hair cut off his ears. Over my father stands the barber—the face I see is pink and fleshy and eager to please—and in the snip and flicker of scissors and the fine rain of sandy hair, my father is talking to his barber about me. He's saying that I'm five years old now and that I'm not bad at home and that I'm pretty nice to my little sister and that I've got me a new dog. But what he's really saying is, "Look at him! Look at him! Don't take your eyes off him! That's my son!" And the barber looks because I'm Harry Brazelton's boy. Room in the town has to be made because I'm Harry Brazelton's boy. I glance down, bashful and proud, and when I glance back up, the barber has spread white lather all over my father's face with a brush.

More men come in. The other barber has gone home for lunch. The barber shaving my father warns these men that they may have a long wait. They say they don't mind. They tell that barber to take his time. What they're saying and what even at five I clearly understand is that they'd just as soon spend that time sitting there talking with Harry Brazelton as doing anything else. What is it they want to talk to my father about? I don't know—things I don't remember. But my father had a way of smiling right up to his most serious utterances, and I saw him do that at various times—smile and smile and then tell the hard truth.

When the barber had finished shaving my father and wrapped his face up in that towel and cranked him back, I thought those men would get up and leave because it was clear that my father couldn't talk. But they didn't. Instead more men came in. It was as if word had passed outside on the streets that the barber (Lacy was his name, I remember that) had Harry Brazelton strapped in that chair and here was the town's chance. They came in and although he wouldn't answer—didn't even wiggle his foot—they kept talking to him. Occasionally, as though to punctuate whatever it was they were trying to convince my father of, they'd reach over and pat me or jostle my shoulder. Fine boy, Harry, they'd get around to saying. Gonna grow up and hit that ball like your daddy or tote that pigskin like your daddy or catch you a string of fish like your daddy catches or go off and find you a wife as pretty as your mama? And I watched my father's feet. They didn't move. His hands—the one I could see— lay palm down on the armrest, the strong, sure fingers hanging easily off the end. I remember thinking it was almost womanish, this lavishing of attention on my father (it reminded me of the attention I'd get when my mother's friends came over to play bridge and I served them their crust-trimmed sandwiches and ice tea). All my father had to do was lie there, feet up and face covered like a mummy. But they'd know it was him. And they came.

Why?

He was honored in the town, certainly. But what had he done to deserve their honor other than hit home runs and score touchdowns and marry a beautiful woman? It was a mystery to me even then. To do those things won you one sort of honor, but what the town gave my father was something else.

The train tracks that ran through the town passed close to our house. After dinner when we sat on the porch, the engineer on the freight train that came by would blow his whistle, and he wasn't blowing it at kids on bikes or dogs or the mule-drawn wagons you still saw on the streets. He was blowing it at my father, who always waved, who floated his arm up above his head and gave the engineer a great semaphoric greeting.

A small town full of pines and pecan trees and sandy sidewalks and creepers climbing the backs of garages and red street-side ditches to catch the heavy afternoon rains and men in seersucker and suspenders and women in linen and voile—and my father on a street corner, at the courthouse, at the post office, at the bank and the drugstore, down at the train station to welcome my mother back from her trips downstate, stopping off at the ballpark to catch an inning or two, sometimes to play.

He sold furniture out of a store he'd inherited when my grandfather retired, but his real occupation was man-about-town.

I remember my father in church. The church was a broad redbrick building, and the congregation sat spread out to escape the eleven o'clock heat the services always seemed to have been held in. The women cooled themselves with fans stuck in beside the hymnals. On the backs of these fans biblical scenes were depicted, and I got my first look at Joseph and his coat of many colors as my mother fanned herself with tidy rhythmic bursts or, during the sermon, with longer, more meditative sweeps. I saw a brightly clad but jittery Joseph standing before a group of dully dressed men, or I saw a Joseph swaying like a willow bough in a breeze. My mother remained cool and distant under her best Sunday hat and veil. The closest I could get to her was the occasional imperfectly blended line of powder just under her jaw. If she wanted to admonish me on these Sunday mornings, she had only to stop her fan or make it quiver like the wings of a hummingbird and tip her chin in my direction.

I turned to my father. The other men in the church sat stiff-necked and as motionless as sacks of rock in their pews, but my father would cross his legs and give me a look at the shine of his shoes and a pat on my shoulder as he stretched his arm out along the back of the pew. With the pat he sometimes gave me a smile, and in the smile I could have read a whole philosophy of life if I'd been old enough and had cared to concentrate. Easy, I suppose the smile said. Let the man doing the preachin' talk to you. He's got a story to tell—

everybody's got a story to tell—and on Sunday mornings we come and listen to Reverend Smithers tell his. Enjoy it. Loosen your collar. If your rear end begins to itch, go ahead and scratch it ... no big deal. He sure knows how to talk, don't he? As I see it now, the smile was both the confirmation of all the church service aspired to be about and its undoing. It humanized the divine, made it local, and I kept waiting for the day when Reverend Smithers would show his offense —for he noticed the smile. A touchy reverend, a man sensitive to the slippage in his control, might have read mockery in the smile and his voice might have stiffened and lost its storytelling flair. But in fact it never did. My father, sitting there in the congregation as if he were lounging at home listening to Fibber Magee and Molly, made Reverend Smithers a success.

After the service he greeted my father warmly. I thought I saw a quieter version of my father's smile on Reverend Smither's face. From one storyteller to another, it seemed to say, today wasn't bad, now was it? Other men filed out into the sunshine of a leafy summer day like men stricken with the loss of an hour from their lives, but my father and the reverend exchanged their smiles and then went on to enjoy a day that had just begun. Frequently we'd go straight to the A&W rootbeer stand after church and my father, licking the brown foam off his lips while my mother lifted her veil out of harm's way as she sipped from her mug, told another story.

They're all stories—every picture I have of my father is a story. But at some point in piecing them together, I cease to see him and see only the town, a town that lived for me only through him. He died when I was ten. In the company of old high-school buddies— Jeff Mayer and Charley Cunningham, plus two others whose names I've forgotten—he went stumping off after rabbits through root-erupting, briar-heavy terrain and accidentally shot himself in the right lung. When he died the town of Clayboro, Georgia, did too—or perhaps it then chose as its standard-bearer a man less versatile and that lesser man simply began to plod or walk so dully ahead it seemed like a death.

So I see the loose and large and deeply gullied area of town known *as niggertown only because my father took me there with him one day and because walking through it he brought the clapboard shacks set up on their cracked brick columns to life for me, gave the neighborhood specific streets and houses where individuals lived. We were searching for a man named Ned because my father had decided he wanted to take me catfish fishing and Ned knew catfish even if he couldn't spell his name. That may have been the first time I learned that a man could "know" something worth knowing and not the knowledge I was being taught that life was pointless without. But Ned took some running down. We saw other white people come and go in their cars—returning maids, picking up wash and the tools some handyman among the blacks might have repaired. But Ned, my father explained, was a slippery customer, about as slippery as the fish he never lost once he got them on his hook. I don't remember much about that fishing trip, but this search for Ned showed me that my father moved in the black part of town as effortlessly as he did in the white. We went to Ned's house and the woman we saw, who may have been Ned's wife, mother, or sister, and who was large and very white-toothed in the obscurity of her shack, said, "Lawd, Mista Harry, I ain't seen that no-count loafer in more'n a week." Then she and my father joked about what a no-count loafer Ned was until she couldn't get enough of it. She came up to my father and stood in the door and laughed for all the neighbors to see just how hard Mista Harry had made her laugh. Then she looked at me and asked my father if I was his baby, and when my father said I was, she said "Lawd" again and laughed at me. The shack was too small and rickety for so much laughter—I didn't understand it. I didn't understand how my father had inspired it. It scared me. I must have sidled up close to him, for he immediately included me in the conversation, making me the center of his attention, and told this woman that if he could ever run Ned down he wanted to take me off catfish fishing. The laughter this time sounded like a long, lamenting, good-natured howl. "Lawd have mercy! Lawd have mercy! That man sure 'nuf come runnin' if he hears Mista Harry wanna take 'im out fishin'."*

We left her laughing on her porch and drove around the block to another clapboard shack. This one my father called Willie's. It was painted white and stained red from the dust and mud, and instead of a front porch and stairs, it had a single cinder block to step up on. Rusted tin signs you couldn't read were nailed up around the door. My father didn't tell me to wait in the car but slung me up inside. Somebody I couldn't see because everything was so dark said, "Sheet, look who done walked in." And somebody else with a slower, groggier but warmer voice said, "There's anutha one behind him, hangin' on his leg." My father stood up to some planks laid down between two sawhorses and drank a beer with these men, although at the time I didn't know what it was since we didn't have beer and whiskey around our house. But the smell in the shack was a fruity, swamp-like odor, with something strange and tart skating around on the surface of that swamp—and that was the smell my father drank. The smell made me dizzy, but I wasn't too dizzy to notice how my father talked of two or three other acquaintances they all had in common before bringing up the matter of Ned. Last time either of them had seen Ned was when he was sittin' at a table over there with a woman named Charleen, so we drove over to Charleen's. On the way I saw some black kids playing with an old car tire and some jays chasing each other around a mimosa tree, and I told my father it was okay if we didn't find him, we could do something else.

Charleen wasn't like the first woman we saw. She didn't laugh and she wasn't fat and she had a pouty grin and a way of standing up to my father that made him square off and stick his hands in the back of his belt when he stood up to her. Her house smelled of perfume and cigarette smoke, and the perfume was as loud as the caw of those jays. I didn't know what was going on except that in this strange world my father had a way of being for each of the people we met, and that his way of being more or less matched each of theirs. Charleen's way was to move her shoulders and hips as if a bug had crawled down her back and she was trying to shake it through while she withheld what she knew about Ned. My father's was to move his eyes around her small, clothes-cluttered room before bringing them back to her and to withhold something she wanted, too. *"Fishin'? Whacha'll wanna do that for?"*

Finally she sent us to a cousin of Ned's, a man who lived out beyond the immediate black neighborhood in a house that looked as if it had once belonged to a tenant farmer until the town expanded and took up most of the arable land. This man was called Lester, and we found him sitting out on his front porch with a leg he'd hurt badly when he fell off a ladder propped up on a chopping block. Three hounds made room for us, and we sat down in the mangy ammoniac stink they'd left behind. Lester wasn't even Ned's first cousin; he wasn't sure what cousin he was. He only knew that as long as he was laid up he needed help around the place and Ned, who'd been sleeping there all right, had yet to hit a lick. What kind of help? my father wanted to know. With this man Lester he was being sympathetic and concerned, and Lester was being concerned and open to sympathy but not asking for it. *"What kind of hep? Hep it'd take to git dat dere truck runnin'."* My father asked what was wrong with it, and Lester said Ned had said he had carburetor problems, but since then he'd taken it apart and walked off. No-count, Lester said, describing his distant cousin's worth. I looked at my father to see if he agreed, since that's what he and the first woman had laughingly called Ned themselves. But my father had already gotten up to look over Lester's truck, soon rolled up his sleeves and, showing none of his usual whistling humor while he worked, he fixed it.

I sat there on the edge of the porch watching him. It's one of the clearest pictures I have left of him now. I watched him, with a great deal of patience and a fine sharing out of another man's mood, master a motor, then start it and cut it twice to make sure. When he returned to the porch, wiping his hands on his handkerchief, all he asked Lester to do in return was tell Ned when he came back that Harry'd been out looking for him. This Lester agreed to do, but as to the outcome, he shook his head doubtfully. My father said to tell him it didn't involve work. What did it involve? Lester wanted to know. Fishin', my father said. He wanted Ned to come out fishing with him so *"this boy of mine can learn how to catch a cat."* That was the only time I saw Lester smile. He hadn't even smiled when my father managed to start his truck, but with his pained yellow eyes he smiled then, and it was a sly smile, as between conspirators who have found a common ground. "You better git on down de road fast," he said, "'cause he be dere fore you is if it's only fishin' you talkin' 'bout."

He came, but I can't remember how fast. And I'm sure we went fishing in a creek out a ways called Turner's Creek and I think we caught fish, although none of that interested me very much. The town—the way my father moved from one actualizing encounter to the next, the special liberties the town permitted and my father, with a sort of disarming boyish inconsequence, took—my interest is all right there. Many times I walked the town with him, my hand in his, which was broad and playful, and my stride doing a quick shuffling hitch to get three to his two. But I seem to see myself now darting from tree to tree so that I might view my father by himself, unencumbered by a son and a stride that didn't match his, although I'm sure I never took such a vantage point during our entire short time together. There's Lanier's corner grocery, where he stops to buy cigarettes and to chat with his old high-school buddy. There's the brick foundations of the high school that burned to the ground. There's the ball field on down the tracks, where the dust seemed to taste sweet and redolent of old home runs. There's Newberry's five-'n-ten and Lewis's Sporting Goods, where my father might shop for something for his willing but less athletic son. There's Walker's Shoe Store and Lanningham's General Store and Jones's Feed and Grain for the farmers and the Clinton County movie house for matinee-goers and their families. There's a cemetery on a low hill south of town, and there's my grandmother's grave.

My father goes there by himself—I know he does—and stands before the gray granite monument that gives his mother's name, dates, and station—a saint, by most people's account, who died when I was barely four and whose image I retain as something fluffy, wispy, and white that is about to collapse on itself like a puffball. From there *my father goes to see my aunt—his slightly older sister, a thin-faced woman left mostly deaf by a childhood case of scarlet fever who cares for her father as her mother had done so that William Brazelton might live out his days without want. My grandfather sits with his cronies under the two large Georgia pines fronting the courthouse, and my father goes there next, his arrival among the old men the occasion for much cane-tapping, snorting laughter, and rheumy twinkling eyes. My grandfather is less effusive. Like his other son, my uncle Edward, he prefers to sit still and be entertained. His younger son's success is both a puzzling and pleasing sort of entertainment to him, I suspect.*

Diagonally across the street from my grandfather's bench, Willard Ewell has his drugstore. My father, on this last leg of his walk around town, frequently stops off there—I know, this leg I've walked with him. We've left my grandfather in the scent of pine and the faint, farthest reach of disinfectant and old paper scent from the courthouse and gone to the drugstore to get a Coke. From all the way at the back of the drugstore where he has his prescription counter, Willard has seen us coming and, unless he's in the middle of measurements he can't stop, is there to serve us our Cokes himself, relieving two chubby girls, Sally and Imogene, of their duties. I like the way he makes the Cokes—with a squirt of cherry and not too much ice— and I don't dislike him, not yet. Like everyone else, he measures me against my father—will I do this like him, or that?—and as everyone else does tells me, disbelieving it himself, that I'll do those things better. But I can't see Willard Ewell. Already he's bald, and with no eyebrows to speak of and eyes hidden behind the drooping lids, he's like a big, wrinkled, sand-colored baby, or something from another species entirely—a turtle or a toad. He talks University of Georgia football with my father. He knows everything there is to know about the team's past performances—in fact, he's an authority on any number of issues. What he doesn't know is the life on the field, in the huddle, poised at the line of scrimmage. My father puts him there easily, good-naturedly—no sweat, step right in. For that Willard Ewell waits on my father—for those privileged glimpses into the heart of the team and for the impulse of generosity that provides them. While they're talking, Willard will wait on me again, too. And the second Coke, like the first, will be on the house.

Those two men with their heads together over the drugstore counter—the golden-haired boy, my father, and the inscrutable druggist, my stepfather—send me a message over the years and the message has nothing to do with what they were talking about, what they looked like, or what their positions in the pecking order of the town might have been. It has to do with desire—desire for something they don't have. The town is theirs—Willard serves as its hub, my father as the most sparkling of its spokes—but it has to do, this desire, with something they don't have and could probably never verbalize but which I heard as a five-, six-, seven-, eight-, nine-, and ten-year-old child in the intensity of their voices, in the sudden snap of their tethers as they strained for something out beyond the comfortable, snug confines of the town. What? I don't know. Women? Sex? I honestly don't know. Perhaps it's only the desire of the next generation speaking through them, perhaps that's all it is—me. I'm there, and it's me who would use that taut tethered snap I heard at the edge of their football talk or imagined in their sexual craze as a means of propelling myself, and not them, out toward the satisfaction of some still unnamed desire. Yes, perhaps it's me and not them, because they knew, without knowing that they knew, that that mysterious desire was unsatisfiable. Better tethered, although they probably never phrased it as such, than senselessly propelled. Better . . . but I don't know.

I saw my father kiss another woman once. My reaction was, the town has given my father a pretty woman to kiss and he has kissed her. I never thought less of him for it. But I have never forgotten that kiss either. Behind my father's store there was a loading dock where customers or delivery men could pull up and load merchandise. This woman's name was Martha Sellers and she had been born and brought up in the town and went to school with my father. She had a head of red hair and somewhere about her—the eyes, the earrings?—there was green. Up on the loading dock she watched my father fit a single-bed mattress she'd bought into the back of her long station wagon. My father had lost none of his strength since those days in high school and college. She noticed this. When he closed the door and stepped back up to her side she told him so, and he said maybe, that she inspired him, or maybe, reverting to schooltime banter and innuendo, they talked about the bed. She laughed huskily, my father more loudly, and the alley they stood in gave off a bit of an echo, left a trace of their laughter in the air. Before it died my father had slipped his arm around her waist in a hefting sort of way, as though he were going to heave her up on top of her station wagon, and she fell back a bit in his arm to give him the full feel of her and to test his strength. Then he laughed again and showed her his strength, bringing her to him as he would, I guess, the live, gradually giving weight of a big fish. She came, holding her head back for last. When the head finally swept forward with a coppery sheen of hair, she and my father exchanged a wet, smacking kiss, her arm—and she was strong too—moving under his and opening to a full, pressing span of fingers on his back. As soon as the kiss was over my father growled at her and, moving his hand to the flesh of her buttocks, threatened to clutch, began to, and then did. She let him, whispering something low and throaty that sounded like "Animal" or "Horrible" or "Call me up" before slowly, again in a fond test of strength, forcing his hand away. They laughed some more, and their lips were wet. Their eyes, before she got into her station wagon and drove away, had a peculiar glint. When she was gone my father remained there on the loading dock in a humid cloud of her perfume and exhaust. It was a warm day. Aroused, he was now getting over it. Where was I? There somewhere. I don't know.

I

He's feinted east, struck west, and beaten a detachment of Frémont's forces at McDowell, deep up an Appalachian draw. Now on Sorrell, his small-boned mare, Stonewall Jackson leads his army back into the Shenandoah Valley and marches it north. No one else, not even General Ewell, whom he will meet that evening, knows the army's destination. God knows, because at Conrad's Store Jackson conferred with God alone in his tent before beginning these maneuvers. God told him that war was horrible and just—*when just*—and that he must strike. Perhaps Jim, his body servant, also knows; the slave at all hours remains faithfully close. Is this desire for secrecy a sin, as some have charged? How can anything a man shares with his God—and that God approves—be a sin? Why not say that this valley is a sin since it, too, bears the stamp of God's approval? He gazes before him at the breadth of field —the grasslands, the grain, the corn—and at the solid, sheltering wall of the Massanutton to his east, through which only he knows his army will soon pass, and he notes the brick and columned homes along the way, the barns that will soon again be full, the stock that will soon again be fat, and nothing disputes his belief that God has blessed these people and this place above all others on earth. Except for the Yankees, of course. And the Yankees, he sometimes thinks, alone in his tent, or stepping out beyond his army in its march north, are God's gift to him, Stonewall Jackson, to punish as he sees fit. But he will not presume to speak for God. The thought comes unbidden, and he will not utter it.

"Close up! Close up!" He passes the command to Major Dabney, his chief of staff, riding just behind him. And the column, 8,000 strong now, closes up.

Moments later, Sandie Pendleton, his youngest aide, spurs up beside him. "Time, sir," Lieutenant Pendleton informs him. "Put them down," his commander replies.

The army halts. For thirty seconds Jackson sits astride his mare, facing north, away from his troops. He permits himself perhaps fifteen seconds more—what he sees on this first day of sunshine in the valley after five in the mountains with rain is so pleasing to his eyes. Cherry and peach orchards in blossom, fields of clover lush as thick green foam. Then he turns in his saddle. Every soldier is lying down. The road and its margins are covered with resting men and their stacked muskets. Every fifty minutes the men have ten, flat on their backs, haversacks beneath their heads—it is the secret to the swiftness of his marches, the regularity of these rests. Farther back he sees the halted artillery, the caissons, the baggage and supply wagons, ambulances, the horses and mules, the cattle he is driving—all with their motion still on them. He can tell by the angles at which they've stopped. During these ten-minute pauses he thinks both of the Union generals he must outmaneuver and of his wife. He loves her, honors her, of course, and to her honor would drive General Nathaniel Banks first out of Strasburg and then out of Winchester, where she wintered with her husband three short months ago. His Anna, his *esposita*. He whispers her name as he allows his horse to crop clover beside the road and his back to slump just a bit. Then Sandie Pendleton rides up again. "Time, sir," the aide says. His marches run like clockwork because he runs them by the clock.

On their feet, his commander tells him, then, as the order

goes down the line, watches his men rise, all of them, as far as the eye can see, and farther—this army he will march to the Cities of the North. For that is his ultimate destination. Once he's cleared this valley of Yankees, he will lead his men down the streets of Baltimore, Philadelphia, and New York. "Ole Blue Light," they call him. Through eyes that notice every impropriety, every breach of conduct, every insult to God, he sees the humbling of these great Cities of the North.

At Mt. Solon, ten miles south of Harrisonburg, he meets with General Ewell, who has ridden fresh to him from his encampment at Swift Run Gap. Ewell, bald and bearded and pop-eyed, is a fighter, but he wastes his fighting spirit in teeth-gnashing over matters he is not equipped to understand. For two weeks he has ill-temperedly obeyed an order to stay in the Luray Valley at Swift Run and threaten Banks's left flank. Now Jackson takes him into his confidence. The others—the members of his staff, his brigadier generals Winder and Taliaferro—he asks to remain outside. But Ewell he includes, informs. It is Sunday evening. Mundane labor on the Sabbath is intolerable to him, but the fighting of battles and the mapping of attacks is God's work, and a man's duty is to work without ceasing in the service of his God. He gives Ewell his orders. He's to detach General Taylor's Louisiana brigade and send it directly to Jackson. With the remaining 6,000 men, he's to march up the Luray and wait at the White House Bridge. Jackson will feint north and then at New Market turn east, cross the Massanutton, and join Ewell. Together they will fall on Front Royal and at the same time outflank Banks in Strasburg.

Ewell, for two weeks confused and inactive, warms to it at once. He's been told the man is difficult, but the difficulty lies, he sees now, in accepting the fact that the man is inspired. Ewell, eyes like overflexed muscles, sees that clear blue light in Jackson's eyes, and although the rest of the face is familiar enough—haggard and mountain-boned—Ewell thinks—the eyes are special. Visionary? Visionary. He's won—but what is he to do with this? And he hands Jackson an order just received from General Johnston instructing him, Ewell, to return east of the Blue Ridge and intercept Shields should he attempt to join McDowell at Fredericksburg. A man's duty is to obey his superior—Jackson believes this with a fervor the depth of which may never be known. Yet with Frémont licking his wounds in the mountains and Shields maneuvering past the Blue Ridge, Banks sits alone, like a fat, oversupplied commissary, at Strasburg. Obey *me*, Jackson tells Ewell, then draws up a letter instructing him, in the presence of conflicting orders, to obey those of his immediate superior. The question Jackson then faces is, Who is *his* immediate superior? The command center in Richmond has become needlessly bureaucratized. Jefferson Davis, commander in chief, has a second-rate military mind. Joe Johnston, the putative commander of the armies in the field, dreams of textbook retreats. Jackson knows who his superior is—he admits to having one. Virginia—this Virginia of his mountain boyhood fastness, of this spacious valley, of that rich alluvial plain—has only one, one man superior to the state he so superbly serves. He will clear it through Lee, he tells Ewell.

That night he will not write to his wife, it still being Sunday. A resolute predawn riser, the next morning he rises even earlier than that. "My *esposita*," he writes, "my pet dove, how I wish you could be here with me when the camp is quiet. I long to hear the sweet music of your voice. I telegraphed you forthwith of our success against Frémont's forces at McDowell. Now I am in the valley, ten miles south of Harrisonburg, and very soon we will commence a march the goal of which I would whisper in your ear, that beautiful small ear that a ring of your hair so winsomely hides. You must send me that ring of hair. Are you listening, my darling? Winchester. Yes, Winchester. Don't breathe a word."

As his army of 8,000 enters Harrisonburg, a small, prosperous, war-blackened city, it seems to bring spring in with it out of the fields. Shutters are thrown open; women in bright, festive dresses appear at the windows along the streets. They throw flowers at members of his staff. The youngest, Pendleton and Kyd Douglas, maintain a teasing, spirited banter with these ladies, although one seems to do as well as the next and the promiscuity of their promises would in normal times earn them the opprobrium of the town. But he doesn't mind. He hears his own name cheered lustily and he hears it spoken—by those expecting a different cut of man—in a surprised, questioning hush. He wears his kepi cap pulled low over his face; he rides as he has since a boy, with his stirrups drawn high. Why this passion to remain nondescript, unprepossessing? Does he really think that classically mounted and resplendently attired he could ever compete with God? No, he doesn't think that. But it all belongs to God—all of it, every plume, button, and braid.

God now gives them the macadamized valley turnpike, and the march picks up. Every fifty minutes Jackson stops them, turns to watch them stack their arms, lay their heads on their haversacks, and rest. When he tells them to rise, they rise. Company commanders immediately assemble them in ranks, and regimental commanders close up the companies. Outside of New Market, after a march of some thirty miles, they make camp and observe the arrival of General Taylor's smartly stepping Louisiana Tigers, whose white gaiters flash in the last light of day and whose regimental music reminds him of Creole airs he heard in New Orleans. He hopes Taylor's men have caught the right eyes. He counts on spies rushing straight down the valley to inform Banks at Strasburg that a reinforced Jackson is marching due north for an obvious frontal assault.

Marching north the next morning, Jackson turns due east at New Market, and it's Taylor's turn to ride up to the commander of the valley forces and express surprise, and then to catch, as Ewell had before him, that special blue of the man's eyes, as clear—should he say clairvoyant?—as the cool dawn sky. Taylor, along with the rest of them, marches east. The pass there through the Massanutton is like a single fleshy fold in an otherwise solid wall of newly leafed trees and gray rock. Approaching the summit there is always fog. At the summit in the heavy damp, the road is frequently mud. Jackson leads his men up the mountain and they pull it well. When the fog is no more than a hundred feet away, he puts the spur to his horse and gallops out ahead, suddenly angry with himself. Because of his desire to keep this maneuver secret, he has forgotten to reconnoiter the pass. Everything he knows about Banks and his lieutenants tells him that *all* the Yankee outposts and pickets will have been withdrawn. Yet he has to enter that fog, and in its shapelessness and colorlessness, it reminds him of nothing so much as a deep dullness of mind.

He enters it with a sense of foreboding gathering around him. No one shoots at him, no one shouts for him to halt; in fact, the silence before him is as absolute as the ruckus behind him is unrelieved. Still, he's moving into something. He senses danger just as certainly as if he'd smelled Yankees—smelled their teeming foreign cities—on the wind. What sort of danger? Not Yankee danger, no. What sort of danger, and what sort of mettle must he call up in himself? Now the mist has thickened on his face and beard, and his horse's hooves have begun to suck mud. He spurs farther into it.

Near the summit the fog suddenly brightens, suffused with sun, but instead of extending his eyesight, it reduces it to the area just beyond his horse's head. The brightness, each speck of moisture a dazzling point, blinds him. There he halts. Discipline and duty, he remembers—it is his disciplined duty to see everything within the context of God's will. He conquers his fear by changing the context from one of an army marching up a mountainside toward an unreconnoitered pass in a blinding fog to the appropriate one of man's suddenly outshone understanding in the glory of God's light. This is right, this is a reminder, he thinks. What I achieve when we march down off this mountain I achieve because it is God, not the Yankees, who lets us pass. He hears his army approach.

It is Aide Pendleton, a loyal and impressionable young man, who comes galloping up into the brightness calling, "General! General Jackson!" and who, had his horse not known better, would have collided with the man he was racing to find. Jackson reins him in. Told that the fog is thicker than Pendleton has ever seen it and as bright as corn silk in the sun, Jackson replies that the road is clear and that he will lead them through. Pendleton is to go back and bring the men up slowly, the light they march in God-given proof that their cause is just.

Below it, off the mountain and into the light of common day, Jackson, as any mortal must, suffers something of a depression. It takes the form of a deep sleepiness. He sinks in his saddle; the angle of the list is enough to cause Major McGuire, valley army surgeon, to break away from the other staff officers and ride up to his commander's side. During the time it takes him to come down off this mountain and adjust to the unexalted state of things below, Jackson is powerless in his strange exhaustion to gainsay the thought that he commands two armies. One he shapes to his will. The other, the army he suspects is trudging down off that mountain right now, is moving in ragged fits and starts, an army like the masses of so-called freed men who with their miserable clutter have already begun to follow the armies of the invading North—the one a shadow to the other. That shadow army he commands needs shoes and uniforms, never has enough to eat. That army is full of slackers and straggles miserably on the march. Nothing more than the promise of a meal will tempt the men of that army out of ranks and into the houses of the valley people, well-intentioned patriots but disastrous to the discipline of the march. Those men will get drunk. They will get diarrhea. They will wander home and back again when it suits them, full of dull longing and dully sated desire, as if they had eaten mud. He can do nothing with that army. He can whip and buck them, threaten to shoot a few and even carry out his threat, and still this second army shadows the first, a cloud of idlers, drunkards, fornicators, homesick louts, that never catches up. His marches, he fears, are like sludge-heavy rivers flooding their banks. When he turns in his saddle to look back, dirty, marginless backwater flooding the fields is what he fears seeing. Sometimes he doesn't see anything at all.

They say he's a visionary—and they don't say it kindly. They say his eyesight for the things of this world has been irreparably ruined by the preachers with whom he surrounds himself. They say Major Dabney, a pastor and professor of theology, can only sermonize the enemy, not fight him. He will say let them talk, that it doesn't affect him, but it does. Crazy, they will mutter as he passes through a town, the cheers for those hometown boys behind him, not for their leader. A religious fanatic. An insanely secretive man. A cautious, not even comical, eccentric. A Southerner (but from the mountains, and always the suspicion of perverse practices up in those hollows, always the accusation of bestiality hovering about their lips), but a Southerner who can't dress and worse yet, can't ride. A dyspeptic who slumps on his horse and sucks on a lemon. No wonder all the young men of this valley flock to enlist in Turner Ashby's cavalry, and no wonder Ashby, with his independent command, refuses to submit to his general's rule. He can't set an example, he can't dash and delight the ladies, he can't dance, he can't command affections, he can't bend a mass of men to the shape of his will, he can't show them a pleasing shape to bend to.

But Stonewall! Stonewall! At Manassas General Bee had

said, "They are beating us back!" And Jackson had said, "Then we will give them the bayonet!" And Bee had said, rallying his troops, "There stands Jackson like a stone wall! Stand with him and fight!" Then Bee had died, the words still hot in his throat. Jackson, standing, had turned the tide, and the fame he had gained and the fame that certain envious superiors had held back—both the fame given and the fame withheld—he'd written to his wife, belonged to God.

Did they still? In moments like this, coming down off a shining peak, he can't be sure. A man fashions a life out of the strongest materials and with the most painstaking exactitude, determined to make it last. Why doesn't it? Perhaps it does. Perhaps in a fit of madness we drive ourselves out of doors while it still stands behind us, unshaken and sane. Then why do we drive ourselves out of doors? Then why do we go mad?

He doesn't know. A man's battle blood rises. A man must fight. Certain men must have an army to fight with, and he is one of these. Certain rare men command their armies as they do themselves. His, dressed in homespun butternut, some dressed in gray, some in captured blue, all dusty, muddy, and verminous, wind down off that mountain in clumsy surges, the artillery and loaded wagons lurching from one hole in the road to the next. The incessant thudding of hooves, wheels and feet, he feels in the ground rather than hears. He hears the squeak of the unoiled axles like the caws of distempered birds, and he hears the tinny clatter of pots and pans the men carry tied around their waists. He doesn't know which army this is—his and his God's or that shadow army which will blunder its way to victory or defeat according to the winds of chance. As he turns back in his saddle Dr. McGuire's there to say, "General Jackson, *there*, sir, *Ewell*," and to point at a long, trailing dust cloud three or four miles distant across the south fork of the Shenandoah River. In that moment other aides ride up. But Jackson sees the valley, the narrow, magnificent Luray, with the Blue Ridge Mountains rising gradually out of the pasture and farmland so that to the vista-sweeping eye nothing is flat—everything is green, blossoming, and curved. This he knows—this valley. This and the thrill of moving bodies of men through it. To the achievement of whose design do not in that moment of doubt preceding his great liberating battles ask him. He says, eyes alight with the flawless spring day, "My God!"

But strictly as a military matter, he must know how simple and masterful his strategy has been. He takes Front Royal at the confluence of the forks of the Shenandoah and cuts off any retreat Banks might make east. The only other lines of retreat are west and north, and if Banks retreats west, Jackson then marches to the Potomac and threatens Washington. If Banks retreats north, Jackson can drive him across the Potomac and still threaten Washington, but with a routed, demoralized army returned to spread panic through the streets. To keep Banks entrenched before Strasburg, Jackson has only to send Ashby's troopers to demonstrate loudly on his front, the sort of thing Ashby's men do best. That Jackson has done, Lee is sure of it.

He has only to consult his map. So much of his map work has been concentrated on the peninsula or the Petersburg-Richmond-Fredericksburg-Washington axis or on spots out of the line of fire where he can secure a haven for his afflicted wife and daughters so that when he turns to the Shenandoah Valley, it is with a sense of release, of escape from a cramped corner. There sits Ewell, too used to the sensible strategy of retreat orchestrated by Johnston to stand contentedly by while Jackson moves against Frémont in the mountains. The letters have come in—letters Lee understands at once, just as he understands Ewell at once, a man whose temper, humor, and loyalty are so tightly bound up that to inspire one is to invite the others. "I don't know where he's gone! He tells me to stay here and watch Banks, and then he goes off—God only knows where!" In so many words he asks Lee to send him off somewhere, too—it doesn't matter where. Lee counsels patience and readiness, meaning faith, of course. He knows Ewell. The South, he sometimes thinks, *is* Ewell, the best of the South, the tough, seasoned fiber of the South—the South he could win with.

"General Jackson must be trusted. He knows what he is doing."

"Yes, sir. I understand. But do you, sir," Ewell asks, "know where he has gone? Does anyone other than the man himself know?"

"Yes, General Ewell, I know. And I approve."

Ewell wants information, and Lee won't give it to him. Headquarters in Richmond is aswarm with people wanting information, some of whom are most certainly spies. Reporters from all the major newspapers in the South are present, and they come to him. He tells them what he can. Sometimes he can't keep them from finding out things they shouldn't, which they then splash all over the front page of their papers, the same papers Lincoln and Stanton, his secretary of war, carefully read. It is, he understands, the deep uncertainty of the times that fires people's need to know. When the laws and institutions a nation lives by are swept aside, when the Christian community of men divides against itself, what is even the most gossipy piece of news if not a plank from the shipwreck floating by to keep a drowning man afloat, until a bigger, more substantial plank floats by, followed by another and another, until somehow one of those planks of that shipwrecked ship of state manages to take the near-drowned man to shore?

Where is Jackson? Where is Jackson? they all want to know. He won't tell them. Jackson's a big plank to ride the whirlpool on, and they are delirious enough already.

For the time being, he will keep Jackson for himself.

Ewell is to hold himself in readiness. In Ewell he would see the whole hot-tempered, high-principled South poised at the edge of that valley, learning patience and self-discipline, and ridding itself of its fatuous pride.

Victory at McDowell—he'll give his inquisitors that much.

Then silence. Banks's apprehension he can feel in Richmond, and he has always had a special sense for Lincoln's disquiet, but from Jackson himself, nothing—it's as if the man marched his army on sound-absorbing dust, dust that did not leave clouds. He waits for a moment when headquarters is clear of staff officers, politicians, Cabinet members, officers of the field come to request transfers, members of the quartermaster's corps, lurking, ingratiating members of the press. With his pointer he walks to the map of the state. The windows are high and a wall of three gives him a view not of the Shenandoah Valley, not even of the James, but of the line upon line of trenches and breastworks fronting McClellan, who is settled down on the peninsula now with his large, unwieldy army as though planning, like the Greeks before Troy, for a siege of ten years.

He is not thinking about McClellan. He is thinking it is wrong, uncivil and uncivilized, and finally ruinous—this craving for secrecy that Jackson has. It is born, he believes, of a deep distrust of his comrades' confidence and an egotistical overestimation of his own powers to perform. He fears for the man, his own lifetime of service having been based on the opposing principles of delegation of authority, consulation of views. His even-handedness is known. It's not a myth or an adornment, he's achieved it through years of self-denial—and now they all come to *him* for news.

His title is Military Adviser to the President. But Jefferson Davis does not like to take advice on anything, and in actuality Lee is little more than the president's secretary or press spokesman. He did not do well the previous fall fighting Rosecrans in western Virginia. That winter he was sent to Charleston and Savannah, where his engineering skills could be put to use rebuilding coastal fortifications. When he was recalled to Richmond he rebuilt the defenses there. The papers called him King of Spades. He has learned not to listen to the papers. For his president and Joe Johnston, present commander of the Army of Northern Virginia, he corresponds with Cabinet members and politicians and other generals in the field. But Jackson he writes on his own. "The blow," he has advised, "must be sudden and heavy."

He walks to the map now. The tip of the pointer he places at the Allegheny town of McDowell, and then, in spite of himself, glances furtively around. The room remains empty. Should anyone enter at that minute, they would see a Confederate officer in front of a map, still elegantly attired at the end of the day—the gray coat long, the shirt collar and cuffs the work of his wife, the invisible socks knitted by his daughters. They would not see a furtive man, but, it would be quite evident from the carriage, the clothes, the face aging impressively under each day's demands, *the* man of the South. Yet here in this high dusty room, he finds himself standing hungrily before a map. They would not see a hungry man either.

He begins at McDowell. "God has blessed our cause in arms with a victory at McDowell," Jackson has wired. Lee knows McDowell—treacherous, broken terrain. In mountain fighting you fight the terrain, and if you conquer it quickly enough, you make it fight for you. Like Jackson, he would prefer to maneuver through the mountains and fight on the lowlands. Due north of McDowell, the bulk of Frémont's force waits at Franklin. Hesitantly, he starts the pointer in that direction, then stops. The rains of those mountains oppress the spirit. For three months the previous fall he watched a world of astonishing beauty sink into a morass of mud, as though only in this way could nature protect itself from the ravages of war. Jackson and his foot cavalry would have started for Franklin and then turned back. Jackson must have asked himself, What would it take to lure Frémont out of the mountains? And his answer must have come in a vision before it came in words. The words come to Lee: A campaign so brilliant and overmastering in the valley that a man of arms must needs come close to admire it. Yes, at campaign's end Frémont will come close and Jackson will smash him. He will draw one Union general after another into the wake of this beautiful thing he's created and in their fearful fascination make them part of the beauty too. That beauty, he will remind them, must be fed. Where is Banks? Where is Shields? Where is Frémont? the newsmongers will ask. Feeding the beauty, Lee will tell them, and they will scratch their heads.

Can Lee say that? No, he knows he cannot. The private, the cryptic, the self-amusing and smug—the words will not pass his lips. He is a public man, and his public, he realizes, is somehow his own, as though by his example he creates them. But now, for the moment at least, he's alone. He steps even closer to the map. Jackson, the worst dressed general in the whole Southern army, leads his men back out into the grasslands and flowering orchards of the Shenandoah Valley, noting with scrupulous attention each rise in the land, each creek, swale, and stone wall, as though the valley itself were his dress. General J.E.B. Stuart could not boast a plume prettier than this. Somewhere south of Harrisonburg—probably Mt. Solon—Jackson stops and enlightens Ewell, who roaringly approves. They will part and meet again—Jackson moving down the valley to New Market, Ewell down the Luray. Strongly entrenched at Strasburg, Banks will read Jackson for a frontal assault and take heart since Jackson's numbers are not overwhelming. If Jackson were to reinforce himself with one of Ewell's brigades, and if this fact were to reach Banks, the whole operation might be made to seem even more plausible, the attack more certain to come directly from the south. But the attack must come up the Luray against Front Royal. It must! It is no longer a matter of anticipating what the daring, convention-confounding Jackson will do—it is a matter of what he *must* do! Lee has seen it now. Once the battle's begun, Ashby can then cut communications to Banks. How could anyone consider doing it differently?

Does Lee back away from the map to broaden his view or because his heart is pounding heavily at such close range? He backs away until he feels the end of his desk against his legs. The desk is piled with papers, petitions, letters, more maps of counties, towns, forts, coastal defenses, states in the West. The room smells of map paper—a musty, ink-edged odor that haunts the imagination. When the maps are rolled up, the odor concentrates to the potency of a drug. He closes his eyes. At that moment an aide enters, his step quiet on the wine-red rug but his boots squeaking obsequiously. President Davis would have his Military Adviser Lee accompany him on a ride to the front to confer with Johnston. More of McClellan's men have been sighted north of the Chickahominy. Is McClellan attempting to turn the Confederate left, or does he simply have so many men on the peninsula that he's forced to spread them around?

Speed, daring, and flawless execution—he sees Jackson's entire campaign tie its dazzling knots before the aide has had time to leave the room and this time, under command, to close the door. It takes Lee's breath away. Jackson's got the best brigade in Virginia, his own Stonewall Brigade. He's got Major General Ewell. For brigadier generals he's got Winder, Taylor, Eleazy, Trimble, and Taliaferro, men resentful of such autocratic secrecy but men who must learn. His batteries under Major Crutchfield are at full strength. His cavalry is commanded by the implacable Ashby. The quartermaster is a mule-driving enthusiast named John Harman. And he's got Jackson, he's got himself, the man inside the man of unswerving regulations and laws. That inside man swerves, he dodges, feints, he dances, and somewhere through the rattle of musket fire and the boom of cannon, Lee hears him laugh. The laugh does not belong in polite company—it may not

29

belong in company at all—but Lee hears it. He tells Jackson, "Take Front Royal," and the whisper is hard, hurried, rapt. "I want you to take it."

In a heat equaled only by the heat of the imagination of the man giving the order, Jackson and Ewell march to within ten miles of their objective. In such a heat there will be stragglers, and those about to suffer sunstroke might mistake the fields of green wheat for cool lakes and plunge in. Lee won't let them. He shepherds the column along the Luray with quick, hounding thrusts of his will as Jackson rides out ahead. The high-walled Massanutton to the west and the gradually gathering Blue Ridge to the east hide this march from the eyes of Banks and all the other Union generals—from Davis, Johnston, and the rumormongers of Richmond, from the eyes of the world. The army fights the heat and the accumulated days of fatigue. Jackson rests it early. But time is short and Lee has it up and in ranks by 5 A.M. By early afternoon it's moved up through a wood and stopped on a low hill looking into the town.

A woman appears, a Confederate spy by the name of Belle Boyd, to tell Taylor and then Jackson that the town, a key station on the Manassas railroad, is guarded by only one large regiment that is lazily deployed. Stonewall can take the town as he pleases, fast or in stages, by stealth or by rout. What will Jackson do? The woman is young, pretty, flushed, eager, brave, exultant in this moment that she stands before the hero of Manassas and the man who is about to liberate the valley. He believes her report. Until this moment he's been keenly composed; now Jackson feels his battle blood start to rise. Lee observes him closely. Headquarters in Richmond is as hot as that valley, but the heat here among maps, petitions and reports—in the full, bloodless breakdown of conscription and commissary statistics, ordnance data, railroad schedules—is enervating. In it, though, Lee's alertness is extraordinary. He can actually smell the battle begin even though the room is airless and every odor hangs limp as a becalmed flag. "Take it, take it," he exhorts his lieutenant, his equally aroused man in the valley. "Take it by rout— now!"

Jackson doesn't bother with artillery. He sends the First Maryland and part of Taylor's Louisiana brigade to drive in the Union pickets, and as the men sweep into town Lee hears the long crackling rolls of musket fire, and he hears, as he will for the rest of his life, until on a day of similar stillness and desire he hears them far off, as though from a more distant valley, the wild rebel yells. They are not human. He could never make them himself. They seem to come out of a man's entrails, they seem to rise with a sudden hot pressure from the part of a man that he shares with a beast, and there, not in the mouth, to take voice. They are shrill, sustained yips. He can't resist them. As Jackson spurs into town, driving Yankees, winning long, howling cheers from the townspeople, Lee rides with him. It is good. The air is hot and full of the odor of powder and horse; the smell of men's fear gives it a peculiarly intimate taint, yet it is as exhilarating as a cool bath. When the Yankees retreat to a low hill northwest of the town and open on the advancing Confederate line with artillery, it gets better. He hears the deep, rousing concussions, feels them where he stands. For a moment the grape-shot is dense, the air luxuriant with it; minié balls sing by him on a high silvery note. This is Jackson's battle, he knows it. And he knows this is Jackson's deep-blooded response he feels, but he will not give it up. Drive them! Drive them off that hill! he urges this man of the mountains, this late-coming convert to the charms of the valley, and Jackson orders his men to sweep the hill with bayonets.

When the hill is clean, Lee sees what the whole battle's been about. They'll ask him this later: "The key moment, General? When did Ole Jack, when did Ole Blue Light, show his stuff?" Their tones will be amused, affectionate, indulgent, certainly admiring, but condescending through and through. And they'll be right. Jackson's genius is suited only for war. Among educated men the best he can become is an inarticulate professor of natural philosophy and math, a humorless target for the mockery of quick-witted boys. But here is this war. Here asking the questions are these quivering, quick-witted sheep. And there in the valley is a man whose wit is such that it will never allow him to understand the provenance of his genius, only to be ruled by it. It takes standing in his shoes. Yes, and standing in his shoes among the waving guidons, the Yankee corpses, and abandoned field pieces, Lee sees what the battle's been about.

A bridge. There's one across the south fork of the Shenandoah that is safe. But the one across the north fork, the one that Jackson will need to capture the fleeing Yankees and drive on into Winchester, is now burning and being fired upon by the retreating rear guard. He gives the job to Taylor—he must get his men across. Jackson goes with them. How many ways can destruction threaten a man? The brown water is high and fast from the recent mountain rains. An armed soldier would drop into it like a stone. The burning timbers of the bridge singe the men's uniforms, the blowing flanks of the horses. Halfway across, the floor is burned through and to continue, the army must crowd into one narrow fiery corridor. There the minié balls strike flesh with a soft piercing thud, pitching men into the burning timbers or the swollen spring waters below. Lee will not let him have it, will not let Jackson cross that bridge alone. There on the map the north fork of the Shenandoah makes a last, convulsive twitch before joining the south fork, and Lee sees it all. Jackson's face is like a mask of war-aroused flesh, and the eyes now shine with a blue so pale and clear it might be the light of eternity shining through. But Jackson is not in his eyes. He's in his swollen flesh, the aroused neck, the straining thighs. His ears are a boiling red. He's in his ears, Lee thinks, and his flared nostrils. Once he passes by, Lee will see that Jackson's also in his broad flexed back, but Lee won't let him pass by—he won't let him have it. He's given it to him but he takes it away.

He's off the burning bridge. For a single, suspended moment before Taylor and his men can begin their pursuit, he sees the blue coats spread out on the plain before him and knows all that artillery is all that is lacking to make the day a devastating success. With a single battery of rifled guns he could eliminate a small army of the enemy. That small army could grow larger. His dream has always been to outmaneuver the Union army so conclusively that he might catch it in a moment like this and crush it completely, have done. As a general in the field, every battle he plots and every attack he orders will have as its object the opportunity to deliver that one master blow. If it's a chess game and his king is hemmed in by pawns, he must find that one configuration of enemy forces that will enable him to end it in a single move—and that move must be bloody, the carnage complete.

But it is not a chess game, and he is not yet a general in the field.

He calls urgently—his flesh swelling, his neck, his thighs, his ears boiling red—for rifled artillery to be brought up.

The aide he has ordered to close the door opens it in that moment to inform him that President Davis awaits him, already mounted.

Artillery! He demands artillery.

"General Lee?"

That bridge is burning—has he forgotten? Still, they must bring the artillery up!

"President Davis, sir."

Now he hears Jackson at that distance of valleys and maps calling for artillery he won't get. That handful of bluecoats

—which in the mind's eye grows enormous, conclusive—escapes over the last ridge as Military Adviser Lee accompanies his president to General Joseph Johnston's headquarters at the front, telling no one that Stonewall Jackson's celebrated Valley Campaign has just begun.

II

It is not over, but for the moment it is done. He lies beneath an apple tree, his kepi cap fallen off to one side. His jacket rides wrinkled up his back and pulls tight across his stomach. It is said that he will never be able to compete with his fellow Confederate commanders in matters of elegance and etiquette because he sleeps in his clothing and where the desire overtakes him, not where he should.

Winchester has fallen, Winchester is his.

He lies beside the road, under an apple tree, with only a low stone wall to shield him from cavalry and foot soldiers still following Banks, and the stone wall might as well be removed along with everything else, Lee thinks, because Jackson now belongs to the entire South. There on one of the tumbled stones sits a Colonel Boteler, ex-congressman and man-about-the-capital, sketching the general. Ten days later that sketch will become the most sought-after item in Richmond. It will show Jackson absolved of the battle, at peace with the grass he lies on, the apple blossoms overhead. To judge by his stillness, he might be dead. Of the two deaths that have impressed him the most—the heroic death of General James Wolfe on the heights of Quebec and that of his mother, secure in her faith, serene—this deathlike sleep preserved in Boteler's sketch might be mistaken for either.

The battle is won, faith secured, restored. But only Lee knows that.

Jackson took Winchester with an all-night march.

First he had to determine that the Yankees were retreating toward Winchester. Banks could have tried to join Frémont in the west or marched south of Jackson and joined Shields in the east. But his frightened homing instinct took him north. Jackson sent Ewell on to Winchester by the Front Royal road, and then with the bulk of his army struck for the valley turnpike. There he intercepted the enemy's train. The question he then faced was how much of the train had already passed through. He sent Ashby and his men to harry the part to the north while he attacked to his south. When it became apparent that he was doing no more than dispersing the enemy's rear, he reversed himself and marched back to the north. Beyond Middleton he encountered all that a fleeing army had sloughed off—muskets, haversacks, cooking utensils, bedding, wagons loaded with supplies and ammunition, most of them already fired. Dead horses had to be dragged off the road and the Union cavalrymen who had ridden them driven out from behind the low stone walls where they cowered in terror. It was Jackson they cowered in terror of—the man was implacable, darkly inspired; it was rumored he flew the black flag. He shot those who tried to escape and imprisoned the rest. His own men, he drove. If he could get to the hills overlooking Winchester before Banks did, the city would be his in a rout.

Commissary Banks, Jackson's men jeeringly called the Yankee general, because he wasted enough to feed half the valley army. But the enemy Jackson faced now was precisely the wealth of things the Yankees had left behind. Surely Banks knew this. Hours before he must have told his men, "Fire those wagons of flour and bacon and let's see how fast Jackson's hollow-sided foot cavalry marches past that." The air stank with gun powder and horse flesh rotting in the sun, and then, suddenly, the army marched into great aromatic clouds of fired bacon and flour. Jackson drove his men. They began to come across looted and overturned sutlers' wagons, and, left behind like scraps too paltry to be swept up, cans of oysters, peaches and pears, boxes of cigars. The fat and treacherous Yankees—he knew the ways of temptation, had battled them all his life. Close up the ranks! Close up!

He overtook Ashby, his undisciplined troopers broken up into small plundering parties now and disappeared. Didn't they know that this was only the start? The coffers and larders of the Cities of the North were full. Didn't they understand that God could kill a man with the best bottle of whiskey and the Yankees' best cigar? Ashby didn't know what they understood. They were riotous and out of control. He was standing there waiting on Jackson because he was interested only in finding Yankees to kill and in avenging a brother's disquieted ghost. They would kill Yankees then! Ashby was to take the men he had left and drive the skirmishers away from the road.

Night now, and the blackness would suddenly erupt with a stitching of yellow flame down the length of a wall, from positions out in a field. Ashby charged the fire, rode down the Yankee skirmishers as if he were stomping the first feeble catch of a grass fire into the ground. Jackson continued at the head of his column. He heard the fierce whining hiss of the minié balls, some, he knew, passing within inches of his head. They would hit him only if hitting him formed part of God's design. He felt no fear. Faith could work miracles. Ashby didn't have it, but he rode down the Yankees in an ecstasy of exposure as if he did. Still, the constant skirmishing slowed the column's advance, and by 3 A.M. when Colonel Fulkerson of the Thirty-seventh Virginia Infantry rode up to inform Jackson that the men would be too tired to fight even if they arrived at the Winchester hills in time, the army was still five miles shy of its objective. Reluctantly, Jackson gave them one hour's rest—on their arms. He himself did not dismount but stood with Ashby, who had also ridden up, peering into the darkness enshrouding the next day.

He prayed. The difference in this war would come down to those who got from their men all that they had to give, and those who didn't. He prefaced his prayer more precisely. The difference in this war would come down to those who got all that their men had to give and those who also got the part that a man gave only to his God. Jackson wanted that extraordinary part, that forbidden part—tonight he had to have it. He prayed to God to give him his men's full devotion and valor. For that hour he prayed without ceasing. But at its close he told Ashby, "I fear that stopping here will cost us lives—Yankee lives we might have taken and those of our men we might now lose."

You gave lives to take lives, but before you gave you took and took—that was the extent of Ashby's understanding. With the troopers he had left, Jackson sent Ashby out to ride down remaining snipers and skirmishers, while he marched his army, his cavalry on foot, to the base of those Winchester hills. Banks had beaten him there, but the hills were not heavily fortified. As dawn broke Jackson knew that with Ewell in position on the right, and his own army forming the left, the city was his, and on the heels of that realization came the keener one that he might enjoy its recapture as he pleased.

He chose to ride into battle with his men. Colonels Campbell and Grisby accompanied him. In a vigorous fire of musket and grape, Campbell and Grisby were soon hit, and something in Jackson, something he distrusted but could not long do without, did a quick, exultant leap. He had not been hit! Before him along the easy ascent to those hills, low stone walls gave the Yankee infantry their cover; over those walls rose puffs of white smoke, out of which shot tongues of yellow flame. Men were falling all around him as he and his army broke with the dawn onto the Winchester hills, but men he had and men he would give. He felt himself swell. As a target he was enormous. Why didn't they hit him? By his presence alone he called his men up, and some of *them* were hit, but impervious to the fire, he walked his horse resolutely ahead until the Yankees broke and ran. Abandoning one wall, they regrouped behind another, and still another, and he realized this might go on and on, this music of near-misses, this exultation of the blood, and for just an instant he knew that he wanted it to. Let there be Yankees and let there be walls and low hills to climb, and men of mine to give so that I might take. Let there be . . . and only then did he hear the din of the actual battle, the moans, the fear-congested pants of the men running to their death. Suddenly sobered, he left them running and withdrew. The men cheered him—they always cheered him—but he withdrew to his artillery commander Crutchfield's position to watch his army turn both of Banks's flanks.

When the way into Winchester was clear, he brought up fresh troops and told them to yell their loudest as they advanced. On the first shrill note of their wild chorus, he discovered he was spent. He rode into town, where the citizens were harrying the Yankees with buckets of boiling water, as if on the crest of a wave. This was the town of his winter quarters. Here among these handsome brick houses, spacious grounds, inside these spare erect churches, he had socialized, shone, discussed theology, in actuality ruled, and gotten, although he did not know it yet, his wife with child. He passed through it now in this moment of his glory, dazed. Once on open ground north of town he could see that Banks's retreat had become a rout and knew that with cavalry he could ride a whole army into the Potomac, destroy it completely. But he didn't have cavalry. Ashby's men had dispersed. The chance lost here was the lost chance of the war. But war was chance, chance after chance like a succession of low stone walls, and he was now tired.

He led his horse through a breach in the wall to his left. His men would pursue Banks until they remembered what a hero's welcome awaited them in Winchester, then they would return. He gave no orders. His horse he left free to graze on last season's apples and grass. The sleep that overtook him there on the apple-enriched earth was like a deep gravitational pull. Piercingly sweet, the smell of apples relieved him of the smell of powder and blood. He was asleep before the blue eyes closed on the blue of the sky, Sunday, he had known all along, and another battle fought for God.

And for Virginia, for the South, for the world's press, even for the bored and discouraged North, for Lincoln and Stanton, Lee thinks, to give them something more than McClellan's dilatoriness to worry about—and for me. Lee observes the famous young general lying there beneath the apple tree, Boteler's sketch, perhaps, already in his hand. Or the hilt of his still undrawn sword in his hand. Or the pen that will write the letters for his commander in chief. Or the pointer that will trace the route of the marches on the map. It is impossible to tell whether Jackson is dead or asleep. The fatigued fall of the flesh from the cheeks looks like a dead man's. The nostrils don't move. A wasp flying between rotted apples lands in his beard, close to the small mouth, and the mouth doesn't twitch. Lee records the massive, rumbling passage of an army on the other side of that wall, records each springy step the wasp takes across the bristles of Jackson's beard; and he doesn't know whether the man lives or dies, or whether in that moment he prefers for the hero of the valley a life of eventual disappointment and defeat to eternal rest there beneath a May day sky and the chaste green apples soon to adorn that tree.

He does the work he's been ordered to do—correspondence, advising incompetent generals in the field, in the name of his president, quartermastering where the quartermaster fails. When he looks back at the sleeping soldier, he knows at once what he prefers; his impatience to escape his office and get under way actually thickens his whisper. "Get up, Thomas," he says. "This is just the start. You must get up. Those Cities of the North—Philadelphia, Baltimore, New York—they are there for you. The Yankees expect you. We shall take them—you and I."

Jackson's eyes are open now, their blue the sky's, two small translucent lakes. There is vision, perhaps perfect vision, but no movement.

"Thomas! It is time."

Still Jackson lies there, the eyes open, the expression on his face both stricken and inspired.

"You must write your wife," Lee says.

Then he remembers that it is Sunday and that Jackson, unlike Lee, doesn't write letters on the Sabbath.

"You must do it for me."

My Precious Pet,

Today God on His holy day has blessed our cause in arms. He has freed Winchester from Northern occupation and given it back to the generous Christian people we both know so well. The assault was made as the sun came up, and whether it was our might the Yankees feared or the rising light of the Lord, they broke after but a short defense and ran, speeded on their way by the townspeople of this brave city. The day continues fair, as fair a day as I've seen, and there is general rejoicing.

If my darling little wife should take it into her mind to pay her husband a visit, I will tell her how to do it. She must take the train to Strasburg, and from there a coach up the turnpike, where but a short time before her husband marched his victorious army, never dreaming that soon thereafter his *esposita* would be traveling along the same road. At the Taylor Hotel perhaps she can find a gallant young officer to escort her up Elm Street to Third. She will pass Mr. Walrimple, the druggist, and Miss Stephens, the milliner, and on the corner she will come to the First Presbyterian Church, whose bells are the sweetest in the city and whose white doors always shine in the Sabbath sun. She will turn to the north—if her gallant escort will be so kind as to remain at her side—on Prospect Street. She will pass Mr. Robert Conrad's gracious home and close by will pause before the door of Mrs. Anne Magill, that estimable lady, with whom my darling spent so many pleasant hours during her previous sojourn. She should hurry now—her escort might have duties elsewhere.

At North Braddock Street she will recognize at once Reverend Graham's house, in whose parlor she and her husband listened to many an edifying discourse and enjoyed the most stimulating company in the city. She must not stop there. Thirty paces more and she will come to the gate of Lieutenant Colonel L. T. Moore of the Fourth Virginia Volunteers. It is a pretty, cottage-style home with a large yard around it. There she may bid her escort farewell and thank him on behalf of her *esposo*, for even though the oak trees are now in full leaf and the wisteria and rambling rose are in bloom, she will recognize the house in which she made her husband the most blissful man on earth. At the front door she should not knock. Once inside she should look in the room to her right, where her husband has his office. He will not be there, but isn't the gilt paper on the walls elegant, and aren't the mahogany tables and chairs handsome? Up the stairs she should come, treading lightly with her quiet, faithful step. She should tiptoe back around the railing up to the front room on her left, and there my darling should peek inside. Will she recognize the brocaded curtains with their tassels and the

Queen Anne four-poster bed? Will she have forgotten after so long a time that man sitting at a slant-topped desk beside the east window reading a book?

She is such a good *esposita* that she deserves a hint. That man is a poor nobody without his little wife. That man is a lowly sinner who dreams only of his angel to comfort him. That man is reading his Bible—*For what knowest thou, O wife, whether thou shalt save thy husband? Or how knowest thou, O man, whether thou shalt save thy wife?* —and when he sees that pretty smiling face in the door, he will know that God has finally answered his prayers. Don't you recognize that man yet? He is your adoring husband. He is sitting at that desk, not reading his Bible but writing you this letter, and he looks up for your face but the doorway is empty.

How his heart aches when he sees that that doorway is empty. When he walks through this town without his darling at his side, how lonely he feels. The sun goes behind a cloud and all the bells from the church towers toll a lament because you, my sweet wife, are not here. Now it is threatening rain. Rumors continue to arrive that McDowell has marched from Fredericksburg with Shields in his van and taken Front Royal. Banks is being reinforced and rearmed in Maryland. Frémont, with his army of 20,000, is said to be but twenty miles to the west of Strasburg. Now the rumors are no longer rumors but verified reports. I am being forced to retreat or fight an army three times my size—if retreat I still can. Once Shields and Frémont unite at Strasburg, I shall be surrounded and this city where we spent such a wonderful winter will be destroyed. My pet, my Anna, what am I to do?

But you are not to worry over that. God will deliver us. It is God, my sweet, who made this valley and God who knows the moment to move His army along its paths. You must care for your health. You must see to our servants, particularly Cy and George, who should never be allowed to forget that the salvation of their souls depends upon our success in arms. You must dedicate yourself to the maintenance of a disciplined, ordered day that once the war is over will serve as an example to those who would roam our land in packs, seizing what they can.

Rain has begun to fall. We are in full retreat. There is little time. Standing in the door, peeking in to the desk where I write, you would no longer see me. Downstairs, where I receive our dispatches and watch our alternatives vanish, I can no longer be found. Reverend Graham, the Robert Conrads, dear Mrs. Magill, can tell you nothing, for our plans have been kept secret and their execution so sudden that the men have barely had time to shoulder their arms. I must drive them, my dove. I don't know how you would get by in your coach, for I must use all of the road. The rain is pouring down. I am a marcher of men, and the Yankee generals who attempt to surround me talk of nothing else but "bagging Jackson," as if they meant to hit me on the fly. But they will not hit me, rest assured, my dear little woman, my life. I will hit them. I will smite the three of them terrible blows. May God deliver us to His chosen spot, and then may God bring the Yankees to me singly so that I can give each of them his sporting chance. Bag Jackson? I say this to you—to all others I remain silent. They shall not! They are not the men!

You are on the train now, you are back in Lexington. It was only a fond and foolish dream I had that I might see your face in that door. This rain tests us all. I cannot stop the straggling. The men do not understand why we marched here and routed Banks out of Virginia, if only to retrace our steps, this time marching for our lives. I cannot tell them. I've trained them to march, not to debate the dark necessities of war. I understand that if McDowell threatens me, he no longer threatens Richmond, and that as long as I outmaneuver three Union armies, I keep our capital safe. I understand that this lovely green valley has become a diversion, a theater to divert attention, and as long as I catch the Yankees' eye, they cannot concentrate on Johnston. The more eyes I catch, the better it seems. But Anna, my darling, you and only you know that that is not me. I have never sought attention. I would be terrified to stand up on a stage, to strut and declaim my lines. That's General Magruder, that's General Stuart. Yet I am here, and if I cannot drive these straggling wet men through Strasburg in time, the diversion shall be over, the theater shall be dark—and all our lives, I fear, as well.

This rain tests us all.

May God save you and ease your troubled mind. This is a letter that can never be written, never be sent.

The rainy day Jackson drove his men to within two miles of Strasburg was the same day—May 31, 1862—Joe Johnston was carried off the field at the battle of Seven Pines. He was conscious, but his wounds were so painful he made little sense. Davis was there, seeking information, assurances, and with him rode his military adviser. As the litter bearers carried Johnston into the gathering darkness and other Confederate wounded limped back from the front, Davis gave the army to Lee. Did Lee want it? It had to be regrouped, refortified. As an instrument of offense and not of strategic retreat it had to be infused with a new purpose, but these were questions a man put only to himself. His president, he obeyed at once.

He accepted his new command, this Army of Northern Virginia, and closed down his desk. Of men used to the lax discipline of Johnston, he now had to make harsh demands. To the delight of the newspaper lampoonists, he put a shovel into their hands and ordered them to build new earthworks and dig new trenches, activity unbecoming gentlemen-in-arms. Drinking in the ranks had become widespread; he drilled the tipplers until they'd sweated the very habit out of their systems. With a firm, judicious impartiality he separated the favor curriers from the meritorious and took away from each man what was not his. More than once he thought of his father, "Lighthorse Harry" Lee, a hero who had died in disgrace, a man for whom self-denial was as foreign a concept as the creed of some monastic order. Was he who he was because his father had been who he'd been? Was he his father's mistakes corrected, his excesses curbed? A narrow view to take of himself, he knew, but these were talented, intemperate men he had to lead, and his father's fate stood before him, as it had all his life, presaging the South's ruin. He stabilized his lines. He called up fresh troops from North Carolina and pressed Davis for a full-scale conscription act. By drilling, by discipline, by the sheer force of his example, he brought his men to a high state of readiness.

Then he summoned his commanding officers and explained to them that McClellan, not being Southern, was content to slowly advance his position and his works under the cover of his big guns and that unless something were done promptly, the city of Richmond would come within shelling range. J.E.B. Stuart he sent on a reconnaissance mission around the whole of McClellan's army, and although the plume-adorned Stuart got the glory, Lee got the facts: The main line of communication to the supply base on the York might be cut if the Union right could be turned. He waited for a battle plan to form, to mature. Under normal circumstances he would have written his ailing wife, Mary, for he'd noticed that in directing his thoughts to the welfare of his family, he sometimes discovered ways to outmaneuver the Yankees that wouldn't come to him during the study of maps, troop deployment, and reconnaissance data. In answering his letters Mary sometimes completed his thoughts for him, and he had learned to listen. It was her arthritic body that had failed her; her mind was extraordinarily sharp. She tended toward the contemptuous in denouncing some of the enemy's leaders, but no one wanted the Yankees driven off the peninsula any more ardently than she. Her ardent desire, she assumed, must have been shared by everyone else. What if it wasn't? If it wasn't, then any leader assuming it was committed a schoolboy's military blunder—equating the will of the commander with that of the last man in the ranks, subsuming the all in the one. But from the start, the South's only resource that exceeded the North's had been desire. Eventually every Confederate leader would have to take Mary Lee's assumption to heart and fight on it, and with insufficient rations and inadequate firepower expect to win, because, as she had made clear to her husband, "If we don't they will, and I won't have them telling me what to do."

Yes, Lee should have written his wife. Also, as commander of the army, he needed a new shirt, two new collars, and a linen coat for this heat—and that would have given his brooding and inactive daughters something to do. But for the moment, Mary and the girls were caught behind enemy lines and no mail could get through. His oldest son, Custis, was with him in Richmond but serving in a governmental post that had left him weak, discouraged, and of no help to his father. It was only a matter of time, therefore, before Lee turned his thoughts back to the Shenandoah Valley and the man he had there—this man whom the press would not shut up about, this darling of the drawing rooms, this Cromwell of the South. His man, Lee's, whenever he cleared his mind and instructed it to speak.

Rain—it speaks rain, a punishing downpour, flooding every stream in the region. And it speaks escape—the Scylla and Charybdis of the Union armies have come together at Strasburg and plucked only a tail feather from Jackson's rear. That feather is bedraggled and wet—a trophy for Frémont and Shields. Jackson pushes up the turnpike, the men dispirited, in flashes rebellious, with Frémont following at a distance, almost every day engaging the Confederate rear. Jackson worries about Shields. He sends cavalry, overseen by the trustworthy Crutchfield, through the Massanutton to destroy the south fork bridge at White House, and the one farther south at Conrad's Store. If Shields is marching up the Luray as Jackson assumes, he does not want him sweeping down on his left at New Market. Let him march the Luray to the end and bog down in muddy roads.

On the macadamized turnpike it is not mud that Jackson has to contend with, and his wagons move through. It is the wet, sullen spectacle the men make—and his fear that one of them in his frustration will unhorse an officer, take to the saddle, and witness that spectacle for himself. He'll see an army poorly shod and clothed, beaten down not by the enemy but by the rain and the rainy realization that they have driven the Yankees out of the valley only to watch the Yankees pour back in; that Yankees are as inescapable and inexhaustible as the elements themselves, as the rain. For that reason Jackson will not sleep in accommodations his aides arrange for him among valley farmers. He sleeps with his men on the wet ground. The rain washes his tent away, too. He refuses to be waited on, catered to. Men survive ordeals like this by restoring the hard edge of challenge to each oppressive minute of the day. His aides offer him spirits. He is tempted. The taste of liquor is incomparable, and it bodies forth to his imagination every being a man might want to become—but all false, all pariah selves to the truth of God's creation. He will not drink. As long as the rain falls he will use it to steady his resolve, sharpen his purpose, as he leads his men.

Then he will use it to give his men a rest. As soon as he has marched his army across the north fork at Rude's Hill, he will destroy the bridge, presenting Frémont with an unfordable stream. Frémont carries with him pontoons, Jackson knows, but it will take him at least a day to get them into place. On that day of rest, the hardest rain yet falls. Fields are awash. Each cow path across a pasture becomes a muddy torrent. Water coursing behind walls debouches through tumbled stones and carries tents with it. How can Jackson put this water to work for him? It's only here in the valley, in this theater to divert attention, that it is raining. Lee in Richmond is dry and hot. How can this water work to destroy the Yankees? Jackson calls his engineers to him, Crutchfield, his cartographer Jed Hotchkiss. His engineers tell him which streams they can and cannot bridge. Crutchfield assures him that the bridges at White House and Conrad's Store, which Shields might use in the Luray to cross the south fork and rejoin Frémont, have been destroyed. Hotchkiss points to the town of Port Republic, wedged up into the confluence of the north and south forks. Command the bridge there and you could keep the two Yankee armies apart indefinitely; fight, if you chose, one at a time.

At Harrisonburg they leave the turnpike and striking southeast, race Shields through the mud for possession of Port Republic. It is a race, like so many others, that Jackson will win. On the same day, Turner Ashby, in a rearguard action, has his horse shot out from under him. Believing himself invulnerable, he draws his sword and leads his men against the Yankees on foot. They shoot him through the heart.

The news staggers Jackson. Virginia mourns, its young women wail for their martyred beau, and Jackson withdraws to his tent. Ashby had thwarted him more than once, but in their courage, in their disdain for the Yankees, and in something else—something maniacal and not subject to satisfaction, to change—they were brothers. Jackson prays for Ashby. He prays to God that God might understand how men like Ashby come to commit the blind acts of zealotry they do, and though misguided, how those acts might be made to conform with God's purpose and be forgiven. He prays long into the night, and Jim, his body servant, spreads the word that the general plans to offer battle the next day since a battle always follows a night of so much prayer. Actually, Jackson won't offer battle until the day after that, but the battle mood is on him and he prays that these Yankee invaders who stomp out the flower of the South might be made to pay a thousandfold for Ashby's death. Praying, his voice never rising above a tense supplicating whisper, he works himself into a towering rage. Somewhere into the night he ceases to supplicate and demands to know why. Not why Ashby was killed, but why he was so fiercely emboldened. Not why he, General Thomas J. Jackson, must soon give battle to the separated Yankee armies, but why he awaits that moment with such anxious anticipation, anxious only that something might happen—a Yankee retreat, a peace treaty signed—and the battle elude his hungry charge like the morning mist.

The occasion for this night of prayer is Ashby's death. But in Ashby's honorable intention to avenge a brother's murder and in his subsequent neither honorable nor dishonorable but simply unquenchable thirst for more and more Yankee blood, Jackson is forced to recognize something of himself. What happens? he wants God to tell him. Why do men of principle, order, and peace—Ashby was a quiet farmer; he, Jackson, a professor and fondly domesticated man—become instruments of blood terror, bloodlust?

During those moments of waiting for God to answer, he hears in the snores and muffled voices of the night-passing army all of humanity crowded onto this wedge of land between the north and south forks of the Shenandoah, and in the flooding rivers he hears the coursing of an implacable desire.

He gets no answer.

He rephrases the question, and repeats it, and waits again. By the time an ashen light has entered the march-soiled canvas of his tent, he is still waiting. He hears pickets coming in and going out, the hoof thud of leaderless cavalry patrols. Those who have it are cooking bacon and coffee. The day, he believes, will be warm, finally free of rain.

Is God deaf to my pleas because when I face the enemy and feel my flesh swell and my battle blood rise it is not the Holy Spirit who is in me, as I had thought, but . . . the devil? Are we God's until the hour to kill, and then does he give us up in disgust?

Suddenly he sits bolt erect. The next question is spoken out loud, intelligible to the slave, Jim, cooking the general's breakfast outside on the fire. He hears an angry, yet cold and desolate voice, too. "Killing the Yankees, am I yours then, Satan?" And he opens the flap to Jackson's tent, saying, "Whachall want, Gin'ral. Y'breakfast?"

Jackson orders Jim to bring him paper and pen.

Breakfast cooling, he writes:

General Lee:

> Turner Ashby died today. By the time you receive this letter, the entire South will have begun to mourn one of its most gallant sons. I have spent this first night without Ashby in prayer. I have prayed that God will forgive

him his fierce recklessness, bloodlust, and pride—and honor in him his firm courage, patriotism, and dedication to our common goal.

I do not know whether God has heard me.

If He has heard me, He has made no sign.

There are many in this South of ours like Turner Ashby, although perhaps none quite so contemptuous of personal safety. Watching young men of this valley and state flock to Ashby, begging for the chance to serve under his impetuous command, I have even been reminded of the great persuasive powers of our Lord as person, as example in the flesh. Yet tonight He gave no sign.

General Lee, what is bravery? Like me, your first experience in warfare was against Santa Ana in Mexico, and you, too, were cited for conspicuous bravery. I have heard it said that you lay for hours beneath a log upon which armed Mexican soldiers were sitting and did not move, barely breathed; that you made of yourself a man of steel. I withstood a galling fire from musketry and artillery at Chapultepec Palace in our successful assault upon that redoubt. Surely if God had wanted to take our lives in Mexico He could have done so in the most probable fashion. From that moment on, I knew that my life was in God's hands, and no sooner had we withdrawn from Mexico than I began preparing myself for indoctrination into the Christian church, finally taking vows in the First Presbyterian Church in Lexington, Virginia. I know you to be as Christian a gentleman as any among us. And I ask you, sir, What is bravery if at every moment of our lives we are in God's hands? Are we not as brave as our belief in God? Is not great bravery, then, no more or less than great faith?

I believe so, sir. I believe that moments of peril are given to us so that in meeting them with bravery we might manifest our belief; that our wars are always wars for Christ. Is it not true, then, that men are sometimes able to perform prodigious feats in battle because they are animated with God's power? General Lee, in those moments of our greatest bravery and greatest belief, is that not God's power surging through us and driving us with a strange sort of delight toward the attainment of even more improbable goals? I speak of slaughter, sir, of killing, of unstinted killing when our bravery and our belief are at their peak and God is strongest in our hearts. Is that not God at that moment swelling our hearts?

I thought so, sir. Yet this long night of prayer I asked Him that question, and He gave no sign.

Turner Ashby is dead. Perhaps his life was never in God's hands, yet his bravery was the equal of yours or mine. In what had he placed his belief? Bravery like his argues, does it not, great belief. Ashby believed the Yankees would not kill him—yet they did.

He has not given me a sign, and I have beseeched Him throughout this night. I write to you, sir. I find intolerable the thought that if it is not God rewarding my belief with brave actions and giving me power far beyond my own to kill these invaders of our land, then it must be the work of the devil. But what am I to think? *He* will not answer. I fear His answer is Ashby's death. In assaulting Winchester, I experienced such pleasure in the strife that for a moment I envisioned an assault without end, where equally brave men fell to my left and right so that I might continue borne on in God's hand —but in that moment I did not feel godly. In whose hand, sir, was I borne? In whose hand are we all being borne, the Ashbys of the South? Who am I, General Lee, when I am this Stonewall about whom so much is being said these days?

This is a letter that can never be written, never be sent.

I shall almost certainly give battle soon.

More than ever, sir, I remain your faithful, obedient servant.

General Thomas J. Jackson
Commander, Army of the Valley

Now a commander in the field, Lee could go to his maps boldly, unfurtively, without mean longings or preemptive, vainglorious desires. The papers were full of editorials questioning the wisdom of Davis's choice to succeed Johnston, but Lee could go to the maps with authority, and then with no abuse of it, tell the roomful of aides to leave. The aides left.

Alone, their commander raised his arm to the Shenandoah Valley. He still wore his heavy parade coat. His eyes moved down the arm, past the gold-braided buttons. His shirt cuff, he noticed, was slightly frayed. His finger had found Port Republic at once, but strangely enough, it was his middle finger that was pressing down on the town. Bending it now, he was able to drive with his index finger around the Massanuttons and into the Shenandoah Valley, and with his ring finger up the Luray. Jackson, he knew, would do that with his army. Without Turner Ashby, and grieving his loss, he could still do it. Two prongs, two days, one army—the Port Republic bridge worked as a hinge swinging a door open onto two fronts. If Jackson could drive Frémont and Shields far enough back up their respective valleys then, conceivably, he could join Lee in Richmond without the Yankees having realized he was gone. They'd have the Richmond press to contend with, and the heromongers, and the adoring and inquisitive women, but if Jackson's great talent for secrecy didn't desert him now, Lee could have him and confer with him before anyone discovered he'd come and gone.

Then ... and with a sureness that was stunning, the whole battle plan fell into place for him. He moved to the map containing the Richmond-Gordonsville-Fredericksburg triangle, but he didn't have to. The map was behind his eyes. He saw Jackson beating Shields and Frémont back far enough to leave the valley with his army unawares. He could pass through the Blue Ridge at Brown's Gap. With no advance warning—since everyone, beginning with Lincoln, would assume he was still west of the Blue Ridge—he could then fall on McClellan's extreme right north of the Chickahominy. Simultaneously Generals Longstreet, Powell Hill, and D. H. Hill with their divisions could roll up the entire Yankee right and drive it back across the peninsula. Before reaching the James, somewhere in White Oak Swamp, it could be destroyed. Lee drew a long, deliberate breath. After the sudden vision he looked for what he'd overlooked, and found it at once—Richmond. While the great part of his army was attacking the Union right, the Union left could assault the city. He drew another breath and asked the next question: Why wouldn't they? Then added: With sufficient demonstration from a small defending force, why wouldn't they? He knew the answer. He phrased it to himself with almost forbidden pleasure, savoring the glimpse it gave him into the mind of his opponent. Because after debating and temporizing for two months, McClellan was not the man to seize his chance when it presented itself. He would not move without conclusive proof that Richmond had been left in the hands of a token force, and by then he would be up to his ears in swamp.

This war was between the grinding weight of the North and these leaping maneuvers of the South. We must leap at him. The second he lowers his musket to scratch and yawn, we must leap at his throat.

So Jackson—perhaps depressed by his long, rain-soaked retreat, perhaps brooding over Ashby's death—Lee would breathe new life into him; he would bring him clandestinely to Richmond and make him twice the soldier he had ever been. He wrote yet another letter—this one eagerly. He congratulated Jackson on his victory at Winchester and his escape from the converging Union armies. He urged him to strike another successful blow when the opportunity arose. He didn't mention Ashby. He said instead that Jackson should make arrangements to impress the enemy with his presence, but should come alone, in disguise if necessary, to Richmond to meet with him. So much would be hanging in the balance ... but in this suspenseful vein Lee would not go on. His letters were well-mortised works of woodsmanship through which only the most discerning eye could catch the gleam of his emotions. Jackson would catch it—and Jackson would come. He signed the letter simply "R. E. Lee" and dated it June 8, 1862.

III

They came for him on that same day, June 8, and again on June 9, with the nation still mourning the intrepid Ashby's death. They came to bag a Jackson. Was their intention (Lee wondered, surmised) to get to him before I could? Had some clairvoyant in Lincoln's pay foreseen the losses on the peninsula, at Manassas, Sharpsburg, Fredericksburg, and nearly a year hence on that first breathtaking afternoon at Chancellorsville, and reported to his employer: We cannot afford to let this so-called Man of God run loose, Mr. President. You must bag him. But Lincoln had the cautious McClellan spread out before Richmond with 100,000 men to worry about; and probably Frémont and Shields, glory hunters both, came on their own.

Frémont came first. Dick Ewell met him at Cross Keys with half the Yankee numbers and pushed the Pathfinder back. The rest of Jackson's army remained at Port Republic, alert for further movements down the Luray by Shields. A Federal cavalry patrol had already entered town from the east and cost Jackson the sermon that Major Dabney was to preach that morning, for it was Sunday and Dabney, instead of delivering the word of God, would fire grape into the Yankee horsemen. Shields would come again the next day, perhaps Frémont, too. Turner Ashby would not—I can only guess (Lee realized, admitted) at General Jackson's state of mind. Cannon toward his west, where Ewell faced Frémont. Shields threatening with his cavalry from the northeast. The flooding north and south forks of the Shenandoah. The one reliable bridge, the no longer fordable fords. Rifled artillery on the heights, but ammunition in short supply. That crowded spit of land between the two forks, a potential bottleneck to thwart any man of speed. And General Jackson, who instead of sleeping had prayed, perhaps every night since the retreat in the rain from Strasburg, but whose nights of prayer would have become feverish and unrequited since Ashby's death. No (Lee repeated), I cannot account for his state of mind. I can only stand by and watch while he prepares to fight two battles on the same day—first Shields up the Luray and then back across the flooding forks of the Shenandoah again to meet Frémont in the west—both battles to be annihilating blows.

Of course he was tired. Bold men sometimes become bolder, less judicious, as they confront their exhaustion, reconnoiter sleep. Certain bold men might look upon the world of their dreams as grand reservoirs, the equivalent of divisions in strength. I dream portentous dreams and know for a fact that General Jackson faced two different armies whose numbers far exceeded his. Nevertheless, I would not have stopped him had I been able. Our whole struggle was predicated on the hope that our enemies would one day position themselves in such a way that with a single unprecedented stroke, we might demolish them before they could reunite. One week, one day, one hour—we would reach a point (Lee determined, concluded) when God's intercession on our behalf became indispensable. I do not know what word General Jackson had from God on June 9, 1862. Bold men make demands of God; they sometimes take Him to task. In a crisis of despair they might believe they supplant him, and General Jackson was bold. I faced McClellan, whose numbers far exceeded mine at Richmond, and addressed God only as my savior whose Son held my soul in His hands. But my attention was fixed on General Jackson, there at the confluence of valleys and rivers, of Generals Frémont and Shields.

What he won the next day, he won by dint of his implacable will. His strategy depended on speed—the speedy movement of sufficient numbers—and on desire. He lost both speed and numbers when the bridge he'd had constructed that night to move his army from Port Republic out onto the wheat-growing plains of the Luray partially collapsed after no more than Jackson's old Stonewall Brigade commanded by the resourceful Winder and Poague's Rockbridge Artillery had been able to cross. General Jackson was, of course, the first across. He did not know that the bulk of his army, including Ewell, who had left a token force to maneuver in front of Frémont, was not following him up the valley. He did not have time to ride back and make sure. In the moment of engaging the enemy, he might not have cared. Across a field of green wheat General Jackson, deeply unrested and possessed of a vision, drove into Shields. He was immediately enfiladed by cannon situated on a hill to his right. He sent the Second and Fourth Virginia to take the Union artillery position, and those two fine regiments failed. He sent Winder straight up the valley into heavy fire, and Winder was beaten back. He looked behind him to call up Taylor, Taliaferro, and Trimble, and the valley was empty. Nothing but a trickle of men was getting across the remains of the bridge at Port Republic, and when finally that trickle began to appear in the valley and to straggle up to his penned-down positions, Jackson knew that his dream of a double victory that day was turning traitor. Before the dream became nightmare, he ordered all men maneuvering before Frémont to cross the north fork and fire the bridge. That decision saved him. It kept Frémont and Shields apart. It left the battle between Shields's and Jackson's vanguards and a trickling advance of men beside a river in flood, in a valley of apple orchards and wheat fields surging with the sap of spring.

The day improved—became bluer, brighter, the very dayness of day—into which the armies could discharge their cannon and musket fire, their smoke, the battle cries of their men and animals. As soon as a handful of reinforcements arrived, Jackson threw them in. The fiddling and bugle-blowing musicians in the Stonewall Brigade exchanged their instruments for arms. Until the Yankees shot their mounts out from under them, Confederate officers pranced up and down lines of huddled infantrymen, exhorting them on. Winder finally got what remained of his brigade up for a ragged charge, and for a moment Jackson heard the yipping tremolo of the rebel yell before three crashing waves of musket fire brought the graycoats down. Only they did not all wear gray coats—some wore blue mixed with brown, and some wore coats of naked, powder-burned skin. They lay flung in the gaping lines of all their unsuccessful charges while their late-coming comrades-in-arms strolled up from behind as though to tap their commander on the back. Jackson feared the nightmare was on him. For each battle-laden breath he drew, he drew another fresh with the promise of spring. There rose the Blue Ridge, there flowed the Shenandoah; there the Luray in fruit and flower. So easy (Lee understood—any general with the courage to see his battle through to the end somehow reached this point) to go to sleep. Or to wake up and call the retreat. Jackson would not. He planted himself. He would no longer admit to the beauty of the day; that perverse trickling forth of men he would no longer accept. If he wanted men, he would have them and smoke thick as thunderheads on the blue of the sky.

No magician (no, in spite of the hyperboles of the press, Lee knew that Jackson performed no tricks), he did not conjure up Taylor and his Louisianans but willed them up. He sent them through dense mountain laurel to silence the Yankee artillery. Winder, slowly falling back, he reinforced with Taliaferro. Trickles be damned. God, if He chose, could damn them all, but he wanted a torrent. He called up Ewell. It was as if he'd reached back and heaved Ewell and his men into place. The strain showed—and the blood rose—in his neck, back, his long ears, his weary face. But there stood Ewell before him. . . . General Ewell, a man wants a thing badly enough and it's not the forces of evil that threaten to undo him—it's the forces of mockery, sir. I will not be mocked. What is a nightmare if not these very forces performing in unison? To Satan you show the cross, but this world mockery, this mockery we carry within ourselves, you oppose with the strength of your will. I will you to crush Shields. I order you to it. Sweep this valley with bayonets. . . . This, the eyes. All that the fierce, laconic Jackson withheld in speech, Ewell had learned (and Lee would soon see), he told through the eyes. Beneath the black brows, in the smoke-darkened face, they were as blue as the spring sky—and keener, colder, less likely to cloud. The dream is only and always the quelling of the forces of mockery. This Army of the Valley will not be mocked!

Taylor captured five pieces of artillery—three Napoleans and two rifled Whitworths—then marched off the hill and into Shields's left flank. Ewell, reinforcing both Winder and Taliaferro now, rolled up Shields's center and right. Frémont stood safe but powerless to help on the Confederate extreme left, beyond the flooding Shenandoah; and as Jackson spurred Little Sorrel forward, it was as if the whole Yankee nation were there to witness what he intended to do to Shields and his army. He intended to drive them, he intended to savor every foot he forced them to yield and, even in the ecstasy of rout, he intended to remember that there were fatter Yankee generals and more punishable armies the farther north he advanced. But Lee called him back. I had no choice (Lee regretted, declared). General Jackson's dream won approval only as it formed part of mine. In the secrecy of maps and furtive hours snatched from petitioners and President Davis's tiresome demands, I approved—I rode with him. But as commander of all the armies of Virginia and North Carolina, I dreamed the annihilation of General McClellan and his Army of the Potomac. To accomplish that goal, I had to have Jackson in Richmond. Left to himself to drive north alone, his appetite and desire were such that he might never have come back. So I called him. I said, "Later, later you and I will conquer the North, but now it is time that we meet. Come to me in secret, Thomas, and we shall see who will prove our match. . . ."

Who were they? They were men without fathers. They were men whose fathers had set them impossible examples, then vanished from the scene. Jackson's was a lawyer. He was a man who had risen out of his rustic origins and chosen the town of Clarksburg, Virginia, in which to make his mark. The house he had chosen for his family was made of bricks, not logs. There Julia Jackson gave birth to her four children. And there Jonathan Jackson, lawyer by day but backsliding card player by night and speculator on the side, sought to set his conscience right by nursing his firstborn, the six-year-old Elizabeth, through a bout of typhoid fever. It killed him. First it killed his daughter, then three weeks later it killed him. A day after that Julia Jackson gave birth to her last child, an ill-starred girl named Laura, who would live to the age of eighty-five. Destitute. It was the first big word Thomas Jackson, aged two at the time, would learn. His father had pursued respectability against the grain of his nature and reduced the family to ruin. When Thomas was seven, Julia Jackson admitted defeat. She sent Thomas and Laura to live with her husband's people on the west fork of the Monongahela, while older brother, Warren, went west to Parkersburg to live with kin of her own. The day his uncle, Cummins Jackson, came to get him, Thomas hid in the woods behind the house until the shadows from the encircling mountains fell over him. The deepest shadow was cast by Cummins himself, a mountain among men.

The house was made of logs. The mill that Cummins ran was made of logs, as was the mill dam. Cummins was made of the same flesh as Thomas's father had been, and years later, in the California gold fields, would die of the same disease. But until then he was this compelling, elemental force who taught his nephew that unprovisioned leaps ahead such as Jonathan Jackson had taken were doomed to failure. He taught him to fish and hunt, to handle oxen and plough. He taught him to ride so well that with his stirrups hitched uncavalierly high, he became Uncle Cummins's favorite jockey in those races where sums of money changed hands. He didn't teach him religion, but in a world where great natural beauty came at a price, he taught him how to survive. Then he took him and his sister Laura to their mother's sickbed, where Thomas taught himself death. At the end his mother touched his face, then sank out of sight—not as a fish does in taking the full measure of its weight and vigor back to the depths where you had to seek it, but quietly, peacefully, leaving a body behind that was no more than the pallid afterimage of sight, vanishing like nothing in this world.

Orphan. A destitute orphan.

By the age of twelve, Uncle Cummins must have decided that his nephew had learned enough to meet the world on its own terms (the world to the west of them, not to the east), for he sent Thomas and sixteen-year-old Warren off on a trip of eighty overland miles to James Island in the Ohio, where Julia Jackson's folks made their living selling wood to passing steamers. After a short visit there, the brothers began to drift farther down the Ohio on a raft. There were relatives in the two succeeding towns. Then there were no relatives, only the river—just as Uncle Cummins must have known. The Ohio as it poured into the Mississippi, the Mississippi as it poured into the Gulf—they spoke to him, entered his dreams, and in the mindless ease of their movement relieved him of everything he'd been taught. Almost too late, he understood where all southern-flowing rivers emptied out; and somewhere near the southwestern corner of the state of Kentucky, he and Warren reached out and snagged on an island where they went to work cutting trees and selling fuel themselves. They stayed there until they'd proved they could do it. Then they went back home. But that island had been malarial. Four years later Warren died from tuberculosis, and by the time Thomas and Laura reached his bedside, he had already cast out on that southern-flowing current and begun the journey that this time would take him all the way to the Gulf.

He had Laura then, and she, sister of his father's death, had him.

It was not how he would soldier, because he would soldier as if another darkly inspired man grew out of his flesh. But he had learned to value the ground he stood on, and he had learned that one unreconnoitered step ahead might just as easily send him spinning off the rim of the world. Uncle Cummins had given him his ground. Now he made his contacts. By his example, not by unmanly pleading, he ingratiated himself with the men who mattered in Lewis County, Virginia. One man tutored him in reading and spelling. Another took him on as an apprentice surveyor. Two justices of the peace proposed his election as a debt-collecting constable. He was methodical but fast. By the age of eighteen he had fashioned of himself a man of principle—resourceful, just, possessed of a pure, almost impersonal ambition, honest to a humorless fault—and a man of modest attainments. He had done it by clearing and cultivating every inch of the ground he moved over. He understood that his father had not taken these precautions. He had only to regard himself through his sister's eyes to know that he had not overstepped himself. When his grand chance came, he took a step unlike any others. It carried him to Washington, D.C., and the office of his congressman, the honorable Samuel Hays, where he wanted to know why he, Thomas Jackson, should not be sent up to West Point since the War Department's first choice from their district had gone and come back unfit—and there he stood, humble and hugely motivated, a destitute orphan in fact, offering himself as a replacement. No one else had beaten him there, had they? No, no one else had. Gray home-spun, heavy brogans, weather-stained saddlebags thrown over his shoulder, he'd ridden the hill country down to the capital and asked—it was closer to a demand—to be chosen. By then he'd inserted his father's name safely between the two of his—Thomas Jonathan Jackson.

Of course there were portraits. A revolutionary war hero, an intimate of George Washington, a three-time governor of Virginia, would have portraits. "Lighthorse Harry" Lee would be a portrait painter's dream. He had stage sense, the means of arousing himself for each occasion. A very subtle mockery that came and went at the corner of the mouth and eyes meant that his portraits lived—he was never the same man in successive viewings. But the portrait of his father that lived longest in the memory of Robert Edward Lee was of a disfigured wreck of a man who had suffered a street beating in Baltimore, Maryland, and then had to be driven home to Alexandria and left in a downstairs bedroom because he could not climb the stairs to lie beside his wife. Lee was five then. Because this interloping father of his had gone to Maryland to take the part of an editor who dared to oppose the War of 1812, a mob had dripped candle wax into his eyes, stuck penknives into his flesh, sliced off part of his nose, and when he did not flinch, had left him for dead. He died for his family when he sailed for Barbados a year later to escape his creditors. He had already spent one year in debtor's prison and, like the most unregenerate of convicts, had sworn not to be taken back alive. Real death came five years later on Cumberland Island, off the coast of the former penal state of Georgia. There was nothing for the Lee family to do except muster the various men "Light-Horse Harry" Lee had been and find a cenotaph large enough to sit squarely on them all. Self-indulgence and enormous self-regard had killed him. To offset this heritage, Ann Carter Lee served her five children daily doses of self-denial. He was the only man she had ever loved. Slowly, over the years, it had begun to kill her, too. Robert Lee had been born into a storybook marriage, in a storybook state, where the pages yellowed as he turned them. Of course he could close the book—he could choose not to read to the end.

For a while that was the choice he made. There was the solace of plantations and homes open to him all over the state—there was Shirley, the home of his mother's King Carter clan on the James. Everywhere he looked there were cousins. The Carters ran separate schools for the girls and the boys. His mother was determined to get by on her trust fund in Alexandria, but Robert began his education at the Carter school of Eastern View in Fauquier County and took his refuge in that world-in-miniature on the James. He was brighter than anyone, and it soon became clear that he was eager to serve. In a climate of good manners and breeding, his personal beauty grew on him like the finest of fruit coaxed from the most favored of stock. What was to keep this world of close kin, good fellowship, and chaste feminine charm from growing selectively larger until the waters of the James met the waters of the Potomac and those waters, unroiled by mean, disfiguring ambition, spread out over the land?

He knew the answer. History was not made by the kind

hearts, the sweet-tempered of souls. On the Potomac sat Stratford, the site of his birth. It had been part of the estate of his father's first wife (and cousin), Matilda Lee, and upon her death had passed into her husband's hands. But when Lee's half brother Henry came of age, it became his. Robert had an early memory of a correct and charitable young man who had allowed his father and second family to remain behind indefinitely as guests. Or was it himself he was seeing —host to a whole host of stricken and improvident Lees? When, summoning its pride, the Lee family left Stratford and moved to Alexandria, Henry Lee the Younger went down his father's road to bankruptcy. The estate was sold and passed out of family hands forever. As his father had done, Henry Lee then courted political favor. For his efforts he was named ambassador to Morocco. Before he could take up his post, however, the news broke that he had violated the bed of his wife's sister, and the Senate failed to confirm the appointment. He lingered on in Italy and died in Paris seven years later—like so many others a boy at his death, history's fool. If Robert Lee *was* seeing himself then, it was a part or version of himself he was seeing to a familiar Lee grave.

Like his father when faced with that mob's penknives and molten wax, he had learned not to flinch. There were backwaters where history hardly reached until the whole world broke apart; and there were strong currents that the thrill seekers and the vainglorious rode into exile and death. The only honorable alternative was to enter the course of history and battle that current as you battled your nature every day of your life—and to open that book. His father had been George Washington's confidant. When he was about to ride off to fight in the French Revolution, it was the Father of his Country who had pleaded with him to stay behind. A speculator on a grand scale, Harry Lee had been privy to Aaron Burr's imperial scheme. The book said that in his father's anxious and elaborate absences Ann Carter Lee, seventeen years her husband's junior, declined. The decline accelerated, and with a sister also ill and two older brothers gone into their professions, the young Robert found himself caring for his invalid mother as he would later care for his invalid wife. She was a woman of gentle breeding and impressive reserves of character made powerless before her time, and it was a lesson her son never forgot. The book had him leading a double life: He still had an education to get, and manly skills to learn. Between hours, in the evenings, on those days without name, he dimmed the light so that his mother could see him and held the spoon to her mouth in case she should eat. On those long, arduous journeys from one room to another he carried her on his arm, matching his virile pace to hers.

He could read only so long. The pages yellowing as he turned them told the tale of a storybook life to the end. His act of trust was to believe that someone would continue to turn the pages for him as he got up and performed his part in the actions described. He collected letters from influential kin; he wrote the most persuasive and impassioned letter himself. Then he presented himself and his credentials across the Potomac in Washington to the Secretary of War, John Calhoun. He was applying for admission to West Point. His father's taste for soldiering had left Harry Lee restless and embittered for almost anything else. Better defended, wiser, not entirely his own man, Robert would soldier the name of Lee back into the honorable course of history.

Who were they? They were Virginians. Virginia was cradle and home shore to them; it was fatherland. To get there they both had to go to places that Virginia was not. Virginia was not Mexico, where Thomas J. Jackson was sent fresh out of West Point. His systematic march through the academy—starting near the bottom of his class he finished in the top third, digesting subject after subject with an unappeasable appetite to know what he didn't—had not prepared him for

Mexico. It had prepared him to wage war. The war he waged in Mexico was illustrious enough. Commanding a battery of horse artillery, he advanced far out beyond his infantry support and then demanded to know why everyone else in his command who had taken to the ditches flanking La Veronica Causeway did not join him in his assault on Chapultepec Palace. Long enough for the right people to take notice, he had stood there alone. He received two permanent promotions and was breveted all the way to major.

But there was another war that Mexico waged against the austere, hill-girt, self-made man from the west of Virginia, and this one involved weapons against which Jackson had no defense. It involved music—in the teasing, lilting language he heard, in the bells that rang at all hours, in the warbling of tropical birds; music was scored in the sun sparkle on the banks of bougainvillea and in the adagioed waft of jasmine; the irrepressible walks of the young men (some surely soldiers he and his conquering army thought they had defeated) were musical. And there were Mexico's women. What they did with their hands and the fans they carried, how they timed the movements of their hips, shoulders, and eyes— they struck chord after chord for him as he stood there. It all came to an orchestrated head during the *paseo*—the finest carriages in the city parading around the fountains in Alameda Park in one direction, while the most fashionably attired officers on their finest mounts paraded in the other. He refurbished his uniform. For the outlandish price of $180, he bought a horse. He, too, paraded. Dizzied, reeling a little from the glitter of gilded spokes and the succession of dark, gleaming eyes, he wrote his sister, Laura, that he might very well stay. He even demanded and got an audience with the archbishop in an attempt to understand what religion it was that encouraged such a sensuous, ceremonial life and bound it all together. But the archbishop responded to him in tones resembling a liturgical chant. The city woke him each morning with a bombardment more captivating and finally more unnerving than any he'd withstood beneath the walls of Chapultepec. After nine months of this he chose to survive, and when his regiment withdrew, he went with it.

To Fort Hamilton in New York Harbor—which was not Virginia, although it gave him a taste of the grandest of the Cities of the North. To Fort Meade in the purgatorial, palmetto wastes of central Florida—which was not Virginia, although it allowed him to regulate his diet, which had been driven to dyspeptic extremes in Mexico and in the banquet halls of New York. Virginia was Lexington, a small town settled in the foothills of the Valley of Virginia, and when the offer came to teach natural philosophy and artillery at the military academy there, he resigned from active duty and became Major-Professor Thomas J. Jackson. Virginia was these hills on his horizon, set at a greater distance than those that had surrounded him when he was a boy, but the distance told him how much he had progressed, measured to the foot the ground he had cultivated, the sum of his attainments. So what if he had worked hard to become no more than a mediocre professor? He joined the Presbyterian church, became the director of a bank, bought a book entitled *The Principles of Christian Courtesy*, and memorized the contents. This was not mindless conformity; these were the tightly concerted components of a life to which he had pledged his fealty. In exchange, Virginia gave him a wife, the daughter of the president of the college Virginia Military Institute lay next to. Before he had become accustomed to his happiness Virginia took her away and, after a proper period of mourning had passed, gave him another. She, too, was the daughter of a college president, and she, too, fanned the flames of his devotion. With her Virginia supplied two slaves, land on the outskirts of town that he could cultivate like any other gentleman farmer, and the brick house at the town's center to which he had always aspired. The house stood two and a half stories tall, solidly squared away, chimney to opposing chimney, its gabled windows symmetrically arranged. Virginia rewarded its own, welcomed its wandering prodigals back. Thomas Jackson had ceased to doubt her.

Then, on Sunday, April 21, 1861, Virginia asked Major-Professor Jackson to march 176 cadets from his institute to the state capital, and Jackson obeyed. Virginia was now Richmond.

Lee, too, served in Mexico. The favorite of commanding General Winfield Scott—the favorite of many commanding officers since his brilliant career at West Point—he was that war's most distinguished officer. By the end, a colonel in the Corps of Engineers who before he could build the roads that would accommodate the attacks had to explore the terrain over which they would pass and time and again found himself in the enemy's rear. In paving the way for heroes, he became a hero himself. His most famous exploit was a solitary night trek through a lava field where he had to feel his way around great, porous blocks and leap crevasses in the dark. Virginia was not this lava waste. He knew where Virginia was—it was at Arlington, on the hills above Alexandria, where in spite of his renewed ministrations, his mother had finally died. It was at the estate of George Washington Custis—grandson of the first first lady, adopted son of the Father of the Country himself—and extended as far as Mrs. Custis's estate, Chatham, on the banks of the Rappahannock. It was wherever his courtship of their tall, frail only child, Mary, had taken him. He had won her despite her father's reluctance. The Lees had lineage, but bad luck. They had a reputation for squandering to live down. Robert presented himself as an engineer whose training had taught him to make provident use of what was at hand, and to shore up. He'd married American history in a nutshell, and the shell was brittle and prickly in the person of his wife; tolerant and

71

charming—if skeptical—in the person of his in-laws; expansive, storied, and perhaps not as vigilantly managed as it could have been when it came to Arlington itself. It was the Virginia of George Washington, fed by his glory still.

It was not these fields of waste that the Corps of Engineers kept sending him to. Lava waste, in the case of Mexico. Or the mud and mosquitoes in which he stood hip-deep on Cockspur Island off the coast of Savannah looking for the purchase for a fort. He had inspected and rebuilt most of the forts up and down the east coast; as well as any man alive he knew how to spot a cracked foundation, he knew what a soaked piling meant. At night the sea lapped its heartless way into the stone center of monuments. He was like a compass with its pivot foot set down in Arlington, where his family grew, but with the public foot, the end that made its mark, stretched out over the continent. He was sent to repair the Mississippi. For more than two years he dyked and dredged and stood hip-deep in mud again in an effort to force the river out of its willful ways and back into its proper channel before St. Louis. He was given more dredging work in the upper Mississippi and the Ohio. He tried to regulate the treacherously shifting channels in the Missouri that Lewis and Clark had recently navigated. At night all banks shelved. He was a master of stopgaps. He did his duty by the land and its system of citadels. But deterioration on a vast and accelerated scale was the secret at the heart of what everyone insisted on referring to as this vigorous young country. There were periods when he almost forgot—office work with the board of engineers in Washington, a superintendency at West Point. Although he had been praised repeatedly for his performance in Mexico, it seemed unlikely that anyone would remember that he was really a soldier. Then someone did: He was given command of the newly created Second Cavalry. That took him to Camp Cooper in the center of Texas.

Wolves howled at night. Frequently their howls caught in their throats and they seemed to be gnashing at their own innards. The ground seethed with rattlesnakes. The Comanche were capable of making any sound and undergoing any sort of villainous transformation. He was there to pacify them, then to push them back. In a theater the size of Texas —but with no spectators—duplicity stood to duplicity until it sickened of itself. While the Comanche were inactive, he rode hundreds and hundreds of miles—Texas, Arkansas, Missouri, Kansas—to sit on court-martial boards and decide the fate of soldiers whose own private foundations and liquor-soaked pilings had given way before the abstract rigors of the law. The waste was local, and it was immense. He thought of the misspent spirit of his father. While out west, he turned fifty years of age.

Then Virginia called him back. George Washington Custis was dead. His wife had preceded him to the grave. Arlington had been left in disarray. He piled leave from the army on top of leave while he tried to grapple with Custis's careless finances and a planting schedule that seemed determined by whim or the wistful assumption that this Virginia soil could do no wrong. By now his wife was arthritic, and although his sons were healthy, his four daughters were not. His own absolutely unassailable health was either his cross or his crown. But he would pitch his battle here; here in Virginia the waste would be made good. It took him two years, but in 1860 he got his bumper crop of corn. As he prepared to hand Arlington over to his firstborn and return to the army, the army came to him. While he was restoring his estate, the country had blown apart. President Lincoln wanted to know, and Lee's friend and champion General Winfield Scott put the question to him: Would he take command of an army of 75,000 and put the seccessionists down?

As he stepped back across the Potomac, Virginia joined

the ranks of the seccessionists. His resignation from the United States Army was dated April 20, 1861. On April 22, he took the train to Richmond. At stops along the way he was cheered. How had it happened that while he was fighting silting rivers, deteriorating forts, and intractable swamps in both the land and men, he had become a man so many could count on? That afternoon he was offered command of the military and naval forces of Virginia at the rank of major general. Virginia was Richmond once again.

Who were they? Lee was born gifted; Jackson was self-made. Lee was urbane and ceremonious; Jackson was recently rural and strict. Lee was bound by kin to the most influential families in the state; Jackson had only Laura. Lee was at ease among boys, men, women, slaves; Jackson was correct and on guard among boys, men, women, slaves, at ease among rules. Lee could dance and play the gallant; Jackson had extra-large feet and a frugal tongue. Lee was not above irony; Jackson abhorred irony, did not understand it, thought doubleness in his fellow man a halving of his worth. Lee delegated authority and kept his autocratic desires to himself; Jackson aggrandized authority and desired a communion not bound by this world. Lee took energy and incentive from all around him, tried to give back better than he got; Jackson, fiercely self-regulated, generated his own energy and incentive, and forced it on a world ignorant of its interests. Lee took refuge from action in thought; Jackson gave to action all the desperate uncertainties of thought and took refuge where others knew terror. Lee, when all wars were over, wanted nothing more than to please; Jackson knew that the giving and taking of pleasure ensured wars until the end of time. Lee was a gentleman, dressed accordingly, and performed acts of courtesy even in the waging of war; Jackson was not, did not, and would never. When it came to the eyes, ears and lungs, heart and stomach, Lee was a healthy man;

Jackson had a hypochondriac's distrust of his eyes, ears, lungs, heart, and stomach.

Still, he came. . . .

But it was not easy to leave that valley with Yankees in it, and before coming, he wondered whether reinforced he might not be allowed to drive two prongs northward to rout Frémont and Shields once and for all, converge on Winchester, and from there rip into the man-and-munition-laden underbelly of the North. Lee said no, although he knew that with an army of 40,000 driving for the Susquehanna, Jackson would have drawn McClellan's Army of the Potomac after him like a vortex. Still, he said no. I did not simply want to liberate Richmond. I wanted to destroy our enemies. We were a state, a confederation of them—a nation. I wanted one massive battle on the peninsula, and then I wanted peace.

For more than a week Jackson remained in the valley, the first two days astraddle the Blue Ridge in an impregnable position at Brown's Gap. When he received word that instead of occupying Port Republic, Frémont had withdrawn up the Shenandoah as far as New Market, he sent cavalry to take Harrisonburg and brought his men out of bivouac to the more restful area near Weyer's Cave. Lee sent 8,000 fresh recruits marching through Richmond under General Whiting on their way to the valley and made sure the Northern spies saw them. He silenced the press to give the illusion of secrecy. To all appearances, the valley army was being reinforced for a drive into the North, but General Jackson he swore to a deeper secrecy yet. From Weyer's Cave, Jackson wrote his wife. He told her nothing. Before the war they had vacationed there in the parklike forests, touring the cave. He asked her whether she remembered. He called her his *esposita* and told her of God's intercession on their behalf at Port

Republic. He asked her to ask herself whether a place as beautiful as the Cave and its surroundings, indeed, as the entire valley, would not prompt an aroused and merciful God to intercede. Then he informed her that he had crowned the army's much-needed week of rest with a communion Sunday for the entire Stonewall Brigade, during which he, like the most humble foot soldier, had renewed his faith in Christ— but he told her nothing. He loved her dearly, he wrote to her as though only the most flattering of language could keep the candle flame of his love alive in the winds of war, he wrote to her as if only she—steadfast, stainless and far away— could satisfy his hunger for heaven. But he told her nothing. The land was aswarm with spies.

He ordered Colonel Mumford with his cavalry to harry Frémont all the way up the valley to Strasburg, to maneuver with such vigor that the Yankees could conclude only that Jackson followed with his entire force closely behind. Shields had already retreated to Front Royal, where Banks was to meet him. One look at the map showed the distribution of forces in the valley to be approximately what they had been when Jackson began his celebrated campaign. As if nothing had changed. Yet everything had. The Yankee generals would not now turn their backs on an undefended area for fear that Jackson would appear there. The forces it had taken to defend an area would no longer do. After Jackson's successes, they needed more. Once again, McDowell would be called away from McClellan's right wing to help contain Jackson's advances. But Jackson would not be advancing north. Frémont, Banks, and McDowell would strengthen defenses at Strasburg, Front Royal, and Winchester, but Jackson and his army would march southeast to turn the right wing of the Army of the Potomac that the reassignment of McDowell had left in the air. Everything had changed. The moment of the South's great opportunity was upon it.

Lee stood before his map. For months, map ranging had been his passion, his consolation, and the measure of his loss. Pittsburgh Landing was a calamity, regardless of what the press and his fellow officers had cared to make of it. Albert Sidney Johnston was dead. Before Pittsburgh Landing, Forts Henry and Donelson had fallen. There was this man Grant. It came home to him through maps. Map plotting had allowed him to keep his wife and daughters out of the Yankees' path until McClellan and his army had spread out over the peninsula like both the James and the York in flood. But McClellan had graciously passed Mrs. Lee and her daughters through his lines, and Lee now had them in Richmond. He had found them lodging on East Franklin Street in a house that a Scotch philanthropist and admirer, John Stewart, had made available. But his wife, so recently mistress of Arlington, did not take well to living on charity, and her arthritis was worse. His daughters had wrapped themselves in a taciturn cloud. Nonetheless, he had them, and for the moment, at least, he knew they were safe. But he didn't have Jackson. Before, without real authority, he didn't have the right to him, but now he did—and this, he knew, as for a final time he studied his map of the valley, was the moment to call him back. He would do it as Jackson at the battle of Port Republic had called up Ewell, Trimble, and Taliaferro with that astonishing display of desire. He would do it now.

And Jackson came. Behind him he left a corps of disgruntled officers who would be told nothing of the army's destination. He would tell Quartermaster Harman, since the men would have to be issued rations and ammunition for the march and battle ahead; and he would tell Major Dabney, who in those moments when Jackson was otherwise occupied would continue to pray to God. But no one else. As at the start of the valley campaign, word passed up and down the column of battle-tested men that Jackson had gone crazy.

They marched over the Blue Ridge and exchanged the lovely Shenandoah for an exhausted littoral of pine barrens and overgrown farms. At Mechum River, Jackson crowded them into 200 small freight cars and rode them down the Virginia Central Railroad to Gordonsville. Off their feet and herded into the airless cars, their speculation turned bitter, mutinous: Washington? Fredericksburg? Some guessed Richmond. Banks and Frémont thought Jackson was driving up the valley toward Strasburg once more. History never tires of repeating itself. The Northern press saw the Valley Campaign being replayed. Lincoln did. Anna Jackson knew only that her husband was revisiting the haunts of their ever-mindful love. She suspected she was pregnant—her secret. Jackson's was not his—it belonged to Lee. For the first time in his life, he was operating in a world of secrecy more tenacious of purpose than his own.

At Gordonsville he sent cavalry down to Frederickshall to stop all civilian traffic. When he reached Frederickshall himself he called a halt to the march, and on a Sunday, June 22, arranged to have Major Dabney preach. During the sermon, as frequently happened, he fell asleep. He dreamed he was writing letters, petitions, requisitions, battle orders, with the same fervor with which he would pray to God. All his correspondence was addressed to General Lee. Every piece of it reached his hand; all of it was approved. He awoke strangely refreshed. That night he asked to have his breakfast served at the usual hour the next morning. Well before that he had stolen out of his host's house and by breakfast time was far along on his way to Richmond, accompanied by two aides and a guide who were to address him only as a colonel. He was at that moment, during that ride of fifty-two miles and fourteen hours, the most revered man in the entire South. His superior was not then revered at all.

Did he, Stonewall Jackson, approve? He did not. At a

depth in himself that he rarely visited, he wanted it—wanted it badly—but at a more familiar depth, he felt only the presumption and discomfort, and longed for an opportunity to cast it off—this reverence the South had shown him. He would be an anonymous colonel, badly dressed, slouched in the saddle, eccentric as a coot, riding to a man who had ordered him to report at the home of a certain Dabb family, in the rear of the Confederate lines on a Nine Mile Road, by four in the afternoon. He arrived shortly after three.

The others—Generals D. H. Hill, A. P. Hill, Longstreet and Stuart—had not yet come.

Jackson dismounted and stood, dust-covered, before a small two-story clapboard house, situated on a knoll, three-quarters surrounded by a split-rail fence. But he didn't report. The man who appeared at the door dressed in long gray and gold, gray-headed and -whiskered, stepped down off the porch and reported to him. He wore no sword, although Jackson would believe he heard one. His walk through the afternoon heat was measured and contained. Nothing about the man was overbearing. The face was compassionate and pained, decidedly so, as though to say, "It's a shame, a shame." What was? Looking straight through Stonewall Jackson's clear blue eyes, what did Lee see? Whose future? Whose life? Whose death?

Uncharacteristically unsure, Jackson began to raise his right hand to the bill of his kepi cap. Lee stopped him by placing his hands on Jackson's upper arms, arms broader and stouter than his.

How did Lee address him? It was well known that he always called his men by their rank. But Jackson was much younger. There was something surprisingly soft about the mouth—in rare moments, it was said, he could smile like a woman. The sternness was gone from the cold blue eyes. At the heart of this man of exacting orders and unyielding resolve there was a beautifully pliable quality—and Lee saw it. In a voice to match his expression, compassionate and pained, conveying that still undisclosed shame, he said, "Thomas, you've come."

And Jackson gave it to him, that gift of the revering South, before any of the others could see.

IV

In my own defense I can only say that I wanted to win this war quickly. It must be understood: We are a brave, generous, and contentious people with a passion to gain favor, to excel. We have no aptitude for hard work. When honor in itself fails to yield rewards and our youthful self-regard deserts us, we are no better than our blustering politicians, our unprincipled press, and our merchants for all sides and seasons. I saw no way the South could arm and provision itself for an extended period, and confronted with our own corruption, I saw no way we could maintain the will to win for long. To drive McClellan off the peninsula, I was prepared to take heavy losses. I had four columns—a total of 60,000 men—to move down the north bank of the Chickahominy and four commanders—Generals Jackson, Longstreet, D. H. Hill, and A. P. Hill—whose abilities spoke for themselves. My problem was coordination and the prompt execution of an order. My strategy was sound, militarily precise, but I had to count on men, and as I sent them out along back-country routes, I had to count on the vagaries of weather and roads. I expected McClellan to retreat from his position north of the Chickahominy; everything consisted in converting his retreat into a rout. But that depended on perfectly coordinated pressure across a broad front, which in turn depended on men, weather, and roads. Jackson, my fastest marcher, arrived six hours late with his army, and Powell Hill, my most impetuous general, led his into battle early. McClellan's forces, instead of fleeing, inflicted heavy losses and retreated, under cover of night, from Mechanicsville to an eminently defensible ridge just east of Gaines's Mill, which looked onto a small and deadly swamp called Boatswain's. The fact that a battle was fought there—a battle we won—may have cost us the war. While so many officers and soldiers were displaying their heroism McClellan, with the bulk of his army, had begun an orderly retreat across the peninsula.

I thought I knew McClellan to be a correct but cautious man who would never attempt a daring counterstroke against Richmond for fear that we would trap him there. But perhaps McClellan knew us better than we knew him. What he offered us at Gaines's Mill was a chance to liberate Richmond —for as his army withdrew from its position north of the Chickahominy, it was clear that he was lifting the siege— and a chance to die gloriously in the act. A rout could have meant the end of the war, but a glorious death meant the end and immediate apotheosis of a Southerner's life. Perhaps McClellan knew that about us and gave us the chance. It wasn't until five o'clock in the afternoon that I was able to complete my line and begin a general assault that would drive the Yankees off that ridge, but until then I watched acts of heroism that took my breath away. I believe that some of my officers went crazy with their courage. When 60,000 men assemble to give battle there is confusion, there is aimless fear, riotous boasting, and desperate speculation, but there is something else. For a man seeking to hold to his wits, there is at the heart of that great uncertainty something as strange and forbidding as another element, and as tempting as an absolute singleness of purpose. There is clarity, but at a price. Men of the mind who live to make war must at last give in to it and swill it from the air as though it were an elixir. I do not give "it" a name—whether courage or madness or emboldened devotion. We are a passionate people. We have decided on the forms that our passion shall take. The drawing room rallying of our men and women is a small, artful drama; it is quick and keen and chaste, and for those who participate in it—as I have—a satisfying whole, means to nothing but the pleasure of its own completion. Yet I can imagine a time when the pleasure of coming to close, chaste quarters shall seem a sham and men and women shall prefer to greet each other in hungriness and gore. I do not wish to see those times. We are a passionate people, and I do not give "it" a name—only a form. I try to.

Yes, I saw acts of heroism that day. I saw men rush to their deaths as if nothing they'd known in their lives could call them back from the promise of the moment before them. I saw men—enlisted men, officers—run into Boatswain's swamp and run out, mud-coated, transformed. What must the Yankees have been thinking? Here come these men, filling the pauses in the cannon and musket roar with their shrill, yipping yell. Here come these officers—mounted, sabers drawn, their faces flush with fierce exultant smiles—and what dark service are we asked to provide them? Astonished, the Yankees shot them; they blasted them with grape. But McClellan knew. These are your brave Southern soldiers; one of them is said to be worth ten of our like. They ask only for their deaths. Give it to them.

How else to account for the heroism of these men? My brave officers knew what I knew—that the South must win at once or burn itself out—and each of them—yes, it was the measure of their devotion, their love—was a South in flames. But how was I to lead them? At Gaines's Mill the Army of Northern Virginia—all 60,000—had made their pact. Battle-sworn, they had offered their lives in exchange for their deaths, and those who survived would renew the offer at the first bugle call. Meanwhile, McClellan and the Army of the Potomac had escaped. Now I would bring Generals Huger and Magruder out of our works at Richmond and in place of pursuing McClellan with four columns, I would pursue him with six. Could I coordinate six? With the taste of their deaths fresh in their mouths—and I knew the taste; it tasted of the log I had lain behind in Mexico; it tasted wonderfully of the lizardy desert and dust—how could I hope to hold them to a plan of attack?

I swung Longstreet and Powell Hill around to march down the James and form my extreme right. Holmes I positioned on their immediate left. Huger, whom I expected much of, occupied my center, striking from the west toward McClellan's obvious route of retreat across White Oak Swamp. Magruder I feared would falter, and I positioned him just to the left of Huger, where that officer, if necessary, could steady him. D. H. Hill's column I combined with the Army of the Valley and put under General Jackson's command. Jackson was to occupy my extreme left. He was to harry McClellan out of the north and, as my other columns struck at his flanks, crush him from the rear. Before McClellan reached the protection of his gunboats on the James and a new base of supplies, I had mapped out his destruction.

He was not destroyed.

The victorious South was. This is history.

Gaines's Mill stirred the blood of all my men except Magruder and Huger, whose blood was stirred by their own ambitions. The peninsula, an ancestral land for both my wife's family and mine, became our enemy, suddenly foreign and baffling to every foot. Roads were missed and roads were mis-taken. Heavy rains fell just as we were ready to ford a stream. The Yankees left loot. They fired their magazines and burned enormous supplies of bread and bacon, but for the eyes of every foot soldier they left something to stop and seize. We marched encumbered with Yankee leavings—this is history. In field hospitals the Yankees abandoned their wounded to try our conscience. We treated them. For every second we delayed, the creeks rose and the swamp that in the best of weather was spongy became a bog. In the battle known as the Seven Days', we spent four of those days in futile pursuit. I studied my map, dry and intricately routed like the veins in a leaf. I thought: There's a pattern there, there are many patterns, and then there's one to save the day. When Magruder stumbled, I moved him over to Longstreet's immediate left. When Huger delayed before an abatis the Yankees had thrown up along his route, I allowed Longstreet and Hill to engage the enemy at Fraser's Farm, an engagement we paid for dearly. But Magruder and Huger weren't the real problem. I looked at my map again. I am not an impressionable man, but as I studied my map more closely, I seemed to be staring down the smokily lit shaft of a nightmare. History. Before the partially destroyed White Oaks Creek bridge, General Jackson sat sleeping under a tree.

My first thought surprised me as much as my vision of the sleeping hero itself. I thought: I knew that it wouldn't work. In the pine forest behind him his Army of the Valley—20,000 strong—lay waiting for orders, and I said to myself, I knew that it wouldn't work because that army's commander is not the man for ensembles. The mistake of this campaign was to think that many men's visions could be as clear and compelling as one's—as his, or mine. General Jackson's sleep was profound and morose. His batteries exchanged fire with Yankee batteries in the swamp, and he could not be roused. His aides tried and failed. He had only to contend with a rearguard Union force, and news was to come that a concealed crossing of the creek could be effected safe from deadly sniper fire 400 feet downstream, but he was to hear that news with a gaze so absent and indifferent that he might still have snored. Awake he slept, more intractably than ever, and I thought: The demands he has made of himself, the rigors of his marches, his spartan diet, his protracted prayers to God, the great effort of keeping the contents of his great heart secret, the pointlessness, the silliness of much of the praise, his fear that he might choke on it, his vigilance in resisting it, his vigilance in resisting so much else—he has exceeded capacity, he has stepped through bottom. The swamp before him was the rack and ruin of forest—spindly dead trees fallen into the crotch of their neighbors, vines like moccasins climbing the trunks, the entangling underbrush, the mire beneath it that meant nothing was rooted, nothing free—and here, I thought, it had happened, here he had stopped. This man of the valley and marcher of mountain passes had surrendered before the turgid unloveliness of this swamp. I watched him the rest of the day as we frittered away our chances, as the horror of Malvern Hill began to take shape. Harvey Hill led a regiment across the creek to show General Jackson that it could be done, and he looked on as though at a theatrical performance he'd seen before and knew to be dull. Wade Hampton rode up to inform him that that crossing downstream had been bridged, and he walked away. Into the late afternoon the expectancy of the day grew dramatically, and then began to turn sour. The men wanted to move. Yankee artillery had been tearing down pine boughs and scattering cone, and the men had spent long enough in their ignominious holes waiting for their deaths. The officers wanted to lead them. The trains were up, and even the teamsters had begun to grumble. General Jackson, unapproachable, led them into the night. At supper he went to sleep with a biscuit between his teeth. He awoke long enough to say, "Tomorrow, gentlemen, tomorrow we shall do something," before consigning the teeth-marked biscuit to the fire and finding his cot.

History.

And I knew—too many men, too much sharing out of secrets. Too many generals wanting more of the discretionary powers I allowed them and too many wanting and needing my praise. Too many and too much, and I had neglected the best of my generals, allowed McClellan to escape and lost the war. For Jackson could have driven into the rear of the retreating Union army and split it like a lightning-riven oak. But I had taken him for granted. And there that night, tragically after the fact, I made a vow not to neglect him again; and another vow: not to make him fight his way—this marcher of valleys, this dancing master of mountains and valleys and their secret passes—through another swamp in his life.

When he fought his way through this swamp the next day—and when Huger got untracked on the Charles Country Road and Magruder returned to his senses and our line of advance, and when Longstreet and Powell Hill regrouped after the fierce, brief battle of Fraser's Farm—McClellan had found the only high ground thereabouts and drawn up his army behind it, the ridge known as Malvern Hill. I make no apologies—except to the restless souls of the men slaughtered there and to their grieving families. I knew what I was looking at. Just beyond this ridge, and we would come within range of the Yankee gunboats on the James; if we were to destroy McClellan on his retreat across the peninsula, it would have to be here, where he had taken an all but impregnable position. Precisely at that moment our chances were the South's, and they were very poor. We blasted that ridge with our artillery, and the Yankee batteries—superior to ours, consisting of more rifled pieces better pitted and deployed—fired back. In midafternoon we attacked. Men who had missed their opportunity to die gloriously at Gaines's Mill got their second chance here. Thousands did. Not a single Southern soldier came within 200 yards of the crest. That hillside was carpeted with our men. Into the night and the next morning, those who had been cheated of their fiery deaths moaned for water, some for a bullet in the brain. I make no apologies. Richmond, city of politicians, gay-hearted scandalmongers, disputatious journalists, lovely short-lived girls, had been liberated.

The next morning McClellan was down on the James. General Jackson wanted to attack him there, in the shadow of their gunboats. He looked refreshed, invigorated. I took him aside. While my other generals rattled their sabers, while General Stuart and that remarkable young artillerist Colonel Pelham threw harmless howizter shells into the enemy from Evelington Heights, I took General Jackson into my tent and said, "No, not here. We've been right, you and I, all along. The best way to get the Yankees off the peninsula is to strike into the North. I want to send you north. I shall do what I have to do here, then follow you. You will find a blowhard named Pope commanding those armies you left beaten in the valley. He is the only one of the Northern commanders for whom I have no respect. We shall use him to draw McClellan after us, out into the open—far from swamps, flooding rivers, and Yankee gunboats. A routed Pope will give us the Army of the Potomac again."

With our dead unburied we had no reason to smile, but General Jackson's small delicate mouth—which I had last noticed opened stuporously on an unchewed biscuit—broke upward on a firm, winging line. I gave him Powell Hill's division. I divided my army into two corps and made him commander of one. I would have Jackson to maneuver and march with, Longstreet to throw in his weight. Why should I have gone on to tell him that regardless of how I reorganized our forces, we would never get the Army of the Potomac as advantageously as we'd just had it and lost it here? He would leave my tent, I knew, and go to his own to write to his wife. Why should I have told her that, the woman who safeguarded his tender sensibilities so that I might have him fierce and unafraid? The fact is that at that moment, I couldn't have told him because I didn't believe it myself. The firm relish in that smile, the excited leap of clarity in those eyes —no, in that moment I believed not in history or my historical forebodings but in him, Thomas J. Jackson, freshly risen from his swamp.

I sent him north. He needed room to maneuver. Without space and screening valleys he could not be in three places at once, as the Yankees believed—and I gave it to him. As I saw him off, he had already begun to suck on his lemon, balm for his dyspeptic stomach and a stinging goad for his mind. He was no horseman. Slumped in his saddle, catnapping, dressed in the plainest of garb, he would be mistaken more than once in the twilight of his marches for a drunken private who had commandeered an officer's horse. A drunken private he would be. He practiced humility as rigorously as most men study their trade. His trade was to be humble and fierce. The press swept past these contradictions in him, calling him phantom, magician, superhuman hero. Let him be humble and let him be fierce; let him continue to be whatever he's been, and the South will win. Martyr him to our cause. His life is strange to him? Life among the Yankees will be stranger—and much less tolerable. Send him north.

I did. Little more than a month later, I would follow. I had divisions to rearm and supply; I had officers to replace and reassign. Beginning with our president and followed by his ministers, I had politicians to assuage. I, too, had a family, a wife who had disregarded the misgivings of her father and married an army engineer who had gotten her with child after child. The males among these children served. They had male cousins who fought for the cause of the North. The daughters felt the acrid war smoke inflame their eyes and crack their cheeks. They watched an invading army trample the only life they had known, and they expected their father to bring it back. Out of the dust, out of the mud, the bowers of their girlhood stripped as grapeshot strips a wood—and their father was to bring it back.

I had first to write my battle report, the battle I now called

'Seven Days'. "The regret that more was not accomplished gives way to gratitude to the Sovereign Ruler of the Universe for the results achieved." The enemy losses, I claimed, exceeded ours. Did I suspect the truth, suppress the truth? Our losses exceeded the enemy's because our time didn't—because our time was short. Did I need to revisit those battlefields to recall the truth? I did not. Images of those first bloody battles would be with me the rest of my life. From my elevated vantage points at Gaines's Mill, Fraser's Farm, Malvern Hill, I saw once more our regimental lines advancing on the run against the Yankee positions. The Second Virginia, the Sixth Alabama, the Fifth Texas, the now-decimated Twentieth North Carolina. I saw the regimental colors, the fixed bayonets, the mounted officers, sabers drawn, the muscles of their horses shining through the drifting smoke. The lines in their advance reminded me of certain elemental motions. Wind rushes over still water in similar surges. Lines of fowl in flight waver and whip just so against the sky.

Suddenly my vantage point changed, and I had to be careful in guiding the hooves of my horse. The bodies were no longer bodies but butchered mass. Here lay half a face in blackened shreds, the remaining half belonging to the bugged eye of a terrified boy. Here strange, ungainly postures for arms, shoulders, necks; strange inimitable wrenchings of knees and undershod feet. Nothing here was at rest. Rest, as a quality of life, had gone out of it and all that remained was refuse. It was the inertness of their youthful wasted matter that appalled me; yet those who moved were somehow worse. The motions of the charge, the sporting spectacle of a man in rhythm with his life, were now dull convulsive shudders, the spasms of a flailing knee, a clutching hand, the fitful digging motions of a body that would bury itself and could not. What moved on the field of battle now were the contemptible leftovers of motion, and I picked my way around them—these boys, these young and middle-aged

men—unable to rid myself of the suddenness of their transformation and the mean interminableness of their dying. The
aides who walked their horses behind me were silent. The
enemy had gone, fled over the next hill. The real enemy, of
course, remained among us, stiffening the contorted shapes
of all that no longer moved, like a vagrant breeze looting the
life of all that still did. I did not write this in my battle report.
I wrote that their losses exceeded ours and that God's sovereign will had been done.

And I ordered another march; I plotted another maneuver
to lure the enemy into another moment such as this. Pope,
whom McClellan had begun to reinforce, had to be flanked.
If we could get in behind him and cut his line of supplies, we
could force his withdrawal to Washington. If we could send
Pope and McClellan back to Lincoln and Stanton trussed up
like truant schoolboys, perhaps we could force them to sue
for peace—if we wanted peace. If we'd be content with it. It
was Jackson, of course, I had to send. Once in Pope's rear,
he could destroy the depot at Manassas Junction and I could
follow with Longstreet in hopes that Pope in his retreat
would decide to give battle. The difficulty lay in getting Jackson, with more than 20,000 men, around Pope undetected.

I joined him at Jeffersonton on a day of heavy August heat.
In addition to Jackson, I called Longstreet and Stuart to my
tent for a battle council, but General Jackson had already
ordered a table to be carried to the center of a nearby clearing
and the clearing to be cleared. We met there in the center, in
the sun, in the dust of trampled grass and flowers, and in the
lingering odor of horses and mules. We were public in our
secrecy, but we should not, Jackson observed, be overheard.
Aides, chiefs of staff, general officers, kept their distance. This
was not my way, but it was of Jackson that I was asking the
barely possible, and it was in that unshaded clearing that we
talked. "Out there," and I pointed beyond the encircling
pines, "there is no swamp, but there are no valleys, secret

passes, and macadamized turnpikes either. The heat will be intense. In place of the Shenandoah to inspire you, you will have pine barrens and untillable soil. Can you get in Pope's rear?" General Stuart, the thrill seeker, the scurrilous wag, boasted that Stonewall could get in Mary Todd Lincoln's rear if he thought he could catch Abe with his pants down, and General Longstreet, the odds rater, narrowed his eyes doubtfully. General Jackson simply asked if I would be coming up with the First Corps. I said that I would. I said perhaps he could have General John Pope primed and blowing for battle, and that somewhere around Manassas we could do it all again. History repeated itself, did it not? Endlessly, if we gave it the chance. General Jackson had already begun to stride off to his staff officers when I called him back to the map. I showed him the route, the shape of my trap.

His men cooked three days' rations. Three days' rations meant they would be marching and although they did not know their destination, they were aroused. They if not their commander read the newspapers and knew they were the celebrated foot cavalry; knew that when feats unprecedented in the history of modern warfare were about to be performed, they were the men who would be called upon to perform them. The rations were all they would have. Jackson would drive beef cattle for later, no commissary. To his wife, he wrote: "The enemy is restless across the Rappahannock, but so, my pet dove, are we." In his predawn prayers he asked God to take this army of willing but exhaustible men and spirit it around the Yankees. He prayed for a miracle, if a miracle it took, or for the simple perseverance of a mule.

Then he was gone.

The first day—marching Ewell's division, followed by Hill's, then Taliaferro's—they make twenty-five miles. The men quickly consume their rations, preferring to carry them in their stomachs rather than on their backs, then to accept whatever nourishment countrymen run out from their houses without breaking stride. In spite of the heat, there will be no stragglers on this march. Jackson has ordered the first straggler shot. This, he has told his men, is what all the drilling and discipline have all been about. They will do their duty. He will march them into the headlines of history. Just before Salem, where they will bivouac for the night, Jackson dismounts and stands on a large rock to watch his men pass. The first brigade by, Forno's Louisiana, laboring after twenty-five miles of heat, begins to cheer him. He gestures for no cheering, for absolute quiet, and sends an aide to explain that the enemy might hear the cheers they raise for their commander, might even from the warmth of the cheers deduce Stonewall's presence. Uncheering, the men bare their heads and wave their caps; silently they mouth their praises. Each brigade by—to the dusty thudding of feet, the squeak of leather, the tinniness of tin—does the same until Jackson can take it no longer. It is self-idolatrous, it is stimulation for the men, and incentive for the next day's march, yes, but it is glory-grubbing of the worst sort and there on the rock, the silent adoring roar of the men swelling inside his head, it is loathsome in the eyes of God.

If God is looking.

The next morning following the route of the Manassas Railroad they cross the Bull Run Mountains at Thoroughfare Gap, where the heat abates a bit, then wind through a region of stunted foothills and small farms where the Yankees, under the marauding Pope, have driven off the livestock and burned the rails. Soon, hungry and hot, they are marching out onto the plain at top speed. With Stuart now covering Jackson's van and flanks, they make for Bristoe Station on the Orange and Alexandria Railroad—Pope's main line of supply. From a handful of surprised Yankee malingerers, they learn that Pope suspects nothing. From quizzing well-wishers along the route, the men learn that only a company of Yankee infantry and another of cavalry are stationed at Bristoe Station, and encouraged by that news, those who are about to faint or surrender to fatigue hold on.

Jackson's first job is to cut the railroad. Once they reach the station, he sends in a brigade of infantry and cavalry under Colonel Mumford to subdue the Yankees barricaded in the town's hotel. A supply train passes that the men try to derail with wooden sills. It crashes through and steams south to bring the alarm to Pope, but within the half hour another approaches, and this one Jackson meets with an opened switch. He has never brought down trains before. When the locomotive leaves the tracks and tumbles down an embankment, the concussion in the ground where he stands is so heavy that the last Yankee citadel among those Cities of the North might have fallen at his feet. The locomotive, he sees, is christened "The President." On its steam dome a picture of Lincoln has already been shot through by a Confederate ball. The men are not so much interested in omens as in loot, but the cars the locomotive pulls after it down the embankment are empty. The next thing they derail is an empty troop train, but the one after that brakes in time and backs out. It, of course, as it sounds the alarm north, will be the last.

Train wrecking has left his men with an enormous hunger and thirst, and seven miles north at the main supply depot of Manassas, there are equally enormous stores of provisions for Pope's army, plus sutlers' wagons in abundance with delicacies the likes of which a Southern farmboy will never have dreamed of—and that their commander, a mountain boy, an abstemious, lemon-sucking zealot of self-surveillance, will only have dreamed of, never touched. He is wary—not of the Yankees but of the ostentatious ease of his success. He is reminded of the ease with which he and his brother, Warren, had floated the Mississippi, the daily delirium of having only to steer. They had floated to a malarial island and Warren's eventual death. Nevertheless, at nine o'clock that same night, he orders General Trimble and two weary regiments from Ewell's division to secure the stores at Manassas Junction before another token force of Yankees there can destroy them. By dawn Jackson is marching the rest of his army, leaving only Ewell behind to slow any major advance of Pope from the south.

At Manassas he counts one hundred new train cars full of food, uniforms, bedding, and boots. Past that he doesn't bother to count. Up and down the tracks at the junction there are warehouses that are likewise full. He posts his guards. These spoils of war now belong to the Confederate army, not to the poor, plenty-crazed Confederate soldier. Pulled up around the main depot like cattle hogging a trough are the sutlers' wagons, and these, he discovers at once, contain goods whose very names seem pagan: canned lobster salad, pickled oysters, French mustard, cakes and wines and Havana puros, lawn and linen handkerchiefs, underclothing more suitable for a dandy of the nights than for a soldier on the march. He posts more guards. He has marched this army on the muscle and sinew of disciplined desire and will not now allow it to sink into the fat of Yankee corruption. When an aide comes with word that the entire second floor of a warehouse is filled with barrels of whiskey, he orders them rolled down into the street and destroyed. Jackson himself remains for the axing open of the first, ceremonially on hand as though for the setting of a cornerstone or the exampled execution of a deserter. The whiskey fumes spread through the dusty depot streets the aroma of dissolution, of all things illicit, and it is with grave satisfaction for these grave times that Jackson watches the contents of the first barrel find the street-side ditch. Before the second can be broken open, a courier from the cavalry he has posted outside of town rides up to tell him that a body of Yankee infantry is approaching from the north.

Soon Jackson has marched a division of men out of town, deployed them behind a low hill, and prepared to annihilate what is now seen to be no more than a brigade of unsuspecting Yankees advancing toward Manassas. Again he is struck by the enormity of his success, by the ease with which one objective after another completes itself before his eyes. Is he like those men he has left behind in the junction overindulging? Is it possible to overindulge in the killing of Yankees? Artillery fire—his own—puts a temporary end to his self-questioning. Had Colonel Poague, his senior artillery officer, waited three minutes longer, the entire Federal brigade would have marched into Jackson's trap. He does not rebuke Poague. He orders the killing of Yankees until the Yankees run, leaving behind as casualities or prisoners nearly half their force. He does not order the pursuit of the remaining half. Instead he leads his men back to Manassas, where the guard he has left around train cars, warehouses, and sutlers' wagons will have been insufficient, he knows, to hold off the hungry depredations of Hill's division. Only his presence— Stonewall Jackson's—would have done that, and he was out of town, feasting on his own.

He returns now to find men swilling whiskey from the ditches. Cavalry have loaded their mounts with stolen goods, sides of bacon hanging off the pommels. Privates are stuffing their haversacks with cakes, candy, fruit, and canned goods of all sorts. He rides right by one soldier seated in the sun, and this young farmboy is so engrossed in the cans of lobster salad and bottles of Rhine wine he is consuming that he fails to see the man above him who could sentence him to death for what he has gobbed on his fingers. Manna, Jackson thinks. Manassas. This—this dusty, overcrowded, supply-laden depot—is *their* vision. Must I make them exchange it for mine?

Beside the private he sees in the dust six empty cans of lobster salad and an empty bottle of wine. "Soldier," Jackson says, and the members of his staff, expecting a tongue-lashing, caution their mounts. But their commander's voice is more questioning than stern. The boy is digging toward the bottom of his seventh can and delays a moment in raising his eyes; when he does they swim up. An instant later, they focus and, "M'god!" the boy says, "G'nral Jackson!" and he struggles to his feet. Jackson eyes him, his back uncharacteristically straight in the saddle. The private is all bones, and only his drunkenness has loosened the squint in his eyes—the sun-and-dust-and-rain squint of the men who make his marches, Jackson knows. He says nothing. His silence is like dogs flushing birds from a field; it flushes speech from the boy. "We done it, we sure done it, G'nral! We done kilt all the Yankees and et all their food! We got 'em comin' and goin' today, ain't we, G'nral! I reckon this is 'bout the best they got!" Then he holds up the nearly empty can of lobster salad. Suddenly grinning and emboldened, with his other hand he holds up the wine to his teetotaling general. Not a little amazed, Jackson asks, "Aren't you full?" Now the grin takes total possession of the boy's face. "Full, G'nral? This don't fill you up. This is like lyin' down in the best feather bed them Yankees got. Try some, G'nral, be mah guest."

And with the can before him, chest-high, Jackson can see the gluey rings the boy has traced around the sides with his finger, see dabs of bumpy white paste flecked with green down near the bottom. He can't see lobster or smell it but he can smell something both bilious and sweet, and he knows he would rather taste his own vomit. "You finish it," he tells the boy. "You finish them all. Make them last the war because we're going to march."

Suddenly the grin dies on the boy's face. The expression that replaces it is so desolate and frank, and makes itself so powerfully intimate with his commander's mood, that Jackson recoils a bit in the saddle. "G'nral," the boy asks, "is this war gonna last long?" And Jackson snaps back at him, although he doesn't feel right about it—he knows he should either pray for him or have him shot. "Long enough for you to eat that," he says, pointing at the three cans the boy still has left to go.

He orders the men to take what they want, what they can fit into their haversacks, and the rest he orders burned. All of it. Warehouses and train cars full of it. An army's staples and its degenerate frills. Word has reached him that Pope has begun to threaten Ewell at Bristoe Station, and he knows he must choose his most favorable ground for battle and march to it at once. Everything has gone according to plan—in truth exceeded plan. Yet everything also seems like an illicit largess, like an outstanding debt payable the instant Pope strikes, and Jackson wants Lee. History repeats itself if we give it a chance, Lee has told him, and he marches his army to the battlefield of Manassas, where he earned the name Stonewall for standing like one. There he waits for the First Corps.

On the first day of the second battle of Manassas, had Pope chosen to overwhelm him he could have—although Hill, Ewell, Taliaferro, Trimble, and almost everybody else fought like demons. Jackson did, too. Still, Pope could have overwhelmed him. A stone wall was exactly how he felt. He would have stood there while Pope blasted away stone after stone, until he lay instead of stood, a disassembled wall that somebody else—a farmer in need of a boundry, a soldier in need of a defense—could have reassembled in time for history in a later year to repeat itself. But Pope didn't blast him down, and Jackson waits not for some future farmer or soldier but for Lee. He doesn't pray that night. Too much has already been given—and perhaps wasted. He does not want to remind God of the fact.

The next morning he awaits Pope's redoubled attack or Lee's arrival along the same route he himself took from the west, the prize to be fought for himself, this utterly undistinguished stone wall. On abused stomachs his men dream of fierce Yankee reprisals, of teams of Yankee surgeons cutting up into the lungs and heart, down into the groin, searching for the sweet smear of cakes and candied fruits, the taint of lobster, oyster, and foreign wines. Midmorning, they spy before the blue silhouette of Bull Run Mountain a rising cloud of red dust. By then Pope has begun his shelling. If these are Yankees coming up from behind, then Jackson's army is caught and every man will die with his vision. If it is Lee— if it is Lee, then the war will go on. Jackson sends Stuart out to meet the van of the advancing force. It is Hood at the head of his brigade, driving Yankee outposts as he comes—Hood heralding the arrival of Longstreet's corps, Longstreet, in that moment, vehicle for Lee. Hood locks onto Jackson's extreme right, and the next brigade, Law's, locks onto his. In that way Jackson's and Longstreet's corps form a crescent-shaped front with a breach left enticingly open in the center, into which the Yankees will later charge only to be enfiladed by S. D. Lee's superb artillery fire. Then the crescent will close. History will have twice come to the plains of Manassas. History, the buzzard, circling patiently above these reenactments of blood.

It is mostly bluecoats I guide the hooves of my horse around now. We charge a retreating foe as passionately as we charge an entrenched one, and these mangled boys in bloodied and smoke-grimed blue are the slag shapes of what our passion has burned through. The plain is full of them. We ran them down. Jackson's corps bore the brunt of Pope's attack, and Longstreet's did the killing as the Yankees showed us their backs. But they showed us their guns, too, and fought as they ran, artillery covering their retreat, so that we lie among them on the trampled earth in a fratricidal wash of blue and gray. It has begun to rain—heavily. The rain will hamper our pursuit and perhaps allow Pope, like McClellan, to claim that he has pounded the enemy and voluntarily withdrawn, but if nothing else, it will cool this excreta of our bloodlust long enough for us to get it underground. We must bury our dead. We must purge ourselves of what we have purged and continue on. The freshly killed men now lie steaming in the rain like offal. We must bury it. Soon I will join General Jackson in his tent. I will greet him at the conclusion of one of his finest hours, the march and the stand off of which future heroes will measure themselves. He will not admit that for an instant his trust in me was shaken, but the eyes will fix me, appeal to me in a way they haven't done before. I will take his hand. I will squeeze through the deference in his grip until I feel him close. Then, Thomas, I will say, now we know how far I can send you and how long you can survive. Marching with Longstreet to reach you was the long, dark night of my life. If it were not for our success, I would keep you at my side. But we have succeeded, Thomas. When Pope and McClellan cross the Potomac, Virginia will be free of bluecoats. We have made this moment memorable because we chose to risk everything. Everything, he will repeat, and in that way discover the true dimensions of what we have risked. I will nod. I will say these things. As night hides the horror of the unresting dead, as rain cools their heat, I will tell Thomas Jackson of the strange mating history has assigned us. He will hear me out, a stone wall with two chinks for the blues of his eyes, knowing it all already, only waiting for my words.

Part Two

LETTER FROM THE
WILDERNESS

You might not remember. There were many days when I caused you pain. It began at the supper table, a summer evening with hours of daylight left. I was thirteen, Evie eleven, Johnny seven, and you had been among us for nearly two years. During that time I credited you with nothing except putting bread on the table. Good bread, I admit. We were having butterbeans, a squash soufflé, and chicken casserole that evening. I remember the dishes because the squash and the casserole were two of Pearl's best. No one was likely to pick at his plate. Yet before supper was well under way I had caused all of you to pick and, before it was over, to stop. In short, I seemed to be able to control your appetites. Once I understood that, I didn't stop until I'd snuffed them out altogether.

Someone had stolen the magnifying glass off my key chain. Remember? If it was you I couldn't accuse you of it, not even in my most father-avenging dreams. But I could accuse Johnny and Evie, knowing full well that you would hear all that I had to say and, if it had been you, quake with your guilt.

I said, "The thief is right here! My pants were hanging on my closet door all the time I was at the pool. My key chain was in my pocket. My magnifying glass that you both like to play with was on my key chain. The key chain is still in my pocket, but the magnifying glass is gone. This is an easy case." I went on in a swaggering, menacing, grown-up tone. "All I have to do is find out who's been here while I've been gone. You, Evie, and you, Johnny, have been here all day. Whichever one of you it was can confess now and save yourself a lot of trouble later on."

Johnny got flustered and those sunny, wide-open eyes of his darted over the table, landing on you. He said you'd come home for lunch, and that anyway he'd gone to the grocery store with Mother for a long time that morning. Evie, with Johnny making such a scene, put up an imperturbable front, remarking loudly enough to be heard in the kitchen that Pearl had cleaned that morning and that she had been in my room.

"Whachall want?" Just that quickly, Pearl appeared in the door.

"Nothing, Pearl," I said. "This doesn't concern you." And when she'd gone grumbling back to work, I uttered weightily, "No, this is a family matter."

At this point I expected Mother to intervene, but she didn't. You wanted to give the appearance of deferring to her, but right there at the start I knew there was more to it than that. You, I decided with my thirteen-year-old's wishful intuition, were staying out of it because you were powerless. As always, you sat like a toad occupying one whole end of the table.

I started on Evie. Like Mother, she knew the trick of absenting herself, but unlike mother, she could never stay gone for long, and when she came back she paid the price. I accused her of showing unusual interest in my magnifying glass, of really liking to swing it out of its shiny red convex shell and look at things like her fingerprints and hair, and in the mirror at a mole beside her mouth. I also said she knew better than Johnny where I kept the key chain and, taller than him, could easily reach into my pants pocket and pick it out. Above all, she knew I would not take my keys to the swimming pool where Johnny, a mere seven-year-old, might imagine I possessed lock after lock.

Suddenly her blank face flew open and then closed in a shaking, protesting fist. She didn't have it! She didn't take it! It was stupid! It was crummy! She never looked at that mole in the mirror!

And I calmly transferred my attention to Johnny, who had never stopped shaking, and thieves shook, I reminded him right off the bat.

Was he going to claim, like Evie, that he didn't like my magnifying glass? Was he going to perjure himself, too? Because that meant lying under oath and, when he finally did get caught, would make things a whole lot worse. Did he take it? Why did he take it? What had he done to it? Where did he have it now?

His face, Father's in miniature except for the rounder cheeks and the slightly protruding ears, grew red. He sputtered he didn't have it, that someone else had it. He swore he'd tell me who.

I laughed at him. Another trick of thieves, I said. They always want to lay the blame on somebody else.

It was then, in response to a pleading look from Johnny, that Mother said maybe it had dropped off and no one had stolen it. Had I thought of that?

Like the most seasoned detective, I smiled and smugly shook my head. "Not the way it works, Mother," I informed her. "It was on my key chain. If it falls off, it falls off in my pocket or in my hand. It's not in my pocket and"—slowly I turned up an empty palm—"not in my hand."

I let a few more suspenseful heartbeats pass and declared, "No, someone in the family's a thief."

Neither she nor you uttered a word to the contrary. Then, as if searching the table for clues, I noticed that the servings of casserole, squash, and butterbeans had barely been touched. I made a mental note to tell Johnny that criminals confronted with their crimes could never eat when I suddenly realized that all four of you couldn't be criminals. I was prepared to admit that the magnifying glass could have fallen off the chain as Mother had said, even wound up in some place other than my pocket or hand, and that neither Johnny nor Evie had necessarily taken it. Yet, like guilty thieves, you were all picking at your food. What did this mean? What if I put my magnifying glass to work on this?

And I found, of course, that I possessed the occasion and the power to ruin your meal. For whatever reason, Mother was not going to stop me. You, I divined, could not. In Mother's and your presence Evie and Johnny might have assumed they had protection should things go too far, but they would be wrong. The only thing that could stop me, I then realized, was for someone to return the magnifying glass or, when I slapped my pants pocket, to feel its silver-dollar convexity where I hadn't before. Surreptitiously, I felt down the length of both pockets again. It was most definitely not there.

If you recall this, you'll remember the rest. I grilled Evie and Johnny. When they showed signs of coming apart, I softened my tone. When they began to relax, I hardened it. I went on until the picking at the plates grew more sporadic and, one by one, as though stricken by a profound sort of listlessness, you laid down your knives and forks altogether. Instead of interrogating now, I began to snipe —drawing annoyed, ouchlike exclamations of innocence, nothing more. I leaned back. I ominously leaned forward. Just as I was about to stretch and yawn, I fixed on Johnny or Evie and demanded a belated "But why?" Finally they only muttered. At the ends of the table you and Mother said nothing. Except to settle yourselves after a sigh, you barely moved. It worked, I said to myself. I may not have my magnifying glass, but I've stopped this meal and the field is mine. It was then that I began to feel disgust for myself, disgust in my empty stomach and, with it, after only an instant's delay, an estimate, already in words, of how vicious and mean-spirited a person I'd become. My only defense against that view of myself was to assert myself more aggressively than ever. And after glancing at you both —you might remember the exaggerated defiance in that glance—I tore back into Evie and Johnny, exclaiming that the time had come to get to the bottom of this, that I was tired of pampering them, that I didn't want to call the police in on this but if they forced me to, I would. Then, some betrayed brotherly look from Johnny or some particularly little-girlish whimper from Evie, and I'd begin to feel sick with myself again. I liked being the bully! The better the bullying, the more I liked it! Shut a whole family down and leave Pearl's best meal cooling on their plates, and I couldn't get enough of myself! Sick! And I'd start to shrivel up in contrition when I'd want to know why. What had this family given me except one dead father, a live one whose ingratiating touch was like a toad's, a mother who couldn't tell the difference, and a magnifying glass that someone had taken out of my pocket. "Goddamn it, give it back! Give it back!" I shouted, including Evie and Johnny both.

Mother didn't send you a signal because even on the periphery of my vision, her stillness was absolute. My shout was out. Evie and Johnny had both started, and my stomach had already begun churning up the bilious remorse that would take the shout back. It was your idea. You said, "I've got a little unfinished business at the drugstore. Like to come along?"

I had never wanted to in the past. You realized, I'm now convinced, that I was rushing back and forth in a cage of my emotions and could only end by doing myself harm. At the time I didn't believe you understood anything and had made the offer with the same slack-cheeked self-deprecation you offered everything else. But I was rushing back and forth, and I jumped at the chance to get away from this browbeating of Evie and Johnny, although I said to them, as if I expected them to sit there until I returned, "We'll get to the bottom of this later." To you I said surlily, "I don't care."

You drove your big Buick like a toad. That's how you sat up behind the wheel. That's how you stopped and started and with a sad clumsy, caution made your turns. I don't remember the evening itself, except that it was summer and all summer evenings to a boy my age, in my part of the world, came on lovely loan from his father when his father came home from work. How I resented your trying to take his place at that after-supper hour. I couldn't lord it over Evie and Johnny for long without despising myself. You saved me from that. But sitting there beside you in a machine you drove like a tank, and my father would have given a twirl, I could lord it over you— it was what you asked for, you lived your life in a servile squat. I only needed the chance.

I expected you to give it to me. "Maybe you shouldn't be too tough on Evie and Johnny ... maybe you should wait till after supper," I expected you to mumble sheepishly. Lacking that, I expected you to offer to pick me up another magnifying glass if I agreed to lay off my little sister and brother. Either way—go easy on a thief or sell your thirteen-year-old principles out for a newer and better toy—I would have an opening. But you didn't give it to me. As we drove through town, the only time you came close was when you asked me what I looked at through my magnifying glass. You really hadn't overstepped yourself there, regardless of how narrowly I had defined your space before you intruded into mine. I probably said, "Stuff—insects and leaves," and you mentioned—no more than a mention—that you had a microscope at your prescription desk if I ever wanted to look at anything through that.

I said no! I didn't want to look through that. I said that I wanted my magnifying glass back! You may have nodded, but wise old toad that you were, you didn't utter another word.

At the drugstore you parked in the alley in back. You said you'd only be a minute or two, but you left it up to me how I wanted to spend the time. You also left the door open for me and the alley flies. When I went in and closed it I smelled you. It was a thick and proper, scared and nauseating smell that those pills gave off—your smell, the smell you'd brought home for two years now. On your desk you'd set out your microscope. To be fair, it may have been there all along. While with a piece of laminated plastic you sat counting off maroon pills, I considered taking the risk. I said I said no! Take that damn thing out of my sight! But the risk of making the sort of fool of myself it would take weeks to overcome was too great. So I said nothing. The microscope looked heavy and much handled, also arcane. There were three focusing dials. To see anything, I would have to let you show me how to operate it. Then what would I look at? Nothing interested me right now . . . nothing—and I frowned as I said it; it was not the sort of discovery that at thirteen I was accustomed to making—nothing but myself.

You did not see the frown. You had already counted the pills out into their bottle and gone to the large black typewriter, where you stood typing out the label. You were like your typewriter—like the bottom-heavy microscope, like your drugstore, like the street of low, close-shouldered stores . . . like the town? Who, you? You and not Harry Brazelton? Now I grinned, but with the grin came a shiver and perhaps for the first time in my life a flutter in the knees. You weren't all those things. How could you be? I began to understand then how one person in a peculiar state of mind could seize on a likeness to such an extent that it generated more and more of its kind, eventually, in the name of that original likeness, taking over the world. Again, that one person was me.

I waited for you in the car. When you locked the back door you had that bottle of pills tucked up in a little white bag and the look on your face you gave to your customers. It was solemn but faintly smiling at the same time. At the heart of it, I believe, was a wish for good health and the understanding that good health would fail. "I've got to run these out to a lady outside of town," you said obligingly. "You're welcome to come along, or I could drop you off at home."

What did I care? Why not? I'd go along.

Instead of backing out, you drove all the way down that alley. When we came out, I was able to see past the intersection of the next street over part of the furniture store my father had owned. It was one street off Main and, along with most of the other stores on the block, had an old rusted tin roof slanting down over the sidewalk. Weather-grayed wooden posts still held that roof aloft. The "ton" of Brazelton was visible in red lettering on the front window, for the man who had bought the store from my mother would have been a fool to have changed the name. Behind the lettering I saw the outline of an armchair, a table, and lampshade, and I recalled that I had had permission to sit where I chose in this shadowy store that smelled of dusty fabric and wood. Then you, my stepfather, who would not back out of the alley and spare me this painful sight, turned left and swung Brazelton Furniture out of sight altogether.

Provoked, I wanted to snap at you, curse you if I dared, and I couldn't. It was the turn you made almost every day of your life, the alley you always drove the length of. When you said, "Think I'll stop off on the way and get an A&W," I did not feel at odds with myself, only strangely weakened and a bit hollow-headed, as if I'd just recovered from the flu. The carhop was a girl who'd drunk Cokes at your soda fountain. You greeted her by name and asked if the mugs were frosty today. She took one look at me, made a prissy sneering face, then smiled at you. After you ordered I said, "Yeah. I'll have one, too."

We drank root beer. I thought as usual you were trying to nickle-and-dime your way into my good graces, too timid to ask for what you wanted straight out, knowing you wouldn't get it, and that the failure would represent lost ground. But that wasn't it, was it? You really did know something about the self-perpetuating war of emotions I was going through. With barely a word, you were prescribing a cure and serving up medicine to me too, weren't you?

You said, "More?" That was all. I shook my head.

You drove us out a narrow road cut in the pines and red clay. When I think of kudzu, one of the images I retain comes from that three- or four-mile drive out of town. I see it leaping in a great transformational splash up over the pines on both sides of the car, as if the road we drove down were a trough between waves. How rich with restful promise movement along that valleylike trough suddenly seemed. It may have been the first time I was struck by the kudzu's beauty, and the first time beauty came accompanied by a yearning for something I couldn't even name. But it—my perception of the kudzu—didn't last long. Mostly I was sulking—and my sulks were losing strength, giving way to a torpid state of watchfulness, like a sentry half-asleep. I watched you. Sleepy or not, I would have sounded the alarm and fought stubbornly if you'd given me the chance. But low in your seat, both hands on the wheel, you drove without looking once in my direction. The same expression—solemn and faintly smiling; resigned, but not to what most people are resigned to. Your presence with me in the car then was like that of a dog, say, trying to take a man's place. If I could accept the switch in species, I would find the dog unobjectionable. For a moment—in the pines and kudzu, in the evening—I think I must have, and as dog, as a subspecies substitute, you became unobjectionable to me. Then you made your turn into a sandy front yard, real dogs barked, and you spoke.

You said, "A ninety-year-old lady lives here with her niece. But *it's the niece who's sick. The niece won't come to the hospital in town because then her aunt would be alone. Sometimes when one person gets sick it starts a chain.*"

You shook your head. Then got out and walked to the front doorstep of the white-frame bungalow, familiar at once to the two heel-sniffing dogs. The niece must have answered your knock. I saw a blue housecoat and through the screen door a shape vaguely like yours, sick in the breakdown of its lines. That shape was joined immediately by a thinner, grayer one. They would open the door and insist that you step in. There would be dessert, homemade ice cream, and stale cookies. You would press the medicine on them and protest that you couldn't. They wouldn't take no, and since they wouldn't, you would have to motion to the car where I sat, taking the liberty of opening the screen yourself so that they could get a clear look. I would see them and they would see me; you would use me to extricate yourself. Probably I would be misrepresented. I was not your son, not even your stepson by consent. "The children need a father," my mother had explained when she married you. But no one had consulted me. I realized then that thanks to those hospitable old ladies —one sick and the other ageless—I was about to be given the opportunity to give you the tongue-lashing you deserved. "I'm Harry Brazelton's boy! Harry Brazelton's boy! I've got nothing to do with you! You haven't even got the right to tell those old ladies that Harry Brazelton's boy is riding in your car!"

But they didn't give me the opportunity because you wouldn't let them. You gave them the medicine. You said no, then something kind to them. The two heads never turned toward the car. They moved in close, becoming one head behind the dark mesh of that screen, and in their fondness and affection looked only at you. Harry Brazelton and his boy never entered their minds.

Driving back, all that you said was, "Said she felt better. But I suspect she just wanted to make me feel good. After all, they've got to believe in me to believe in my medicine."

I said nothing. I was tired—hungry, I suppose, since like the rest of you I had only picked at my food.

At home, thinking perhaps of the offer of ice cream you'd turned down, you said, "I should have had a float at the A&W. A root beer float. How 'bout you?"

I said no. Then I told the truth. I wasn't hungry. The fight had gone out of me. I felt no affection for you and wouldn't, voluntarily, for years. But I wanted to make peace with Evie and Johnny. I especially wanted to make it up to Mother. And I did, never suspecting at the time that that had been all you'd intended, all you'd allowed yourself to hope for. I thought then that the best that could be said for your behavior was that you hadn't antagonized me; the worst and most pertinent, that you'd staged just another flop. One of many. Yet why, then, lying on my bed, tired and unhungry, learning to live without my magnifying glass, did I walk the length of the house to the kitchen to stick my head past the swinging door and observe you digging vanilla ice cream out of a gallon carton with a battered old spoon Pearl used to stir the soup? I didn't look long. In fact, I think I pulled my head out with something of a start. But why look at all? Why worry about the hunger you were left with after another unsatisfactory outing with Harry Brazelton's boy? I don't know. I was thirteen, Willard, and not in my right mind. . . .

V

It was not pretty. This time it would have been better if it had been. The army that crossed the Potomac in early September of 1862 came to liberate the oppressed people of Maryland, whom Lee expected to rise. But that army was badly depleted by stragglers. Many who had sworn to defend their homeland would not fight in the North. Many were ill. Those that crossed were forced to subsist on green corn, since it would not have done to raid the larders and barns of the very people the army had come to save; diarrhea, fatal and farcical to marches, was the result. Few shoes, few untattered uniforms, and the sharpness of autumn evenings coming on. No, not pretty.

Because of minor riding mishaps, both Lee and Jackson crossed the Potomac in ambulances. Once in Frederick, Jackson, hero of the press in both the South and North, was besieged by admirers. The populace did not rise, but the women did. They oohed and aahed over Lee, they rallied with Stuart, but they became aggressive raiders of talismanic scraps from their hero Jackson. Armed with scissors they cut the buttons off his coat, locks from his thinning hair. When they could no longer get to his person, they cut strands from his horse's mane. He was driven to his tent. For one entire day he remained there. The following day, disregarding the advice of Longstreet, Lee sent Jackson back into Virginia to take Harpers Ferry. Perhaps he wanted to make Jackson a gift. Perhaps, recalling that Jackson had been a young artillery officer on the slopes of Chapultepec and a professor of artillery at Virginia Military Institute, Lee wanted to make an artillerist's dream come true—for Harpers Ferry was commanded by three heights. He drew up an elaborate but not impractical plan to take it, drive into Maryland, lure McClellan out of Washington, reunite his army, engage McClellan and defeat him on open Yankee ground. Wrapped around three cigars to keep them fresh, a copy of these plans—Battle Order 191—came into McClellan's hands. How is unimportant. The pettiness of how makes historians blanch. The Northern high command smoked the cigars and McClellan, deliberate to a fault, tried to race now before Lee had his army back together and his ground chosen for a fight.

Jackson did not know Lee's plans had been discovered. Once he had reached Harpers Ferry there were problems getting divisions in position on Mary's, Loudon's, and Bolivar heights, but still, knowing no reason to rush, Jackson may have savored the taking of the place one day too long. To his wife he wrote only that God had entrusted it into his hands. It was rich in men and munitions. Those men were superbly outfitted. The commanding Yankee general, when he rode forward to ask for terms, glittered in his brass, boots, and epaulets like a pagan prince, and Jackson, dressed in the clothes he slept in, his cap pulled self-effacingly low, demanded an unconditional surrender. Once he got it he provided generous terms, as though attesting to God's munificence, savoring, too, his surrogate's role. Who can pretend to know a man's mind in the warring emotions of his heart? Perhaps he lingered that extra day because he wanted to make sure. Or perhaps he lingered because he understood it was General Lee's desire that he both savor this gift he'd been given *and* make sure.

The town itself, built at the confluence of the Potomac and

Shenandoah rivers, the streets cobbled and tiered, the houses made of the reddish stone of the area, may have held him. Or the rivers—spume-scribbled, broken by sun-whitened boulders. He was, we remember, a man of the mountains, snug towns, shallow flashing rivers. Perhaps for that day he was a boy again. His sister Laura, playmate of his youth, may have spoken to him. His dead brother, Warren. . . . Perhaps it is possible to succeed so gloriously in war that the world offers itself to you as though the first blow had never been struck, exactly as though the conquering general had forever remained an unbloodied and uncovetous little boy. An illusion, perhaps, of one day. . . .

That day for Lee had been the most anxious of his command. McClellan had moved on him as McClellan had never moved before. Harvey Hill, with a force of 5,000, had been ordered to slow the Yankees down at Turner's Gap in South Mountain while Lee maneuvered to the west and Jackson accomplished his mission. The night before the day of his sternest test, Hill watched the campfires of tens of thousands moving toward him over the plain. An army advancing by night would extinguish one campfire as it lit another, but Hill, fixed on the farthest line of the advance, would see no lights go out. It was as if campfires bred campfires, soldiers soldiers, and the Yankees knew no limit to their numbers, no death. When he had overcome his amazement, he sent a courier to warn Lee. Puzzled, suspicious of the veracity of Hill's vision, Lee, nevertheless, sent Longstreet to his aid.

Thousands of fires moving over the plain at night, fires shadowily suggesting masses upon masses of men. . . . Lee would have read what Hill would not have, and might have wondered, however briefly, about the supernatural working-out of a curse. When Birnam Wood to Dunsinane came. But he was not MacBeth. The South steeped in its own blood, as was the North, but he wanted only an end to the hostilities and an honorable peace. If at the instant of engagement when his battle blood rose, he appeared to want something else, he would not be deceived by appearances.

The next day a fierce battle was fought at that pass, and Hill, before Longstreet could reach him, held off the grandest army any Southerner had seen. While the issue was still in doubt and passes to the south and closer to Harpers Ferry were also being threatened, Lee must have doubted the wisdom of the entire invasion. Men grew out of that mountain, which they then sought to overrun. Jackson had not yet reported victory at Harpers Ferry. How much could his men and that mountain take before his entire front collapsed? If the Yankees got between him and Jackson, what recourse would he have but to run? Where, caught north of the Potomac, could he run? Questions he must have asked. And the question that underlay them all: How had the cautious, self-doubting McClellan become another man? For we are one man, are we not? And the man we have shaped for today will be the man we awake to tomorrow, will he not?

But dramatically, Hill held. Lee pulled back off the mountain that next night and took the best ground that the circumstances allowed—Sharpsburg, with the Potomac at their backs in case a sudden retreat into Virginia became necessary, turned to face the broken terrain around Antietam Creek. Now if Jackson would only come. Then, leaving Powell Hill behind to process prisoners and captured munitions, Jackson on a night's forced march came. Now if McClellan, finally confronted by his reassembled enemy, would only revert to the man Lee knew him to be and hold off his grand assault until the next morning, when Jackson would have his men and batteries fully deployed. Then McClellan reverted and held off.

The battle broke with dawn and ended with the fall of night, when crazed or cold soldiers fired the haystacks scattered over the field and roasted alive the wounded who had crawled there for relief from the day's smoke and sun. At day's end lines remained essentially the same. The earth, however, had changed. The creek water. The woods on Lee's extreme left. A cornfield that Jackson gave perhaps 3,000 men to get, or simply not to give up. The dry, autumn-tinged air had changed, soured by the smell of powder, burning flesh, and blood too heavy for any breeze to dispel. The battle moved from left to center to right—morning, noon, and afternoon—and by the time it was over, hardly a Southern soldier survived who hadn't withstood a Yankee assault. The battle was a draw; 20,000 died. The next day no one wanted the field.

Not that earth, water, and forest; not that trampled, blood-ied corn; not that air.

There were heroes. The North will know its own, but on the Confederate left Jackson was a hero; Jubal Early wanting only a throat to claw, an ear to hear his imprecation; John Bell Hood, the fearless, joyless, saturnine Texan. In the cen-ter, Harvey Hill repeated his showing on South Mountain; Robert Rodes, with the very force of his self-regard, shored up a crumbling front. On the right, Robert Toombs and David Jones distinguished themselves, but there the waning afternoon belonged to Powell Hill, marching up from Har-pers Ferry in the red hunting shirt he always wore into battle, his men dressed in new, captured Harpers Ferry blue. Before the Yankees realized this march-weary but battle-fresh divi-sion was not their own, Hill had mended the breach and driven the enemy back beyond Antietam Creek, where the battle that cloudless day had begun.

Only the ground had changed—now and for time imme-morial planted with canister and shot; and the water—run-ning then and thenceforth over a bed of abandoned weaponry, horse, and human bone. The foliage in the shred-ded forest would grow back, but out of what mutilated fiber, nourished by what blasted root? Men would eat corn again, but on that field where the few stalks left standing resembled the standing dead, nothing would grow again that a man would dare to put into his mouth. It would take a change in the battle-laden air, something to indicate a curse had been lifted. But the air has not changed. . . .

It was a battle unlike any Lee had fought, and not the battle he'd wanted to show Marylanders, whose imagination he was trying to excite and whose loyalty he had hoped to win. It was fought with a series of dull, bludgeoning blows, and he learned that day how dull and fearlessly inflamed men can be. He was grateful to them. Rushing from front to front behind his reserve-depleted lines, he orchestrated the battle as best he could, shifting brigades as alarms sounded and breaches appeared. He knew the enormous danger in which his country stood. Routed, badly beaten here, and Lincoln would order his army to Richmond. He knew how thinly his lines were drawn. Nothing short of genius would keep them patched together until McClellan's characteristic caution overtook him and he withdrew. Shuttling brigades, even divisions, Lee displayed genius. The lines held. With every moment a crisis and with ammunition almost gone, the lines continued to hold. Still, Lee must have been bored. This was time-marking of the most aggravating sort. There must have come a moment during the day—perhaps there at Bloody Lane when the center almost collapsed, perhaps when Burnside stormed his bridge and threatened to roll up the Southern right—when Lee understood what drudgery killing was, what dull and daily fare. He was a soldier, and he did it. He sweated heavily in his parade coat and, racing from front to front, lathered his horse. He loved his men—this roused and ragged South—but the dull swap of men killing only to be killed must finally have worn him out.

Did he show it to the younger man? Battle blood raging that morning when they conferred, would Jackson have seen it even if Lee had allowed it to show? . . . A stand-up fight. Unfortunately, Thomas, this too is war . . . It is unlikely.

Even when they were looking at Lee, Jackson's eyes were on that cornfield. Into its head-high camouflage he had sent Lawton and Hays. Hooker's first furious assault had driven them out. He had called for enfilading artillery from his left, more from his right, and then had sent in Hood's division, reserving Ewell's division commanded by Early for a flanking maneuver on the left. Hood and Early had driven back Hooker, but Union artillery preparing the way for Mansfield had stopped their advance. From the vantage point of Dunker Church on the Hagerstown pike, Jackson observed the battle—that harvest of men and corn, each man in his death fall bearing a stalk with him to the ground. How could he have had eyes for the philosophical resignation he might have seen in Lee's? The battle count was the corn count—it was that simple—and for that morning portion of the battle, both sides concentrated their fire there. With the stalk-shattering thud of artillery and the hissing of ball and shot through the leaves, how could Jackson have heard that note of somber consolation Lee offered for their shared fate? He couldn't have. In many ways that morning the two men did not meet. Only when Lee asked him, "Will you be able to hold here?" would Jackson have seen and heard his commander clearly. Then, intensifying his ardor for the fight with his devotion to duty, he would have answered, "We will hold."

Later an aide will bring him fruit, and Jackson, eating apples and peaches, will watch the battle conclude. When the Yankees withdraw, it will be to put pressure on the center, but he does not know that yet. Instead he contemplates an advance. He sucks a lemon now, a sure signal to those staff members present that he is studying how to strike a blow. But he has almost nothing to strike with. The cornfield belongs to neither the South nor the North, but to the dead, and all that he can do is order the wounded to be brought out. As men go in to get them, the Yankees shell the field once more. Most of the remaining stalks disappear. Some writhing wounded no longer writhe. The men running in must run nimbly, for bodies cover a large part of the ground. Some fall and cover ground that those running in behind them will have to run around. Still, wounded are brought out. Mounted, Jackson watches them being carried into Dunker Church. Their faces are smoke-blackened; around their mouths there's a ring of deeper grime where they have bitten off cartridges in their frantic attempts to load and fire. Many are insensate, groaning out of some deep reservoir of pain. Instead of a cross over his laboring chest, one still-uncynical boy clutches an ear of bright yellow corn—a rare find for someone who's been forced to eat his corn green. It is then that Jackson turns to one of his aides and says, "God has been very kind to us today," an assessment the aide will ponder for the rest of the battle—if he survives it—and into the night, when the cornfield, the Bloody Lane, the area around Burnside Bridge, will be alive with the scuttling sounds of men scavenging shoes and clothes, the deliberate, more desolate sounds of men searching for their fallen friends—and always, the moaning of the still-undead for water, water. How has God been kind?

For some the following day is worse. With very little left to withstand a concerted Yankee charge, Lee is still reluctant to order a retreat. McClellan is not known for being able to concert much of anything, and should he decide to renew the fight piecemeal, Lee would be there, happy to oblige. But McClellan does nothing. Instead he decides to stand his ground. His army exhausted and unprovisioned, and facing another at least twice its size, Lee now calls for a retreat. It is a hard decision to make, its effects harder and bitterer still on Jackson, the culminating logic of whose every thought has been to strike into the North. Does Lee order Jackson to see to the evacuation of the rear guard, or does Jackson take the duty upon himself? Lee withdraws his army at night. Dawn finds the last infantrymen—soldiers from Ewell's division, men who have survived that fierce, bloody harvest of corn—splashing across the Potomac, and Jackson sitting his horse in the center of the stream. A masterful retreat, he's been taught, can be as efficacious as a masterful advance, and as beautiful a thing to see. This retreat has gone uncontested. All the men—when these last few cross—are safely back on Southern soil. Yet it is foul. It is a walking death. With the rising of light, Jackson sees streaks of blood in the water from the opening wounds of the men crossing above him. He hears their tired mutterings—no words. No one stops there in the center alongside their famous general to deliver a judgment on what it's all been worth. They are, he knows, brave, obedient and God-fearing men who would follow their leader to the gates of hell, and their blood—pale and pink in water the fast-clarifying color of steel—they will willingly give again, but none of them now raises his head to see who it is that is overseeing their retreat. Jackson waits until the last one, the runt of the last company, steps up onto Virginia soil, before reining his horse from north to south and crossing himself. Instantaneously, the mountain-cooled water of the Potomac washes clean and the brief invasion of Maryland is over.

VI

For the next two months the Second Corps of Lee's Army of Northern Virginia became the Army of the Valley once again. Jackson camped outside of Winchester—city of beloved memory—with orders to slow down McClellan's advance should the Yankees choose to move south through the Shenandoah Valley. When it became clear that McClellan was advancing south east of the Blue Ridge, Jackson was recalled. The march to Lee's right on the heights above Fredericksburg covered 178 miles and took five bitterly cold days. At Fisher's Gap the Army of the Valley converted back to Lee's Second Corps. At Gordonsville Jackson received word from his sister-in-law in Charlotte, North Carolina, that his wife had given birth to a daughter, Julia. The birth date was November 23, 1862. True to his nature, Jackson kept the happy event a secret. A month earlier, Ann Carter Lee (like Julia, named after her father's mother) had gone to the same North Carolina to escape harm's way and been stricken by a mysterious fever. Lee's secret had been his daughter's death. But birth and death were in the air, and neither secret could be kept for long. Annie Lee made way for little Julia Jackson; at Warrenton the Yankees paused in their advance and McClellan was replaced by Ambrose Burnside. The big battle to come would be Burnside's affair and fought on Julia Jackson's behalf. Alone in his tent at Culpeper, waiting for Jackson to come, Lee understood that only now had Annie truly escaped harm's way. Life, his grief instructed him—and his service to his country confirmed every day—was both priceless and contemptibly cheap.

But Annie had been special. She'd been conceived in St. Louis during a period when Lee had had his wife and the rest of his family with him. His other children he had conceived on the run between fort-inspection assignments or the surveying of coastal sites. He'd always managed to find time to get back to Arlington and get his wife with child. It became a joke among the house servants, and although Lee never encouraged the familiarity other masters permitted among their closest slaves—that his father-in-law, for instance, did—he could not censure them or deny them their little joke at his expense because he himself could not reconcile the exigencies of profession and fatherhood with his own conscience.

After the arrival of her first child, George Washington Custis Lee, Mary contracted a pelvic infection she never completely overcame until she was well past childbearing age. It left her partly lame and finally arthritic. But she insisted on having his children. It was her duty and desire to give birth to Lees; the South needed Lees. Her little joke at his expense was that she rarely called him anything else. He was "Mr. Lee" to her—good day and good-bye, sir, as the world called him forth. He tried the other extreme and teased her affectionately as "Mim." There were times when it was a comedy routine or, in spite of her condition, a spritely dance. On those first days back, Mim and Mr. Lee would rally with each other through the whole of Arlington. In the dining room Mr. Lee would eat with a wolfish appetite and Mim feared for the sheep within her fold. In the sitting room Mr. Lee tisked her as Mim sharpened her tongue on those glory-grubbing politicians across the river in Washington who were no match for her and whom she generally despised. Out on the veranda in the evenings, the fireflies winking over the broadly sloping front lawn were all of Mr. Lee's unrewarded good deeds and were Mim's salty little spots of humor sewn in her husband's wounds. In the bedroom she said nothing. She waited for him with her gown folded neatly above her aching hips, and all her keen-tempered spirit went toward the consummation of their mutual goal. She never wrapped her arms around him or clung to his neck. At the moment when her husband—this Mr. Lee—began to gallop, she placed one hand on each of his broad shoulders and with measured urgency pressed home, as if to hold him to the straight and proper course.

This was the great-granddaughter of Mary Washington. She was not beautiful. Her chin was too heavy, her nose too sharp, and her mouth too thin. Her hair barely had the body to sustain the ringlets that fell to each side. In certain moods she tended toward the slovenly. Lee himself was a paragon of masculine beauty. While he was assigned to Cockspur Island the belles in Savannah, many of whom were stunningly beautiful and perfectly schooled, fought for his attention. His attention he gave—through the years nothing would amuse Lee more than innocent flirtation with lovely young girls— but his deep interest, his fascination—he would not say his virginal love but he would say his mysterious desire—he reserved for Mary Custis. He came to understand that what attracted him so strongly to her was the way she violated most of the strictures his mother had set out for him yet left inviolate the values that gave them common ground. If Lee had been taught to hold his counsel, she volunteered hers. If Lee had been taught that watchfulness, self-denial, and close accountability were virtues to live by, Mary Custis, every inch the aristocrat, took by natural right what she assumed was hers. It disturbed and delighted him, this assumption of hers. It excited him. What saved her from being offensive or from spending herself in a stream of opinionated scorn was her extraordinary sense of limits. She *knew* just when to mute an attack or veer off from a point driven too hard. Each of her conversations—perhaps each of her comments—obeyed an artful form, and as long as the form was respected she might press it at every point before desisting and say what she pleased. She pleased to say a lot. When the country split apart and the barbarians from across the river confiscated Arlington, she said it in the most unappeasable way. But she never broke loose, she never cut her lines of communication entirely. Where had she learned this? Lee didn't know. He assumed it was innate which meant that it was a sense brought forward and refined. At the start of their married life there were times when he feared she might sally forth and never come back, times when that mysterious desire for her was at its strongest. His love, perhaps, was born in those instants when she said just what she had to say and stopped, making of a form of behavior she'd inherited something as close-fitting and personal as her own skin.

And because she asked for it, because this, too, formed a part of who she, an only child, must be, he got on her child after child. Then he went away. He'd come back to find them all sick—the diseases that children got, whooping cough, chicken pox, mumps, except that his wife, in addition to her long-standing ailments, got them, too. The house, their wing of it—for he saw no sense in setting up a permanent residence if he was such a transient in their midst—echoed with their long, croupy coughs. He relieved the house servants and attended to the sick himself. He applied compresses, administered emetics, held head-clearing vapors under their noses; he cleaned, cooled, and swabbed. He tried to rally his wife's spirits, but her spirits never seemed as sorely taxed as his. She was just sick. She was broken out, swollen up. Her breath trickled in and out of her congested lungs. He couldn't escape the association that his wife was being worked on by forces that were just as inexorable as those that crumbled forts or silted in rivers, and there were times when the engineer in him should have despaired.

He himself never got sick.

With her face polka-dotted, or her spare cheeks puffed girlishly plump, she would tease him about it: "Mr. Lee, if you weren't such a marvel of manly stamina, you'd have the good sense to take a little rest yourself. You're looking a little piqued, Mr. Lee. I recommend a light case of these mumps." Relieved by her humor, he made his rounds of the rooms. Her humor never entirely rescued him from the understanding that his daughters had inherited her sickly disposition— they had certainly inherited her thinly drawn features and undemur eye—but it softened the blow and gave to his efforts, which might have been as thankless as guard duty or as fruitless as a rote-performed penance, an acknowledgment of gratitude. When he had his wife up and about, he would take her to one of the many warm springs thereabouts. Until the times turned ominous, the conversation would animate her as much as the mineral water, which she drank in enormous quantities. There were Randolphs and Carters and Fitzhughs, plus more Custises and Lees among the immediate cousins, and those they didn't see at these mineral spas they visited at plantations up and down the James. She insisted on her mobility, helped along by Mr. Lee. When she returned to Arlington she was returning not just to a plantation where she was mistress but to candelabra that had shone on George and Mary Washington, and to china that had been presented by the hand of Lafayette.

Then the times did turn ominous, and the Yankees took it away from her. Before someone could put a stop to it, Yankee soldiers had looted the Washington artifacts and spread them over the northern half of the land. The trips the Lees had taken for Mary Lee's health and amusement, General Lee now plotted out for her survival—how to keep Mrs. Lee and her daughters one step ahead of the marauding Northern armies? She refused to leave the state. He reasoned that the closer she stayed to home, the more painful her awareness of Yankee depredations would be and the more precarious her health. To himself, at least, he insisted on that connection. But she insisted that McClellan had driven her from her home once, and would not do so again. It sent him back to his maps. He was a military strategist, and he was a pastor shepherding his flock. The two roles overlapped, intermeshed. A father to his family and to his country—it was not vanity, not boast. In his mind's eye he revisited the sickrooms of each of his children. His three sons had not been sick for long and now served. But his four daughters and his wife—they would never be entirely well; they had not been raised for the rigors of war. He could stand at their bedsides just as he stood before his maps and see the same story told again and again—death if he did not move them quickly and well, not just out of the path of the oncoming enemy but out of a world whose history would always be told from one war to the next.

Finally he had failed. When McClellan overran the peninsula, he had trapped them at the Carter plantation of Shirley on the James—his wife Mary, their daughters Mary, Agnes, Mildred, and Ann. Then he'd passed them through the lines. But because he had not taken Richmond, and because he had not destroyed Lee in Maryland, McClellan had been replaced by Burnside. And Annie Lee, leaving the state to seek safe haven in North Carolina—in actuality she was simply visiting girlhood friends—had died.

She had been his favorite. She had been conceived in the heat of a St. Louis September, when he carried around the smell of river mud in his nose. It took him two years to lure the Mississippi back into its proper channel, and in addition to that mud's stink, he carried around a sense of himself as a sort of Herculean impostor: His success with the river would last only until the next flood. There was a prairie out there

—their bedroom looked out on it, heaving up to the horizon like the breast of the sea—where the river could cut any channel it chose. His response to those finally unmasterable elements was to get his wife with child—at least he could do that. He could even get her back to Arlington before the next St. Louis summer set in. But he could not be in two places at once. He had returned to St. Louis to repair the previous winter's ice damage to his dykes when word came of Annie's birth. He had been present at the births of his other children; it would be seven months before he saw this new daughter. For that reason he would feel like a visitor in her presence, or one of the fond uncles passing through Arlington of whom there was never a shortage. And even though he gave her his own mother's name, he knew there was no way to get those missing seven months back. His wife and other children would tell him stories about the endearing little tricks she'd learned during that time; he could witness for himself the wilier and somehow more endearing tricks she'd learned since then. She remained the most mischievous of his daughters, and because she had the largest, most melancholy-seeming eyes, she could take you by surprise. From the start she got more than her share, and she took it, but not as her mother might have with that naturally entitled air. She took it with a sort of theatrical guile that let anyone who was curious enough see just how she did it but which didn't shame her into giving a bit of it back. She became the family's pet thief; puckishly, she flaunted the code of honor the others sub-scribed to, and no one, least of all her father, held it against her. She was Annie-the-Outrageous, Annie-Who-Lived-by-Her-Wits. She mimicked her brothers' and sisters' honor-bright expressions and turned up with their charms and keep-sakes, the most secret of their treasures, and the most trea-sured of their secrets. Later she would outgrow it. Her face would assume the drawn and distanced, vaguely resentful expression of the other Lee girls—their father didn't fool himself, it was the expression of exile—and the eyes would become as melancholy as they seemed. It was as if the eyes had stagnated. Lee watched that winning, duplicitous light go out of them and grieved for his daughter before her time, vainly hoping that this was all the grief for her he would ever know.

His wife's grief now would be sharply indignant. How much is enough! When will the Yankees go home! In the midst of so much death and desolation, Lee's grief came freshet-clear and fixed on those missing seven months. He had always assumed—he didn't know how—that when this war was over he could make those seven months up to her. Only in that way could he cease to be the most intimate of her visiting kin and become a father. And only a father, he now understood, with seven months at his disposal, could hope to win back from the doom of embittered spinsterhood the young girl who had flaunted them, bedeviled them, provoked them in the most delightful and disturbing ways, and had robbed them blind. None of that was possible any longer. His grief was for life deferred, made permanent now, not for the death of his daughter. It was the sort of loss he had not experienced before, and he didn't know what to do with it.

By now Stonewall Jackson had moved into position on Lee's right. Here at Fredericksburg a big battle was about to be fought, and somewhere within the pounding reach of its guns lay Julia Jackson, newly arrived in this world. Julia Jackson now lived in Annie Lee's stead—that was one way to understand it. Those tens of thousands that faced each other with their cannon and musketry bowed to the same power and the same fate as that fragile little head. That this child might be allowed to live in peace they fought this battle, fought this war—and that was another way to make it make sense. But the gaily aggrandizing spirit of the girl his dead daughter had been still lived in his memory, and studying the foolhardy positions the Yankees had taken, Lee knew there was another. He was not happy with it, it hinted at too much he'd been taught to suppress and promised a bounty that threatened his capacity to humbly receive, but it was not beyond the bounds of understanding that in honor of his daughter and in exchange for those seven irretrievable months of teething and teeming life, this battle had been given to him to fight as he saw fit, given to *me*.

It is cold, cold enough in early December to chill even the Yankees to the bone. Yesterday morning there was half an inch of ice on the Rappahannock. The men are rested, if not warmly clothed and shod. Below us beneath the gelid fog lies Fredericksburg. When the fog lifts I expect Burnside to make his first charge, as if in shelling and taking the town, the Yankees assumed they were entitled to the hills that overlooked it. I *gave* them the town. I sniped at their pontoon layers just enough to make them think that when they marched across the river they'd taken Fredericksburg by force. But I gave it to them and asked God's mercy on those inhabitants too intrepid to leave. The hills, the Yankee officers will be telling their men, belong to them, too. This Lee there above them, that braggart Jackson, that dandy Stuart, that laggard Longstreet—these were the scarecrows they'd run out of Maryland. We did not run. Faced with an enemy that would not renew the fight, we conducted an orderly retreat. The company commanders can lie as much as their press, as much as their vainglorious generals, but the Yankee infantryman will know the enemy he faces.

We did not ask for this war. These thousands who die so that a few chosen children may live—we did not ask for that! They come to us with their might, with the deadlines Lincoln has set for taking Richmond, Mobile, Atlanta. They talk of the abominable practice of slaveholding, and come to set an

131

enslaved people free. Mine they will find free; my slaves I held, knowing that if I didn't they would starve. But that is not the real reason they come. Constitutional questions estrange us, and questions regarding lands as yet unsettled, but that is not it either. They come because even though men among us have grown corrupt and opportunistic in the prosecution of this war, long ago when the Northerner was dedicating himself to the acquisition of wealth and the debasement of nature, we dedicated ourselves to certain civilized standards of living. They come because they cannot tolerate in the countinghouse of their riches our measure of their loss.

They come for our life. We will give them, humbly and with God's blessing, their death.

Our life *is* their death. The terms of this war were decided long ago.

I watch the fog sink into the Rappahannock, the spires and rooftops of Fredericksburg emerge. Across the river, on Stafford Heights, the Yankees have already opened on our positions with their heaviest guns. But our works are well built, our men well entrenched, and we run no great risk from their long-range bombardment. At my side Generals Jackson and Longstreet peer into the fog as keenly as I do for the first glimmer of mustered blue lines. General Jackson would have fought this battle elsewhere, where, after repelling the enemy attack, we would be in a position to ride the last Yankee down. I do not explain that before it begins, this battle of Fredericksburg is all but done. He assumes we are fighting here to protect the supplies afforded by the lower valley of the Rappahannock from Yankee depredations, and so we are. I, too, am the South's commissary, am I not? But what I have not bothered to explain to him is that this battle, the charges the Yankees will mount up these treacherously exposed slopes, will measure to the man and last foot of bloodied earth how badly the Yankees want what we have. That is my secret. Although Stonewall Jackson will fight at his serene and savage best, this is my battle, given to me, for whatever unsearchable reason, by God.

Humble and grateful I watch the fog give way to Yankee lines, batteries, caissons, supply wagons, ambulances. As we can see them, so they can now see us and they open on us from the town with the full force of their artillery—Napoleons, Parrotts, Blakelys, as many as 150 pieces—joined by the thirty- and twenty-four-pound siege guns from across the river. Not even at Malvern Hill have I witnessed such a fierce cannonade. Major Taylor informs me that they're getting off fifty shots a minute, these explosive Yankees. We answer a few of the batteries in town, but mostly we wait. Men will die from this shelling, but the men who will give the Yankees their deaths will live. They stand, Burnside's mustered infantrymen, before the town where Longstreet awaits them on Marye's Heights, and against our right, where Jackson's corps invites their charge. The artillery show is being staged for these poor foot soldiers who will walk into Richmond over a carpet of blasted rebel bodies—so they will have been told.

The fog has now vanished; the day is sunny and cold. Through rifts in the blowing smoke I peer with my glass into the ranks of those infantrymen. The relentless thudding of shells into the earth that shakes them shakes me. Entire lines jitter like men of glass; or it is my glass that jitters. They are young, of course. Their faces are lean and long-chinned. Some have the coarse, burly look of rivermen. Many seem jarred loose from their senses and strike out wildly at their fellows-in-arms, kicking their heels like colts. In the cannon din I imagine I hear their hysterical "hi-hi-hi." Actually, it is the sound I *see* throbbing in their throats. Then—some time has passed—I hear the sound itself—a high yapping pant— and in the sudden silence of artillery on our right, Yankees are moving against Jackson. They advance unopposed to within one hundred yards of our lines, then all our batteries open on them at once. They pull back and try again. Some-body from the horse artillery—it will be Pelham, Pelham the darling who seems to grow younger with every fight—is enfilading them from the extreme right, shifting positions adroitly when they get his range. Then I hear the musket volleys like great jagged rips in the firmament; moments later I hear the men firing at will. Yankees have broken through a swampy gap in Jackson's center. I wonder whether in his desire to come to close quarters, Jackson has given the enemy that gap on purpose. Yankees slog into it, and for a tense quarter of an hour I peer into gray leafless wood and smoke. Then I see the Yankees stumble out of that gap and once in open field, where our artillery can blow holes in their fleeing ranks, they run. And that is their death—small stick figures in blue, running in puppetlike jerks, faceless, facedown in the mud.

No, I am wrong. That is not their death. Not only God's ways but the magnitude of His works is unsearchable. I re-main humble and now, as witness to God's intercession, truly amazed. I recover my senses by recalling that child . . . by recalling those children: the one that God in His mercy has taken from this sinful world; the one that God in His mercy allows to remain. No, not their death. Only a rehearsal. Burn-side now moves the bulk of his army against Longstreet. Just before town, a canal runs parallel to the river. From that canal to a sunken road within which our marksmen crouch four-deep, there are 400 unobstructed yards. The terrain slopes upward. Behind the road there's a steeper slope—Marye's Heights—where our guns are well pitted and trained on that open ground. That's where Burnside makes his charge. He sends his men not in a flood of blue but in waves. I have stood on a beach and watched waves break upon the shore, wondering at the thousands of miles that each wave has traveled in the making; then at my boot tips I have mea-sured the inches—the inches!—by which one exceeds or falls short of the other. Spume expired on the sand, and what was left of each wave dragged rock and debris with it as it withdrew. That is the battle that Burnside fought that cold afternoon. He sent his men in waves. The artillery decimated them; during some charges the marksmen crouched in that road got off no more than a single volley. The Yankees came from before noon until dusk, and members of my staff simply lost count of the charges. We measured them instead by how close they came to that sunken road, and except for one crazed boy shot only after the marksman could count the freckles on his face, no wave came closer than forty yards. My men did not even get their boot tips damp. Breaking uphill, the entire Yankee assault then poured back down in a tide of human carnage, and it was the wave makers—Generals Burnside, Franklin, Hooker and Meade—who were swamped.

And again I am wrong. The waves were not waves but men. The men were mostly boys going "hi-hi-hi!" with their last, terrified lungsful of air. They ran not just over open ground through a "galling fire," a "withering fire," a "plunging fire," but over their own men, trampling the wounded and dead before they fell. Humbled, grateful, and amazed but also fascinated, for the entire afternoon I watched them come on. I know that during that time General Longstreet reported all to be under control, and that Colonel Alexander of the First Corps artillery assured me that nothing living as we knew it could cross that field, but I don't recall my instructions to them, if I gave any. The killing at Sharpsburg was butchery. This was masterful, predetermined, clean, classical in its staging, satisfying in its ease, and repeatable as often as Burnside cared to send his men and his men cared to obey. He did until dusk. Trampling their comrades-in-arms—they had only to look down at the mangled limbs, the blackened heads, and see themselves one second later when they fell— they obeyed. I understand ocean waves. Sacrifice of this sort, reenacted by boy after boy after boy, I'm afraid I do not. God delivered Burnside to us, but what did Burnside say to deliver those boys? What did he tell them—boys, after all, with the most grievous of their sins still before them—that we had that they as Yankees could not live without?

And am I wrong again, yet again? Is it blue I insist on seeing and gray that I should? Is it gallantry of this futile heroic sort in blue that I find so incomprehensible? If our places were reversed and I told my men to carry that road, take that hill because those Yankees threatened to destroy all that we held dear, my men would leap to it, determined to die in the act. They leapt to their deaths at Malvern Hill, did they not? Aroused in their ardor to the point that only their deaths would satisfy them, what wouldn't they do? They would do this, I know. They would climb the bodies of their countrymen in search of their own incandescent extinction. Would Yankees? Would those cold-eyed, cold-faced boys?

They have. They lie there blanketing the frozen ground as the sun sets behind us. All shelling has stopped, and the senseless groaning of the wounded has risen from those 400 yards as though the earth itself agonized. God has been good to us today. He has stopped the enemy in its advance on Richmond and inflicted losses it will not soon make up. But in His goodness He has also been provident and wise. The thrill of victory has had at its deepest register the thrill of watching ourselves fall. What else but the distanced dying image of one's own self can ever arouse such fascination? God has allowed us to see it all—victory and defeat—and from one vantage point—mine. It was my battle from the start. He gave it to me. He put General Burnside there before the town and me here on this hill. Already the men call it Lee's Hill, for here is where I've stood.

General Jackson, joining me now at the close of day, has not understood the battle it's been. So many emotions I see in what the press persists in calling an inscrutable face. Foremost among them is a thwarted sense of exaltation. He still wants to drive them. He urges a night attack with our men wearing white armbands to distinguish us from them. I shake my head. We would not be distinguishable. It is time to pause. Restraint as a virtue, as a rare sort of pleasure, he has never understood, not in the waging of war. "Thomas," I tell him, and of all those assembled at that moment there are just the two of us—proud, enraged newborn father, father to the newly deceased—"Thomas," I say quietly so that only he of all the living, dead, and dying on these hills can hear, "Thomas, it is well that war is so terrible," and he knows its terror, I watch the blue eyes tense, behind them a dream of domestic bliss about to shatter, "otherwise, Thomas"—and why speak shared knowledge, why utter the superfluous word?—"we should grow too fond of it."

He nods. Why even nod? He bows his head.

VII

My precious darling,

I must now accustom myself to saying "my precious darlings" for you are equally precious to me. Dr. McGuire, medical director of the corps, to whom I have described our Julia's symptoms, agrees in the diagnosis of chicken pox and cautions you against administering an emetic unless the fever rises precipitously. Instead you are to apply tepid compresses of vinegar and water to the face and neck. You may also apply a mild mustard poultice to the soles of the feet. A feather bed will only exacerbate the fever; Julia should lie on a mattress. The room at all hours should be kept at an even, moderate temperature with chloride of soda evaporating to purify the air. By the fifth or sixth day the watery fluid in the pustules will begin to drain away, but Dr. McGuire warns that this is when the danger of pitting is the greatest and, to keep Julia from scratching, recommends a salve of beeswax and sweet oil applied to the face and neck. He is an able man, Dr. McGuire, who for some time now has unfortunately been surgeon to the war-torn and shattered. He deeply regrets that he cannot be there to care for that delicate child himself, for with a patient so young the utmost vigilance should be exercised.

I, too, regret that I cannot leave my men, but this army is plagued by absenteeism and Burnside may soon move again. Some wives have begun to visit their husbands, and if we remain here in winter quarters long enough and our dear daughter's health improves, my only desire would be to see my *esposa* again, and now little Julia, whose letters I read with devotion and whose lock of hair is the trophy I prize the most.

You must not worry about me. Our cause is just, and over the last year with God's bountiful blessings has emerged victorious. We inflicted heavy losses on the enemy at Fredericksburg, heavier by far than the Northern papers were willing to admit. Their troops sacked and pillaged many of the lovely homes there, and I take consolation in believing that those responsible for the depredations fell in the Boggy Wood and on the slopes to Marye's Heights. They came bravely, but as if animated by their guilt, seeking their death in atonement for their sins. Our losses were slight. The men are in good spirits but unused to inactivity. We drill and march them regularly, but the weather has been forbiddingly cold and wet. I am reminded of our march in the snow to Romney of almost one year ago. Shortly thereafter, you visited me in Winchester and our daughter received the first loving warmth of our devotion and the first divine spark of her life. Oh, that you could visit me again! Oh, with what fervent prayers I pray that our daughter may recover and give to that divinity within her the example of a long Christian life.

My own health is fine. Only my ear troubles me, and for that reason and because Dr. McGuire insisted, I have left the tent and moved into the outbuilding the James Corbins here at Moss Neck used as an office in times of peace. Mrs. Corbin has been most gracious, and she has a daughter of six years named Janie who is the angel of the camp. Their house is exceedingly long and elegant. My quarters are warm and comfortable, small but large enough to share with our Corps chaplain, Dr. B. T. Lacy, who joins me in frequent prayer. On the walls hang pictures of James Corbin's favorite dogs and horses of the hunt. General Stuart delights in rallying with me about "the great decline in my moral character," assuming that I am a man who would take pleasure in the hunt. Others, perhaps assuming that as a corps commander I need to make more of a display of myself, have given me a splendid saddle and bridle and a magnificent bay stallion. General Stuart himself had a glittering uniform made for me, as handsome as any of General Lee's. That is not the man I am—you of all people on earth know that! I ask for the prayers of the pious, and not their gifts. To know that my countrymen are praying for me fills me with a sweet and inexpressible delight. For myself, I desire only to stand low before God and do His bidding. "Duty is ours; consequences are God's." He may take my life for the cause of my country if He chooses. In exchange I ask for His blessing on you, my dove, and for His merciful vigilance over our stricken child. Pray, my darling. War is terrible. Pray for peace and that this killing may stop so that I can join you. Pray for our daughter, that she may never hear the roar of the cannons. Pray for our government, our president, General Lee, for our Christian South. Pray without ceasing.

Your humble and loving husband,
Thomas

He prays. Praying in his tent, he's got the servant Jim at the flap ready to sound the alarm that the general's going to battle. There won't be a battle until Burnside tries to cross the Rappahannock, and after trying once and bogging down in mud he's been replaced by Hooker, who is content to hold the lines until spring. But praying in the sturdy brick outbuilding that serves as the plantation office and sportsman's den, Jackson asks not so much for victory in battle as for success in bringing the sinners among his soldiers into the fold. Frequently Reverend Lacy, mountain-boned like the general although Shenandoah-born and bred, prays with him. The upsurge of religious activity first observed the previous fall in Winchester has increased in the cold and poorly rationed camp by the swollen Rappahannock, and they pray for a continuation of that. Both believe in the well-spokenness of prayer. They pause at length to shape their words, offering nothing to God that is not well made. And once on their knees, both are tireless. Jackson is a soldier. He prays in salvo after salvo, beseeching and besieging God's throne, never aspiring to ascend to such an eminence, only hoping that after a long, faithful cannonade God will take notice of one lonely sinner down on the plain. Reverend Lacy learns of the soldier from the supplicant and is impressed.

But praying alone, Jackson is a different man. The sentry at his door he has sent into the yard with orders to keep visitors, officers, members of his staff, at a like distance. In this small temple of brick, hung with paintings of fine-blooded animals, he abases himself, he weeps, begs forgiveness for all acts of arrogance and rebellion, for all vaunting of his meager military might. The war with the devil is more arduous than the war with the Yankees, and he asks God to forgive him his lapses. Then through the pain in his right ear he listens for God's reply. Although he would not tell Dr. McGuire this, he believes that pain in his ear comes from straining to hear God's voice, from asking a miserably flawed organ to attain to the divine. He hears nothing. He hears the wind of his waiting as though through the whorls of a conch. He pleads to know why and immediately pleads pardon for his presumption in pleading to know anything. He waits, the

Yankees across the river kept busy by Stuart's and Hampton's gallant cavalry raids. Lee is encamped five miles upriver at Hamilton's Crossing. In one sense—again he scores himself for his presumption—they are so positioned and engaged to give him this opportunity for prayer. Assurance, he prays for. A sign of forgiveness and salvation. Onto the wide-planked floor how low can he go? Prayer. Pray without ceasing. Without patience and fortitude, without a nakedly bared heart, he can expect nothing from God. Baring his heart is like peeling back the tissue-thin layers of an onion. He peels back.

He's been proud and vainglorious in the minutest particulars of his life. He's curried favor with superiors and denied it to those who've asked it of him. He's secretly rejoiced at the misfortune of his critics. He's made secrecy not only a military tactic but a means of personal aggrandizement. He's enjoyed the bewildered expressions of his officers when they cannot read through his impassive face to the workings of his mind. He's relished their submission to him on faith. To be unprepossessing and crabbed in dress, posture, and speech he now admits can be as offensive as the preening of a martinet, a way of gathering mystery about himself, a way of competing with God. He's done that. And in humbling himself, he has not always humbled himself before God. He's stood humbly before General Lee, duty but duty to man in that moment his highest good. Has he peeled back the last layer? He's assumed his salvation won. Presumption, the vilest presumption. His heart, he believes, is bare. Listening, waiting, his ear begins to throb. Pain or sound? A message or the dumb animal hurt of the carcass he will become? He hears nothing, only, like insects on a summer night, the busy-work of thousands of men waiting to resume the war against the North. In waiting on God, heart bare, he becomes aware as always of those thousands of men and then of himself— but of himself as though they, his men, were looking in through the unshuttered window at his weeping, kneeling form on the floor. A powerless, unrequited man.

With the eyes of his men on him (although the shutters, he knows, are closed), he takes a bit of his power back and wraps it around his nakedness like a poor undergarment, around his heart like the tissue-thin skin of an onion. He *has* the obedience and devotion of his men—he must never forget that. Powerless in the eyes of God, he can lay claim to a certain miserable power here on earth. He picks up another garment, a frayed collarless shirt, perhaps, and puts it on; his heart he clothes in a second slightly thicker skin. With that power he has confounded various Yankee armies, insignificant, perhaps, when compared with Napoleon's campaigns, and contemptible in light of God's victory over Satan and his traitorous hosts, but a feat valuable to his country's cause, earning him praise. With all due respect—the pants now, soiled and weather-shrunk, the heart more richly veiled—he deserves God's attention. Even the Yankees cheer him. They cheered him at Harpers Ferry as he marched in to accept the town's surrender. "With Jackson at our head," they declared, "we should not now be laying down our arms." He is not negligible, he is not! And the boots now, like a boy's the outgrown coat, the heart in its glossy wrappings a rare fruit —he has something to offer, does he not, and God has something he, Stonewall Jackson, a wretched sinner but a man of means nonetheless wants. Will God listen? Will God suffer Himself to be approached?

Jackson listens to God listening. He listens through the pain he does not feel to the humming expectancy of a tiny vastness that he interprets as a sign of God's willingness to come to terms. But he will not gloat. If he believes he has an advantage and presses it, he will find his mouth stopped with dust. He has no advantage. He has a moment's miraculous grace. With due deference and profound gratitude, not as though he were addressing the Lord of Creation but as though he were talking to one of his own kind, an even-tempered, exemplary man, he says: "Let us collaborate. I say nothing of the Yankees and our military campaigns. You have blessed our endeavors in arms already, and I trust we will continue to win approval as a nation in Your eyes. I speak of something perhaps dearer to us both. I have the devotion and obedience of my men, 30,000 souls to the glory and enrichment of Your reign; You hold in Your hand like a fragile fledgling the life of my infant daughter. Until the Yankees force us into battle I will dedicate myself to my men's acceptance of Your Son and our Savior Jesus Christ, and You, if it meets with Your pleasure and design, will save my daughter's life. I wish it. I wish it for dear Anna's sake, and I do not disguise that I wish it most fervently for my own. The men, I give to You in exchange. I have aroused their capacity for devotion and faith, and I pledge now to fill it with Your presence. If You find favor with my proposal, can You respond with a sign?"

The sign comes at once, pain in his head so pure it's strung from ear to ear like an incandescent wire, blinding him with its flash. The flash itself is unapproachable; it is to the after-flash he draws near and reads as a sign. "Thy will be done," he utters solemnly, recalling in the breath and after-ache in his head that God's will had made itself known as his own. "*Our* will be done," he solemnly dares to amend.

He is trading 30,000 converted souls for his daughter's life, and he begins at once. Waiting with the sentry beside a fire beneath a shorn sycamore in the yard are members of his staff. The day is wet and uninspiring. He sends the newest member of his staff, the aide-de-camp James Power Smith, a young Presbyterian minister who's replaced the battle-fatigued Dabney, out to collect all the regimental chaplains he can find. It is immediately apparent that there aren't enough; almost half of the regiments are without. None of them is paid, clothed, and horsed by the government, and the first order of business will be to lobby the politicians in Richmond for money for these men of God. The next will be to urge churches throughout the state, indeed the entire South, to send the army their best preachers, for it is eloquent persuasion that Jackson now needs. And the third will be for those chaplains now present—pale and pious men, almost all young, clothed with the patchwork of their impoverished congregations, their jaws locked against the cold—to do the work of double their number and organize prayer meetings, hymn sings, Bible studies, services of all sorts to meet the needs of God. Jackson is not a man of long speeches. The men now standing there in the muddy, trampled yard know this. After learning the three orders of business, they wait for a peroration as laconic as their own might be long. Those who have been with the army during the last campaign—Manassas, Sharpsburg, Fredericksburg—will have seen their commander's face darken and his eyes burn with the blue of a great, stormy depth. Before battle they expect it; here the change is so quick and the context so unlikely that they are startled. He exhorts them: "While the Yankees remain across that river *this* is my war! We shall win it!" And his failure to invoke God's name or ask for His aid as he has before every battle he's ever fought startles them anew.

But they perform. This is a war for which they have arms. They organize, they shepherd, they enlarge their flocks. They quote Scripture and sing hymns. They preach. Some are fine preachers and become better, surpass their limits, caught up in the enthusiasm of the day. They preach the endangerment of Christianity, they preach the prospect of hell everlasting to the unregenerate soul. The sinner's foot may slide in due time, but the war is there to yank him into the pit of his endless agony at once; God need arrange no timely accidents when man arranges so many of his own. Yes, these ministers, chaplains, and divinity students who come suddenly of age trade off of the war to win their war. But they also trade off of the weather, which day and night chills with the chill of the final hours, and off of the men's hunger, which cannot be sated by starvation rations and packages from empty larders at home. Some of the brigades build their own log chapels, the proud eponymous Stonewall Brigade the first among them, but it's as if all these sermons, all these dire admonishments and calls to everlasting life, were being delivered in the out-of-doors where the men could draw up close to the conflagration of their own great fear and need, where all that they suffered and went without could through some miracle of combustion fuel the fire.

They come in massive numbers. Jackson appears among them. As always they begin to cheer him, but now he will not permit it. His countenance is stern, its meaning unmistakable. All their devotion must go to God. He does not neglect their military readiness—it is after drilling and marching and standing picket duty that they attend services. Nor does he neglect his own work that has been allowed to accumulate over the heat of the last campaign. He has battle reports to write, fallen officers to replace, promotions to award and deny to men whose egos in the lull between battles can reach enormous proportions. He has depleted regiments that must be brought up to an acceptable minimum, and he has his precious few pieces of artillery to protect against the requisitioning demands of his fellow commanders. Shoes, clothes, food—these creature comforts he wages war with Richmond to procure. For his army, for himself, he instructs his cartographer Jed Hotchkiss to prepare a map of such scrupulous detail that from where he stands in Northern Virginia all the way to Philadelphia, first of the great Cities of the North, he will know the location and name of every hamlet, every significant farm. In unguarded moments he dreams about this map, its fabulous fidelity to the miles he will conquer, the high dryness of the terrain it bodies forth to his mind's eye—but his unguarded moments are few. He is campaigning for his men's souls, his daughter's life, and as if on the longest of his forced marches, he sleeps as it were in the saddle, never resting, only shutting his eyes. Dr. McGuire, ten years his junior, a studious yet impressionable man, warns him against overworking and, knowing the general's deeply religious nature but nothing of his pact, goes so far as to suggest that it is the providence of God that has given him this long recuperative pause in their country's fight. He should take advantage of it. Reverend Lacy, ignoring the demands of the body, wonders at the stamina of the general's soul. They pray.

When Lacy can pray no more, when he is actually persuaded that God for the moment has heard enough, Jackson goes out to pray with his men, or to read them Scripture, or to lead them in hymns. "How happy are they Who the Saviour obey,/And have laid up their treasure above," he sings gravely. "He hath loved me, I cried,/He hath suffered and died,/To redeem such a rebel as me," he intones in a voice measured against both presumption and unmanly pleading. Wednesday and Sunday evenings, he invites the members of his staff to his own quarters for additional prayer. They, too, come—even the gallants among them. Who is this man, this inexhaustible force? they wonder admiringly, but also like men held in puzzling thrall. He is as chary with words as the pulpit-ranters are prodigal—explain to them, they never quite demand, the secret to his success. They leave their commander convinced once more of his greatness. Outside the dampness off the river, out of the saturated ground, works up their feet and hands, and wraps a fine freezing scarf around their throats. Mud, bare trees and underbrush—everywhere the ashen-brown of a great natural stasis. Thirty thousand men lie out in this, their tents ashen-brown, their bodies, their animals. Only the pines remain green, but a stony, recalcitrant green that mocks a man's yearning for spring. Through this their general marches, marshaling his forces against the devil of the dying year.

They see him relent only in the afternoons, when after dinner he entertains little Janie Corbin, whose silky blonde head flits like a luminous spirit in the yard before his door. He bends down to her, inviting her to touch his face, his beard. If she plays hard to get, he might sweep her up. If the wind isn't blowing, if the horses, mules, and wagons they pull are quiet, if they themselves are soundlessly quiet, they might hear him coo to her. Usually she recounts in a breathless itemizing voice the things she has done since she last saw him, and he chooses one of the things for praise. Some assistance she gave her mother, a special prayer she said. Occasionally, and most out of character, some piece of pure self-indulgence she has gotten away with. She ate all of a forbidden jar of jelly, then put jelly marks on her cousin's napkins and clothes. Wasn't that clever? It was, Janie. Sly and clever. She smiles, and even though teeth are missing and the lips are cracked from the cold, he gives her everything, finds nothing to forgive. Before she leaves, he tries to match her brightness with something of his own. She takes away pins and buckles, bits of quartz and colorful stone he's found. One day when he says something she particularly enjoys, she squeals and leaps to kiss him on the forehead. It leaves him smiling, but thoughtful and still bent as though stricken by the kiss. When he straightens up, he goes back into his quarters and returns with the hat that General Stuart gave him to match the glittering uniform he was too embarrassed to wear. He carefully detaches the gold braid encircling the crown and places it over her head like a coronet. Then he gazes at her, wistful, it seems, for something he can never have. A moment later, snapping the two of them to a sort of self-reproving attention that she understands intuitively and forgives, he forces himself to send her away.

He cannot relent for long—it is not in his nature. Or rather it is—at perhaps the fondest and profoundest depth of his nature—and he must guard against it. Even more likely, it is that fond relenting to his heart's pull that he has enshrined and must guard against intrusion, not allowing himself to enjoy it until all of his enemies are subdued. Her nature, he knows but will not put into words, is as delicate and dear as his daughter's must be. Why shouldn't his life in every minute be the crowning of a child?

The Sunday General Lee comes to attend services in the Stonewall Brigade's log chapel marks the culmination of Jackson's efforts to Christianize his army—a rare day of sun. Military matters, the two generals leave for later. With their staff officers serving as trains, Lee and Jackson ride along a recently cut road to the chapel. Ostentation, like the cheers and rebel yelling, is to be avoided in Jackson's army, but the image of the splendidly mounted and splendidly dressed Lee, and the somberly dressed and mysterious Jackson, dazzles the men of the Second Corps. They don't cheer and yahoo. Instead they step up to the road and gawk, then immediately follow after. The Stonewall chapel they fill to overflowing, and the overflow spreads out over the mud and sun-brightened patches of snow like the widening reach of a whirlpool. At an altar of rough-planed boards, Reverend Lacy preaches a sermon drawn from First Timothy, verses five and six: "Sinners all, we have been abducted by the devil and held for ransom." The chinks in this chapel's walls broadcast the Word into the freezing tents of the Second Corps, across the river into the Yankee camp. "For our sakes God has paid the devil's ransom, forsaken, *for our sakes*, his own beloved Son. The *ransomed* Christ! Why, Christ suffered *for our sakes* as any spy privy to the secrets of the high command would suffer if caught behind lines. But ransomed, we are free! We must ask ourselves: 'Was what was done to our ransomed Lord by the devil in unregenerate man done in vain?' It shall not be so!

His wounds have paid our ransom! His suffering unlocked our chains!" The text is not one he and Reverend Lacy have prayed from or discussed. Rather Lacy preaches—and preaches magnificently, Jackson knows—in honor of General Lee. Accustomed to the honor, Lee sits composed, nodding solemnly, and perhaps it is only Jackson at his side who notices a moment's weariness in his commander's face, as if all the subtle tensions and fine knottings that manifest the man's intelligence had snapped at once. Lee at that moment looks as though he suffered the world's shame; then his face recomposes itself, his discriminating intelligence returns, and he nods.

When they leave the chapel, Jackson sees the masses that Lee's presence has drawn. Once again the Yankees are assembling a mighty army, stockpiling supplies, but Hooker gives no indication of wanting to move soon. Lee prefers to counterattack once Hooker does. Jackson listens, concurs. They are back in his quarters now. But through his mind's eye he is still marveling at that army Lee assembled at the chapel door. Vast numbers and rapt, redeemed faces—he knows that his daughter's life is saved.

Not only saved. Reanimated, allowed to flourish. The letter from his wife comes that very night, and Jackson relaxes one of his oldest restrictions to learn the news. God's day is not a day for the writing, reading, or transporting of private correspondence, but he justifies himself by remembering that this is also God's news. She smiles, she eats heartily, she kicks and snatches, she babbles incessantly—if only they could understand. She is their radiant cherub! He would not have her called a cherub lest God, chiding their presumption, take her to His side too soon. She is the joy of their lives in this world of want and war. Yes, he understands. After midnight—a Monday now—he writes to his wife. Give thanks to God, only to God, although in dedicating himself to the conversion of his army he, Jackson, merits perhaps as much of her gratitude as the Almighty. But he does not tell his wife that. Writing to Anna, recalling the four years of their married life, he feels particularly close to the Giver of All Gifts, since such a sweet and temperate bliss he knows he could never have earned on his own. Now that his daughter is well, he longs to see them both. Is that yet another gift that God has reserved? Pray that He has. But afflicted once more by treacherous weather and word of new enemy activity, Jackson cannot take the risk of bringing his family north. Instead, with an almost swooning affection, he reads his daughter's letters—for they come now as though written by her hand—and he continues to see to the physical and spiritual well-being of his men. When Jed Hotchkiss is back in camp, he examines the progress of his map as though like a hawk he overflew every inch of its terrain. Janie Corbin visits wearing her coronet. Her mother apologizes, but the child gets loose and down to Jackson's quarters she comes. Mrs. Corbin should know better than to apologize. Yes, the general is very kind, but she also knows that little Janie can be a pest, especially when she is fond of somebody, and she's become dotingly fond of their distinguished guest. He asks Mrs. Corbin to grant him but one more favor: Allow her to come.

She comes. Then one day in late March she doesn't, followed by two more. The third day spies and pickets bring him word of ominous Yankee movement north along the Rappahannock, and with the campaigning season upon them he knows that he must move camp closer to Fredericksburg. It takes a day to assemble his men into marching formation; that day Janie also fails to appear. "You have benefited the cause of your country immeasurably by your hospitality," Jackson intends to tell her mother as he takes his leave, hoping also for a good-bye kiss from his second favorite little girl. At the sight of Mrs. Corbin's haggard face he tells her nothing. Janie, he is told, has scarlet fever, and out of shame

Jackson does not mention what he knows Mrs. Corbin will have discovered for herself: that scarlet fever has broken out in the camp. But she has begun to recover, their doctor has assured them. May God give her life! Jackson pleads and then remonstrates, "You should have told me sooner. I could have done something." No, he is reminded, he was busy with his army and defending his country's cause. The child has taken enough of his time. There is nothing he can say. In exchange for the Corbins' hospitality, for the spirit-refreshing visits of their delightful little girl, he has drawn with his army a pestilential circle around their house. He excuses himself by promising to return in better times, and by promising to bring with him for Janie to wear the brightest star he can find in those Cities of the North.

At Hamilton's Crossing, five miles from Fredericksburg, he learns what he feared to a certainy as he moved the 30,000 men at his command: She has died. The next day he receives word that her two cousins, whom he remembers only as those playmates she often escaped to come see him, have also died.

Death has been his profession, his métier. As commander of an army he has stood up in death, growing in stature as it grew so that he could always see beyond the bodies he gave for any particular piece of ground. The ground itself—he barely recalls what it looks like. He's been trained to view terrain for the battlefields it offers; from the start he's viewed those battlefields with their fallen soldiers in place. But the ground—first spring flowers, wheat, corn, rolling upland meadows? He thinks of the Shenandoah valley. Can he respond to the beauty of a place only at the head of a marching army? In his own defense he recalls the quiet beauty of his home at Lexington, the plots of flowers and vegetables out back, the two acres he owns and tills just outside of town. Unbloodied ground—it was then. He made it grow. The tender white bean sprouts breaking through moist black dirt always gladdened his heart—and with that vision before him, in that instant alone in his tent, he finds he has begun to shake. It's as if he has never known death before. Or as if all the deaths he has known have been a bloody sorting-through to the deaths he will finally have to face. Janie Corbin—who grew every day for him, exactly like those bean sprouts seeking the sun. With her winning generosity, Janie once more gives him his daughter.

He has begun to pray. Suddenly he stops, and the sensation he has is of speaking indiscreetly, of becoming drunken in his grief. He feels as if he has just disclosed valuable secrets to the enemy. The next moments he sits there impassively on his camp stool, knowing that God, unlike the members of his staff, will not be thwarted by his blank face but knowing nothing else to do. He had made a bargain with God—an army for his daughter's life—a bargain both sides kept. Then God took Janie Corbin's life and, for good measure, those of her playmates. Why did that make it seem as if God had bargained falsely? He can't accuse God of that, but he finds he can't trust Him either, and since God is as privy to these thoughts as he is, he can't control this base and unmanly feeling of betraying his own and his country's cause. Suddenly his much-heralded privacy is as public as those observation balloons the Yankees send up and as indefensible. He has nowhere else to turn. He picks up his pen and writes:

Dear Anna,

Hooker is moving, and we will certainly be forced to give battle soon. If you would see your husband before this season's campaign, you must come at once. Julia must come. There are dangers, I don't deny it, but those against which an army of 30,000 can defend you I count as nothing. Of the others, I say no more. I miss you terribly. There are days, my dearest, when I wonder if our brief years together have ever been. They appear so fragile and faded. On those days Julia is like a mocking dream, so sweet but cruel to bear. You must come at once.

She arrives on a day of April downpour, the cherry, peach and dogwood blossoms clinging limply to their branches. Jackson finds her diminished, strangely and subtly remote from the person she has become for him, and hence somehow threatening, like an impostor or spy. In the instant of their reunion he draws back. His daughter Julia is robust, her open mouth, tongue, and teething gums wet and alive for him; and he pulls back from her, too. In the onset of conflicting emotions he stands there dripping rain off his rubber overcoat in the coach's aisle. This is Anna, this is Anna, he reminds himself, until gradually, as though awakening to the confines of a familiar room, he sees that it is so. He holds her then, she welcoming the wetness off his coat. Love, that great longing for her caretaking presence in his life, he now experiences as a deep sympathy for what time and the privations of war have done to them. This is Anna.

"Anna," he whispers. And in that moment it seems inconceivable that he will ever again call her his dove, darling, precious, or *esposita*. "I have feared for you so," she tells him through tears, only at last and very briefly able to look him in the eyes. He sees then that she is the same Anna, after all, and appears diminished to him only insofar as she has lost the power to protect him. Unwittingly, his hand goes to the ringlet of hair beside her right ear. Its luster, its richness, is spent. "You have said nothing, Thomas." And she draws him away from her hair to his daughter, whose hair is a gossamer brown. "Take her, hold her." No, he is wet. They must keep her dry. This rain has paralyzed armies. She is only a five-month-old child.

Outside, as they enter the covered carriage that will take them from Guiney's Station to Hamilton's Crossing and the home of William Yerby, the men are waiting for him—men who for the three months of their winter quartering have known his express desires. Nonetheless, in the presence of his wife and infant daughter they now cheer him. They stand in the rain while the general and his family pass by in their carriage and cheer him devotedly until Jackson no longer raises his hand in protest. Word spreads down the road faster than they in the mud can travel, and the cheers greet them as they take each turn. Powerless to stop them he turns to his daughter, who with a bold, amused, suspicious, and inquiring expression in her eyes looks up at him. He realizes that he knows no more about the contents of her mind than he knows in truth about his own. "They love you more now than they did in Winchester," his wife says, drawing him back to her. She speaks with deep regard and admiration, but also as though charging her husband with a grave responsibility. She means the men.

At the Yerbys', Jackson's entire staff is waiting for him. Having given his raincoat to Aide-de-Camp Smith, in the Yerby parlor he holds his daughter in his arms for the first time. She is applauded for not crying. Jackson hears Sandie Pendleton remark that there are grown men in this world who would die of fright if they found themselves in the general's arms, and in the muffled laughter and the lingering murmur of approval, Jackson takes a sort of refuge. For a moment there is nothing that keeps him from pouring out the full measure of his affection on his daughter—except his fear for her. Only Christ, he thinks, could be held in licit worship; only Christ given unrestrained praise. What a relief that must have been for his God-fearing parents. He smiles soberly, uncertain but undismayed, and in that instant Julia matches him—smile for smile—only hers takes possession of her face like an eruption. In a rush of inexpressible joy, he seems to draw back from this child in his arms, as though to view her more clearly. But in the silent second that follows, at the trembling reach of that distance, he knows he adores her.

Has he committed a sacrilege? He doesn't know. It is little Julia's sudden stillness, sudden seriousness of expression, that prompts him to call for Reverend Lacy and the baptism they are gathered there to witness. Anna has not been told that there's to be a baptism, but like one of her husband's uninformed lieutenants who are quick to move when the general's strategy becomes known, she appears at his side. Reverend Lacy steps forward with his familiar leather-bound Bible. He reads the service. In the moment of great expectation when the reverend places his moistened, mountain-boned hand over the baby's skull, Jackson is once again assailed by his doubts. The hand of that man of God blessing his daughter could, if it chose, crush her with the full, closing force of the fingers. He has seen that hand raised in prayer. He has seen the entreaty in the hand. Now he sees its crude red strength. When Reverend Lacy finally lifts it off Julia's head, it is as if he were giving back life, life he might just as well have taken. And that was God. In that moment the hand lay over his daughter's head, those reddened knuckles and long, taut tendons were God.

He has given his daughter back. Julia must rest after her trip, and Anna must clean up. He rides to inspect the readiness of his men. That night the Yerbys host Jackson and his wife, the gallant and superbly mannered members of his staff. After dinner, casual conversation gives way to speculation about where Hooker might choose to strike. Some fear a feint to the north followed by a massive attack south at Port Royal. Jackson, if only because his corps occupies the southern front of Lee's army, expects the blow to fall farther to the north. It is then that Anna excuses herself. Moments later Jackson finds her feeding Julia in their room. He is almost shocked to see how vigorously his daughter sucks. About to close the door on the two of them, he walks instead to look down over his wife's head. He stands stiffly, aware of himself both as a military commander and as a boy peeking furtively down at the breast and the small sucking child. The breast is full, fleshy, and white; he sees the watery milk drool out between Julia's lips. Again he is about to depart when Anna looks up at him, the contentment she would share with him shot through with apprehension, giving her face the false look of an ingratiating dog. He reminds himself: Anna, this is Anna. But that night he lies with her and it does not happen. In the master bed of the vacated master bedroom they listen to the exchange of picket fire up along the Rappahannock until finally, with a discreet sigh as though releasing the one breath she has drawn since lying at his side, Anna asks, "Thomas, how long is this war going to last? I will believe it if you tell me." He responds irritably, as though the question had come from a prying reporter—he doesn't know why. "I shall have to ask General Lee," he says.

In the middle of the night he wakes not to the sound of musket or cannon but to the sound of his own voice sobbing her name. He buries himself in her, stifling the sobs. The final cry he withholds, then releases with the burning of his seed, after which she holds him—his head—saying nothing, until he has gone back to sleep. The next morning he awakes before she does to the uncertainty of what he has or has not performed. Her sleeping face tells him only that she has not rested. The features seem drawn to a concentrated point, as though she listened for the distress of her daughter or a word of his own. "Anna," he whispers to himself. "This is Anna."

That day he does not believe General Lee tells him the truth. "This year, Thomas, 1863, mark it. We shall drive into the North and make them see that devastation and suffering of the sort we have undergone is the price of their persistence. I know the people of the North. They will not pay as we have. Nothing they have or can envision for themselves will be worth that price."

"I cannot tell you, Anna," he tells his wife, "how long this war will last."

She nods in resignation and lifts from her cradle the daughter he converted an army to save. She then hands the child to her husband, meaning, he believes, that for Julia's sake he should end it soon. She is a symbol—what they make of her—expressing herself now only in absent little whines. He wants to hand her back—it would be a way to protest, to clear the air—but his wife shakes her head. In both the tide and undertow of his love and fear for his daughter, he stands there caught. Then the tide takes him. By cooing to her, making nonsense faces and nonsense noises, he manages to replace the whines with a sputtering laugh. He finds himself showing her his watch. Then they gaze at each other, she with a long musing, peaceful smile in her eyes. She resembles him. No, she resembles his mother, her namesake Julia, who took just such a long peaceful, musing look at death. When on the heels of that look little Julia starts to cry, he doesn't understand why. He does what he did before—make faces and noises, dangle the watch—but this time to no avail. When he looks up for Anna he finds he's alone, his daughter crying now in utter opposition to her father's desires. The sound is raw. He turns on her an obdurate face. She reacts to the change in his expression with a questioning catch in her cry, then screams again. It is a contest of wills, he sees, and decides to wait her out. When Anna returns he learns that it is not her feeding time, but that, yes, she is probably wet and *would* cry then; he is not to be surprised. Still, he will wait her out. When she quits, she does so from exhaustion—trailing off in snuffling little peeps. Once she is perfectly quiet, her smile comes back—wanly, questioningly, perhaps, but wiser, he believes. He has lost no love for her. He has given her a place in the world. Her mother now takes her off to be changed.

She was wrong. "Not wet at all."

"Just trying me out." Jackson smiles.

"She has a variety of tricks. You will see when you know her better."

"She's a Jackson, I'm afraid," he says with pride in his voice and no pity that the pride can't at once conceal. "We shall have to break her will."

He rides off to headquarters. That day he spends not in long consultation with his officers but with his map. Hooker will try to flank Lee's left as it pulls in to anticipate a strike against the South. A full, flanking sweep would take the Yankees across both the Rappahannock and the Rapidan, and into an overgrown area known as the Wilderness. A battle there would be savage, and he turns away from his map. But on a cot in his tent he spends the night, the next day working with his quartermaster, Harman, well into the afternoon. The trains are up, each wagon full after a winter of requisitioning. Jackson instructs Harman to point the mules north. The men have already cooked their three-day marching rations. He waits there at headquarters for this war that will not go away, the date of whose final battle no man can predict. Late in the afternoon he rides back to his wife and daughter.

Approaching the Yerby house he performs an exercise of the imagination. He blocks out Aide Smith, who accompanies him. He blocks out the limb-splintered gashes in the forest, the trenches and gun pits in the earth; he blocks out himself on horseback, in camp-smelling uniform, the smell of powder and blood that remains in his nostrils, and the cries and comatose groans that remain in his ears. He tries to block out all the dark and eloquent detritus of war and to imagine himself, an admired but not yet accomplished professor, returning home to his wife and infant daughter in an untroubled little town. Passing through the Yerbys' front door, he passes through his own. It is five o'clock; two blocks up the street, the church bells toll the hour. The season is spring, and the members of his staff who await him phantoms from a time

160

neither come nor gone. He does not acknowledge them, but they are used to his eccentric behavior and are not offended now. From the Yerby foyer he mounts the Yerby stairs—his own. This is not war but a day home from his duties at school. He will walk down the hall to greet his wife, who at this hour will be feeding their daughter so that her parents, too, may eat at their appointed hour. He will open the door, and beyond her—from door to mother and daughter to the open window admitting a breeze full of flowering fruit—will stretch a vista of the valley and the Blue Ridge Mountains, which he will take a moment to contemplate, for in the serenity of its light and shadows, crops and woods, it will give him a picture of his mind. In it, occupying that nearer space, he will find his wife.

Anna. This, too, is Anna.

"Anna," he says, startling her—although she is not feeding the baby but sitting beside the window, gazing not at the horizon but at her lap—"we must pray!"

"Thomas!" she utters, recovering from her start but not from her disappointment. "I worried you had already gone."

He strides over to her and, in the act of falling to his knees, compels her to kneel, too. "We must pray!" he repeats, his voice hoarse with the baffled urgency of his command. He does not know what to pray for, even why they should pray. His imagination has failed him and now, it seems, so has his faith. Pray with me for my faith—in shame he will not ask that of his wife. His faith will come back. Pray that you, Anna, can serve me until it does. But his wife is not the woman he left to go to war. She is frightened and confused, made pitiably small by the massing of men and events. Nor is he the same man. He has been made larger, but perhaps just as pitiably—like the dinosaur that far outgrows the powers of its mind. Only their daughter thrives in this world at war, and she was born to it, Jackson remembers. She sucks its great uncertainty like an elixir from the air.

"Pray that we have not forfeited our right to God's mercy," Jackson instructs his wife, his own prayer a sham.

Sunday the officer corps from Lee's entire army assemble in a tent at Hamilton's Crossing for service. Again Reverend Lacy is to preach. The enlisted men spread out over the fields, standing or sitting on makeshift benches. They are there waiting and cheering when the officers arrive. To please his wife, Jackson has worn J.E.B. Stuart's glittering uniform. Stuart flirts with Anna by overpraising her husband. General Lee congratulates her on Julia's birth and on the great courage with which she, his Anna, inspires General Jackson. Others are there—Hood, Rodes, Early, Taliaferro—to play up to her. She never releases her husband's arm. Before Lacy has begun to preach, in the eyes of his men and fellow officers, dressed in resplendent gray and gold, Jackson manages to go to sleep. In his dream he mixes his battles and sees himself running wildly over terrain that is alternately Winchester, Port Republic, Manassas, Sharpsburg, following an anonymous trail of blood. He is alone, although never unaccompanied by cheers. Leaving the tent, it is as though he has not left his dream, and he approaches his commander. Were those field pieces he heard? No, Lee gives him a Sunday wink, perhaps his own snores. Very elegantly attired, General Jackson. When would he hear them? He does not ask when the war will end, but when—no sense of humor today, his wife attached tightly to his arm—it will begin.

Sotto voce, amid the jubilant exhortations of his men, Lee mouths the word "soon."

That night—God forgive him if God concerned Himself with Thomas J. Jackson anymore. Actually, two more nights pass. It is the third, then, although the three together count as one dark night in his soul. At the close of the third, birds —two whippoorwills—are booming in the trees outside his window. The adjutant from General Early's division knocks on his bedroom door, and Jackson, crowded in his skin, neither awake nor asleep, knows the message before the adjutant can state it. In restraining himself, the excited young officer almost crashes in the door.

"Hooker has crossed the Rappahannock."

"To the north?"

"Yes, with his full army. The Rappahannock and now the Rapidan, to the north."

The baby has begun to cry. Dawn, empty and ashen, shows Anna Jackson sitting up in bed, an arm extended toward her husband. "Thomas?" she questions quietly, her voice one sound he hears, clear and bodiless, as though it originated inside his head. His daughter's crying is the other. "See to Julia," he says, then dresses quickly (his clothes have been left at hand). When he finishes, Anna has Julia at her breast. The arrival of the adjutant's horse and now the commotion in the house have silenced the whippoorwills. The sound he now hears is his daughter's vigorous sucking and his wife's shallowly drawn breaths. He stands there for a brief moment gazing down at them. He wants to fix them, not as a portrait he can carry into battle but with the visual impact of something akin to meaning itself. Once again, and for the last time, he discovers that he cannot. Frightened, Anna reaches out to her husband with the hand she has used to hold the breast up to her baby's mouth, and Julia loses the nipple. She cries at once, a squalling of want and greed.

"You must leave immediately. I shall ask Reverend Lacy to take you to the station."

"Thomas," Anna utters (again, the voice in its desolate clarity seems to sound within his head). "What is it?"

"We shall fight a big battle soon," he replies just as quietly, into the teeth of their daughter's furious demand. Then assuming his bearing: "What is it?"—he both asks and answers her question—"It's the war."

VIII

Yes, Hooker has crossed, but not with his entire army. He's left General Sedgwick with perhaps three divisions on Stafford's Heights overlooking Fredericksburg and forced Lee, on the first day of the 1863 campaign, to divide his already divided army. Longstreet's corps fights in North Carolina. Now Lee puts Jubal Early in command of no more than 9,000 men on Marye's Heights with orders to keep Sedgwick out of the Confederate rear. The rest of his army, less than 50,000 to contend with the 100,000 that Hooker commands, he marches northwest into a good-for-nothing area of pine, second-growth hardwood, and brush known as the Wilderness, where Hooker, after crossing the Rapidan and the Rappahannock and marching southeast, has unaccountably stopped. The point of contention is Chancellorsville, a large brick house built on the macadamized turnpike, once a baronial mansion until the Wilderness overran the plantation it served. Now a tavern, hardly a town. There the Yankees have dug trenches, thrown up earthworks, built abatis. Lee, joining Jackson along a three-mile front, wants to know why. Why has Hooker conducted an impressive flanking march and crossed two rivers with numbers the Southern commanders can only dream about to suddenly stop here? Hooker is ambitious, Lee knows; and intemperate. Every general Lincoln has named to command the Army of the Potomac has flown to his charge on the wings of a boast, and Hooker is no exception. "Lee's army is now the legitimate property of the United States government—mine!" he has declared. Five more miles and he would have been in open country, where his superior field pieces would have been of great use. Yet he's stopped here, and pulled in his forces around Chancellorsville, an insignificant crossroads tavern in the Wilderness.

Why?

Does he really want to fight Lee there? Doesn't he know how hopelessly confused an army of his size will become fighting in that undergrowth? Hasn't he looked?

The first day of May—a beautiful day of peach and cherry, anemone and bloodroot, and Robert E. Lee and Thomas J. Jackson both look. What they see on peering into that Wilderness is the secret to their histories, perhaps to the South's. Neither has said. The soil is Virginian. The youthful tangle of scrub oak and pine, creeper and briar, might just as easily be found in the North, and in its air of sudden depletion and rank regrowth belongs to the nation as a whole, the whole that was then rent. But it is into themselves and their embattled country that they peer as they work their way from light green leaf and lithe gray twig deep into the swarming loveliness of the self-engendered and the self-consumed. Jackson believes that Hooker has stopped because he plans to withdraw that night. The Southern army, for once outflanked, did not retreat toward Richmond as Hooker had expected, but turned to fight. For the very reason Hooker has stopped, Lee believes he will stay. Something has spoken to him. Something in that Wilderness where not one living thing is half his own age yet where at any given moment the impression is of immemorial age and futility, something has told him: "Swallow your bluster, take truthful stock. You're one man, not one hundred thousand. Find a clearing and stay there."

Chancellorsville.

The battle begins with Lee and Jackson peering into that forest and with Hooker falling back to a crossroads tavern where when it is night he can see the stars. Then it is night. Abandoned, overgrown land now hosts 150,000 soldiers, plus thousands of horses and mules, and the sound of their presence—so disgruntled, so alien—quickly becomes the voice through which the Wilderness speaks. In a grove of red pines, Lee and Jackson sit on cracker boxes the Yankees have left behind and warm their hands over their fire. They burn pine wood and smell pine, the eager, inspiriting fragrance of pine, and ask themselves how. "We've got to get at those men before Sedgwick tests Early, Thomas." Jackson still believes Hooker has conducted a feint only to pull back around Chancellorsville and withdraw, but Lee, who has reconnoitered most of the Yankees' crescent-shaped front, knows that Hooker's left is anchored all the way to the Rappahannock, that his center is protected by heavy earthworks, and that his right extends miles out to the west. Yet—Lee's question there in the vast congested breathing of the two armies and the quiet sap-popping of the pine—is Hooker's right anchored or up in the air? If it were up in the air, could a man march an army around it, come in behind it, and give battle that same afternoon? A man could—one man could, and an army willing to march for that one man.

Lee, bareheaded, studies Jackson, whose face is hidden by that brow-obscuring kepi cap. The night is sharply cool. Jackson's jaw is unquivering, firm. The small, delicate mouth is also pressed firm. A stern face, Lee thinks, whose sternness is each day's achievement. The man is a masterpiece of self-denial. Behind the sternness Lee reads through to Jackson's doubt, which is also his own—the questionable wisdom of dividing a twice-divided army once more, and this time in the Wilderness—but also to his daring: that they must. And perhaps past that to something else, something seldom glimpsed in Stonewall Jackson but that Lee sees, knowing exactly where to look: the wistful, powerless protest of a child at the harshness of life in the adult world, at yet another cruel parting. Fatherless almost from the start, too long unmothered, old beyond his years, yet young, as though Thomas Jackson were still waiting for his rightful start in life—yes, Lee knows where to look. At every crease and smoke-squinted line; at the bone wearing out the skin. It shouldn't be. We fight this war for the children in us all.

Then Jackson looks up. General Lee knows best. Jackson will do it if it can be done. He will do it eagerly. Soon they admit a third to their circle of light. J.E.B. Stuart can testify to a great chance, and does so as though dancing through the embers of all that was pensive and private in the mood of his great commander and famous lieutenant. Hooker's right is, indeed, up in the air! Hooker's right is hung out like Old Glory flapping on the line! And there are ways to get there —back roads and lanes, narrow but concealed—that will allow you to walk up and tap ole puff-'n-strut Joe on the back. Tomorrow mornin' first thing, he'll have a guide there. They were talking—gentlemen—about an outflanked flanking march, just the sort of thing legends were made of, and if General Lee didn't have any plans for him, Stuart would be happy to provide cavalry cover himself. For secrecy's sake, he'd even leave Willie, his banjo player, at home.

"General Jackson?"

"My troops will move at dawn."

Lee returns to his tent. It is after midnight. Jackson, whose ability to sleep in the saddle—wherever he stops—has allowed him to conduct his most exhausting marches, also allows him to hold his most troubled thoughts at bay. His wife and daughter are en route to safety in North Carolina—he can do no more for them than that. If he thought he were entitled to it, he would ask God's blessing for them; provisionally, he does. Then he lies beneath a pine tree on the bare ground, sleeping at once. When he awakes in the early-

168

morning dark—a time of surprises, a time of stolen marches —he orders his officers to ready their men. Wearing a black rubber raincoat against the chill, he sits on the cracker box he occupied with General Lee and pokes at the remains of their fire. He hears no guns. Opposing pickets no longer exchange boasts or taunts. For an hour before dawn, at the end of a long, anxious night, the Wilderness has won. Tens of thousands of men sleep as the animals and insects of the forest do, as he has. Then he hears the sullen muttering and clumsy rising of his soldiers as company commanders move among them; he hears the restive snorting of the cavalry's mounts. Sandie Pendleton brings him a steaming tin cup of coffee from the first mess now up and about. When he offers to build up the general's fire, Jackson orders him to bring the cartographer Hotchkiss and Reverend Lacy. He drinks the coffee, scalding and bitter. He knows the Yankees are still there. He hasn't heard them, but he has awakened with his faith in his commanding general entire and intact. It's like this ground he sits on. It prescribes his duties; lends a subordinate's clarity to what he must do.

When Lacy arrives to sit beside him on the cracker box, Jackson asks not about the latest news of his wife and daughter but about what Lacy knows of the backroads of this region. His ministry once included this Wilderness area, did it not? Lacy tells him what he can; about the roads, he knows little. They are dark and narrow, but so are the passageways of a virtuous Christian through this life of sin and sorrow, and Jackson cannot trust the minister to reproduce a faithful map of this world. He sends him off to pray. Hotchkiss comes with more exact information. Except for one stretch of perhaps two miles, he can show the general how to march around Hooker without being seen. The roads are damp enough to hold down the dust but not too damp to impede the wagons' progress. He can march on them, his secret his own. But, yes, they are narrow, and under low arching trees, dark. Moving over them will not be like moving through the Shenandoah or the Luray. The men can march no more than four or five abreast; the mounted officers will barely be able to squeeze by. Does the general remember the races they had with the Yankees up and down those spacious sloping valleys beyond the Blue Ridge? Does he remember the rivers, fruit orchards, and the vistas of wheat, with the mountains on the horizon and the unsuspecting Yankees beyond? A man of maps, Jed Hotchkiss can live with them just so long—and Jackson stops him. He's to show him those dark, narrow roads and the two-mile gap he cannot fill. Then Stuart comes with his guide, looking rosily rested. To fill the gap. In exchange for those two miles, visible to Yankee outposts, Jackson is offered three more under cover, curving out from the first road as the bow does from the string, but returning, as the bow does, taut and tested, perhaps, from the passage of so many men. Yes, gentlemen, and strung. It is Stuart in his glossy beaver-tail beard and his pheasant's plume who smiles, Stuart used to raids along the narrowest of ways, to brief savage joys. Major Hotchkiss is to take this guide aside—he's little more than a boy—and draw a new map. He's to make two copies.

When Lee has his in his hand, he nods his approval and asks, "How many men do you propose to take?"

Jackson doesn't hesitate. "My entire corps."

"I see," Lee replies. "I'm to be left with only two divisions to face Hooker's force."

"He will not attack you. Before he finds the courage and the resolve, I will have driven into him from the rear."

Lee regards his corps commander with a fond and solemn look. "I first admired you, Thomas, through the medium of a map. It was a grander map than this, and you served it grandly, marching men unlike any soldier before you had done. What a virtuoso you were! This map is but a scrap of that. The route it traces is close and crabbed. But it is the map you must master, or we are all doomed. If Hooker breaks through here, he falls on Richmond."

"He shall not!" Jackson swears, but quietly, as though conserving his righteous wrath.

"No, he shall not, Thomas," Lee says just as quietly, placing both hands just below the younger man's shoulders. Yes, Jackson is the younger man, but in some ways—the terribly fecund and disruptive ways of this Wilderness, perhaps—the older. Lee presses his arms, his voice gathering emotion, itself taking on age. "Go get in his rear! Make him pay with his last drop of blood!"

And he is gone. Suddenly, down dark, narrow ways, two-thirds of my army is gone. There is little I can do with the 14,000 who remain. I make my dispositions. Along a line of more than three miles, I place my guns to cover the most likely approaches. I send out skirmishers to keep the enemy busy but not to provoke attack. If he attacks, I have sections of line with men stationed as much as six feet apart. Generals Anderson and McLaws are good men, solid soldiers, but they wonder how long I can violate military convention and escape a beating. I wonder myself. I sometimes think the South's only hope lies in Lincoln sending more and more conventional men out to get me—more McClellans, Popes, Burnsides, Hookers—who will overestimate our strength and show caution when they should strike boldly because they cannot believe I would divide my army so often in their presence unless I possessed superior numbers.

Or unless I were mad.

I am not mad, not for a minute. I simply want to make sure Thomas Jackson can hear me. Left here to be routed, I want to be sure Thomas navigates this Wilderness and strikes by this afternoon.

So I accompany him. On this map drawn onto ash-smudged paper with a blunt black pencil I follow him and his three divisions—Rodes's, Colquitt's, Hill's—out onto what Major Hotchkiss has marked as Furnace Road. It proceeds in a westerly direction until Catharine's Furnace—an iron-smelting operation for which most of the wood in the area has been cut—before turning directly south and then swinging back to the west, where it then meets the more frequently used Brock Road, running north-south. The day is blue and sunny, but the cover is good. Is it so good that a single Yankee picket won't detect a marching column of 30,000 men? On the narrow and roundabout route that column, with its guns, wagons, ambulances, and infantry, extends for miles; and is there nowhere a Yankee picket with sufficient vigilance to discover its movement and report it to his superiors?

Jackson worries about that single Yankee picket. If he is discovered, Hooker might very well let him march to his westernmost point and then overrun Lee, leaving Jackson with an army in the Wilderness and no one to fight. Into that worry runs the reverie of his great Shenandoah marches that Jed Hotchkiss has touched off and that these wagon-size roads—like skulking byways, like a sinner's low-tunneled path, like, it doesn't occur to him in so many words, our cramped, blood-obscured entry into this world—almost certainly reinforce. To kill the enemy in God's eyes—along His rivers and valleys, under His peaks—has been his duty and his desire. It has somehow instructed him in the beautiful. Nothing is beautiful that has not been won back from Satan, and in restoring the Shenandoah to God, he and his men have made it beautiful once more. Can he make that claim? He doesn't know, doesn't really make it. It is part of his reverie of past accomplishment that, as it runs into these knots of present apprehension, gives to his face a look of extraordinary conflict and ferocity. The men see it and march silently ahead. It is the silence of an imminent struggle, and it works back to men far down the column who can't see their leader's face or his now-rigid posture atop Little Sorrel, only the patched backs and shaggy necks of the men in front of them, the bare heels.

They come to a slight eminence open to the north, then quickly descend to a shallow creek they must cross, just beyond which sits Catharine's Furnace. Rodes's and most of Colquitt's divisions have crossed and turned south when Yankee artillery opens on the column at that low, exposed hill. Five miles farther to the east Lee hears the shelling, knows the risk he runs of being cut off is now greater, yet still urges Jackson on. Just as Jackson expected Hooker to retreat, Hooker now expects Lee to; and there's reason to believe that that column marching south will be interpreted by the enemy as the first stage of Lee's fallback around Richmond. Jackson comes to the same conclusion but bristles at the thought that for him to succeed now Yankee presumption and stupidity will have to play their part. He's been seen! Unseen, he could have fallen on the Yankees with all their explanations for him, like their suppers, caught in their throats.

He marches south, then west. Before he reaches Brock Road, his road, this pariah's path, narrows still more, and he can feel the men shouldering in close and hear in the close-compassed thud of their feet their desire to break loose and run. It occurs to him that if the roads remain narrow, he can march his men into the Yankee rear with their bayonets fixed and their desire to break loose at its peak. All depends on the degree of Yankee readiness. At Catharine's Furnace the artillery fire has now ceased, indicating that for whatever reason, Hooker has not chosen to press Lee at that point. If he believes Lee has begun to retreat, he might be planning to move Sedgwick against him from the east, his own force from the west, and catch the whole Confederate army in a sort of moving pincers before they reach Richmond—in effect routing the city out of the city, the government, the war department, the women and children. Jackson does not envy Lee his decisions; his own orders are clear: He's to make this march and attack the army he finds at its conclusion; and in the obscurity of these westward-angling roads, he clings to the clarity of those orders as he would to a talisman.

He takes out Hotchkiss's map. Although this one is quick and crude, he recognizes in the draftsmanship the hand of the man commissioned to draw the map that would take Jackson from Richmond to Philadelphia. This humble map precedes that grander one. Isn't it always so? Does he who eschewed the regalia of rank have to be reminded? From Brock Road at that moment, General Stuart comes galloping up to report that he and his men have driven off Yankee cavalry stationed north on the road, although they will almost certainly return. But since Jackson and his army will turn south on Brock Road and pass from sight before following their bow's route back to the north—and here Stuart makes use of the map himself, the fingers ruddy and thick, like the fist they form, like the irrepressible man—it might be to their advantage to let the Northern cavalry get an eyeful. Brock Road is the road to Spotsylvania, directly on the route to Richmond. Jackson says nothing. When he and his officers emerge into the open they do, indeed, see Yankee cavalry to the north, sitting their mounts, content to observe. Jackson worries more about the sudden broadening of the road than he does about the Yankees; about the relaxing effect it may have on men until now angrily pent up. Down a hill and 500 yards south, however, they do a near about-face and march north, back into the shadows and narrowness and the sudden close-shouldered-ness of men who until the Yankees came had wide fields to range over, space to fill.

It is noon. Lee maneuvers in front of Hooker's left and center, battery commanders like the Confederate skirmishers firing just enough to hold the enemy's attention but not enough to provoke a cannonade. The wind is from the west. It blows into Jackson's nostrils not the smell of gun powder and smoke but that of vegetation; there's honeysuckle in it, for a moment, like the achingly unobtainable in dreams, honeysuckle gushing in waves. What will honeysuckle do to his men? Jackson wonders. Or to himself, their commander, leading an army in one long, snaking advance into another army's rear so that in the presence of dogwood, cherry, and peach, and the evening's full fragrance of honeysuckle, he can fall on it tooth and nail? Nothing, it will do nothing. In fact, he doesn't know. But, of course, he does. To the man susceptible to the smells of spring, it will do everything. It will enter him through every orifice in his body, inebriate him, and with long perfumed fingers, unknit him stitch by stitch. That man is not the commander of this army. Then who is he? Who is that man who would surrender to the first wafting advance of the honeysuckle? He doesn't know. He knows only that he carries that man inside, and that as strange as it may seem—and to Stonewall Jackson in that moment of close, fragrant passage through the Wilderness, it seems surpassingly strange—he must fight for him, although *he*, whoever *he* is, would surrender at once.

Fight for the right to surrender at the first grazing touch?

He thinks of Mexico. He thinks of Mexico as if the life he lived there had been immersed in another element. He understands then that he needs open ground.

On the heels of that understanding comes another: Closed ground, close, self-perplexing passageways, and nothing else, will allow him to get into Hooker's rear.

When this narrow, bow-shaped road rejoins Brock Road past the eyes of Yankee pickets, Stuart is waiting for him again. Stuart will give him that open ground he's just dreamed about, and give it to him with a view. He must come quickly and alone. They, only the two of them—and if a stray shell were to find them now, both the abstemious and the profligate South would mourn—part hanging boughs and walk their horses to the brow of a low hill. There Jackson sees what he's marched for. Behind shallow trenches and abatis of recently leafed trees the Yankee soldiers, their arms stacked, are lounging about, while to their rear butchers are slaughtering the cattle that will provide them with their evening meal. From a regimental flag atop an officer's tent Jackson identifies this as the 128th Pennsylvania, belonging to Howard's Eleventh Corps. He's caught them more than just off guard. Farthest from the noise of the battle, they are deep in their ease and a number are sprawled on the ground playing cards. He watches one, a red-haired boy, get to his knees and brandish his winning hand in his opponents' faces. Jackson makes out three face cards, perhaps three kings. He hears the boy's laugh—a loud, snickering pant. Shortly this boy will be dead, as dead as that side of beef hanging in the sun —beef nobody will eat.

"General Jackson!" This is Stuart's disbelieving whisper, for once alarmed, as Jackson edges Little Sorrel out from behind the last hanging bough and into the Yankees' view. Like these arrogant idling troops there are more and more, and Jackson has unaccountably given them their chance. Stuart has even stepped out beside him, the two of them there to be seen on a low hill to the west, but they won't be, Jackson is somehow certain, and if seen, perhaps even better, for who would believe the sight? "Yeah, I seen yer kings, but look up thar and see if that ain't ole Stonewall Jackson and Jeb Stuart looking straight down at you." No, they would not believe the sight, just as they would never believe that the battle off in the east was about to come west and this would be their last hour on earth. Jackson's lips move. Is he now going to call out? Stuart must wonder, although a glance at the peculiar light in his commander's eyes and the duskiness in his normally pale skin would tell him that Jackson was praying to his battle god. But loud enough for the Yankees to hear? "General Jackson," Stuart again cautions. But Jackson will not be observed. If he has been rash in exposing himself, he has also been rash in leading a march into a sight-less wilderness, and one act of rashness answers to the other. He steps out into the open in order to step back, for what he and Stuart are looking at is not the Yankee rear but its extreme right front, and to get in the rear they must enter the Wilderness again.

I don't hold the delay or Jackson's foolhardiness against him. I sent him out there. I wanted to rout Hooker into the Rappahannock, but I also wanted to see. To see what? The men of Howard's corps amusing themselves, cocksure and unprepared? I have seen enough men idly engaged one minute and dead the next to wish to see more of that. No, I wanted to see whether Thomas could do it—and what it would do to him. His route now will take him north to the turnpike, and from there on a broad two-mile front driving back to the east. I will know when I hear the sound of his cannon and musket, perhaps the yell of our men smoking out their game. I wanted to see what it would do to me. My mind has not been clear. Like Thomas's flanking route, it has been shrouded by second-growth doubts and anxieties—what has grown up since the war tore my first-growth beliefs down. The Virginia of George Washington and Thomas Jefferson I once thought a great master, as much a spiritual as a geographical force. I actually believed that a land of such valleys, mountains, rivers, and coastal plains could arouse in man an instinct to wonder, and wonder-struck man, I postulated, was forever a stranger to meanness. I was wrong. The mob that stuck penknives into my father's flesh and poured candle wax into his eyes would have abused him as badly in the Shenandoah Valley as they did in the streets of Baltimore. Nothing, I am now certain—neither the healing powers of nature nor a woman's virtuous example—can bring peace to that war we wage inside. I *do* believe those who wage that war most vigorously will henceforth become our great men, all the energy and compelling force of personality being theirs. And like Thomas I, too, longed for that clearing to step into, even at the risk of being seen by my sworn enemies, even at the risk of being cleanly shot and killed. I mark it on the map. Here we stood in full view of Howard's lounging soldiers, beef drovers, and butchers, J.E.B. Stuart, unafflicted by such dark impulses, apprehensively at our side. Here we rode back to our waiting army. Here we marched again into the Wilderness, and here, facing southwest and stretching at least a mile to each side of the turnpike, we made our dispositions—three lines of attack, ten brigades.

And I wait for the cannons and the wild hunter's yell. By four o'clock I am still waiting, and I know that Thomas is desperately trying to get his men and guns up off the march and into their lines. Word reaches me that Early has pulled back from Fredericksburg and allowed the Yankees up the heights. I send a courier off at once, ordering Early to hold the enemy at Salem Church, to die there if need be. If Sedgwick gets in my rear and Jackson in Hooker's, who in the treacherous gay density of springtime green will know Southerner from Northerner, friend from foe? Thomas understands this. On the brink of attack his great fear is that the lines will not hold, and that the first breakdown will instantly spawn others, until the Wilderness imposes its own laws. Those laws are neither man's nor God's, and Thomas Jackson will not accept them. The men must remain silent, and silently, in a deep fog of green, they must form their lines. When given the order to advance they must move straight ahead, pausing only to allow the artillery to smash whatever obstructs their way. They are not to stop. They will stop when they feel the muddy waters of the Rappahannock wet their shins. It will be night then. The Yankees who survive the rout through the Wilderness will be swept up in a great biblical torrent and carried out to sea. Morning will break on a Wilderness no longer in enemy hands, and hence no longer wild, but a paradise restored to God.

Yes, I understand Thomas. God's sign to him has been that low hill, that suddenly clear view of the lounging enemy, caught, even for Yankees with the arrogance of their numbers, astonishingly off guard. God, far from deserting him as he had feared, has forced the enemy to look with eyes that do not see, listen with ears that do not hear, and has given to Thomas such preternatural keenness of eye and ear that he has been able to discern the red-haired soldier's winning hand, hear his idiot's snickering laugh. Then God said, "Step out, Thomas, stand clear. They will not see you." And they did not see him. Then God said, "Now drive them, Thomas. Drive the enemy into the Rappahannock." And Thomas galloped down to his men, pushed them the last curving leg of his march, and against their instinct for aimlessness, for disorder, set his God-given command.

Yes, I understand him.

May the God we fail in every hour clear this land of its invaders. May He choose for this purpose Thomas J. Jackson, who wants so badly to serve.

At five o'clock across a two-mile front drawn up in three battle lines, the Second Corps advances. It's the bugles I hear first—a faint, contained clamor off to the west. The wind is out of the west. The skirmishers have met the first Yankee pickets, and the next sound I hear is their musket fire—little spent pops, curiously spaced, as though the marksmen were chatting as they advanced and fired during the intervals in conversation. Yet I know this is the beginning of the fiercest onslaught we may mount during the entire war. It begins out to the west with a tinny clamor and a string of quiet, muffled explosions a child might set off. Then, with the first line advancing through the undergrowth, the second crowding it, and the third already breaking down in its eagerness to join in, I hear our men yell, a chorus that will strike panic into the Yankees but at this distance sounds as one voice and that, clearly, belonging to a slightly demented, sensation-crazed child. When the battle has begun in earnest, I will order Anderson and McLaws to attack Hooker's center and left, but for the moment I listen to that laughing child and the little puffs of powder he explodes, the frightful little racket he makes blowing all his bugles at once. I look into his face, such blue eyes, unnaturally bright, and so many lines—like a map of the terrain that his fiery little imagination throws up before his mind's eye. What must those lounging card players think, to be attacked by a child? Why do we ask the children to fight our wars when it is the children we must save? I do not know. Why do the children so love to fight, killing in their make-believe game merely a way to keep score? I do not know. The questions are vitally important, but I do not know the answers.

Jackson drives into Hooker's rear. He overruns their camps and, with his long whipping lines, catches them front and back and enfilades their avenues of retreat. He will not allow his men to stop. His officers have orders to shoot plunderers. The Yankee suppers must remain uneaten, the uniforms and boots they are caught without left behind. Jackson drives the men of Howard's corps onto the thorns of the Wilderness. If they stop to regroup, he pounds them with his fast-advancing horse artillery and envelopes them with his longer lines. Soon they no longer stop to regroup. I have already ordered Anderson and McLaws against Hooker's center and left, but it is Jackson's advance I attend to. His left, north of the turnpike, commanded by Rodes and Colston, has outraced his right, commanded by Colquitt and Ramseur, and I worry about a break into which Hooker, with his abundant reserves, can drive a wedge, failing in that moment of anxious exhilaration to take into account the psychology of rout—what any soldier's nightmares will have taught him. Hooker will make no strategic choices. He will either dig deeper into that clearing where the Wilderness has driven him or, like the most terrified of his thorn-flayed and smoke-blinded soldiers, he will run. I believe he will dig deeper, caught between two great fears. He will want to see the stars. Above all, he will want to die with his wits about him—and in the calmly configured constellations, he will imagine his wits restored. As the pounding of Jackson's artillery approaches, and the musket volleys, and the shrill, heckling yells of the men, I know all that can save Hooker from complete rout is night and the quiet swinging clear of the stars.

Then it is night. In the clearing at Chancellorsville, with his breastworks and abatis frantically refortified, it is the evening star Joe Hooker will see first: Venus, rising brightly through the smoke clouds drifting east. He will begin to master his panic by breathing something of the distance and something of the serenity of that star down. I will not see it. For the moment the clearing at Chancellorsville belongs to Hooker, and I, here in the Wilderness, must content myself with Stonewall Jackson.

He struggles to reform his lines. Rodes' and Colston's are badly entangled, and if he can separate them and get the men back to their proper regiments, he plans to call up fresh troops from Hill's division and order a new attack. He will not believe the first one is spent. His battle blood has risen and with no Yankees for the moment before him to fight, he attacks that Wilderness of scrub oak and pine—that dark, disorienting sameness of scrub oak and pine. The men must reform their lines! Somehow he manages to ride down Generals Heth, McGowan, Jones, and Pender. "Form lines! Move up! We must move ahead!" Into what? they wonder. That darkness? "Into whatever resists, whatever opposes you!" they are told. Jackson means not just the enemy, our Northern brothers, but the overgrown land itself—the brush and trees, even the darkness. "Sweep the field clear with bayonets!"

My map tells me nothing now, although I still carry it folded in my hand. It's a memento, I fear a memento mori. Yes, he means the darkness itself. Can he see Hooker as I do, feeding desperately off a pale point of light? And can Hooker see Jackson dreaming feverishly of a radiance restored? A combustible Hooker is part of that radiance and for the star-gazing Yankee, Jackson, of course, represents that onrushing night. Can they see that? Can their men? Does each side know why the other fights? Why, then, asking only for light don't we lay down our arms? My map is no good. It's my longing and sadness, and my great admiration for the man who wages that war of wars vigorously to its end that gives me Jackson.

He will not relent. He has fought masterfully and fiercely any number of days, and now it is night. If he can't find cavalry to reconnoiter the route to the U.S. Ford on the Rappahannock, he will do it himself. A young courier, David Kyle, who knows the region, accompanies him. On the way they meet General Lane, seeking confirmation of the order to press on. Jackson confirms. He's to press on at once, attacking the enemy's right and driving it north. His staff officers begin to appear—Wilborne, Boswell, his brother-in-law Joseph Morrison. Names become memorable now. Will Young Morrison mention Anna and Julia? Will he know something Jackson doesn't, or will he inquire? No, there is no time. General Hill himself has ridden up, accompanied by his aides. It is Hill's men that Jackson will send to cut off Hooker's line of retreat to the ford. Kyle, the guide-courier, is about to show them a road they can take. A road in this jungle is worth seeing, Hill will answer, and go along. Bullock Farm Road, it is called, branching off to the left in a northeasterly direction. Parallel to the turnpike and moving east through the densest darkness is Mountain Road. The names we are left with. General Lane will attack along the latter. The Yankees are close. How close? Why this compulsive curiosity to know? Why this ungovernable desire to steal into the camp of your enemy, to hold your face bare inches above his? Jackson leads a reconnaissance patrol grown now to perhaps twenty men through the lines of the Eighteenth North Carolina and out into the star-shrouded blackness of Mountain Road. I don't know why.

He is warned by one of the horsemen in the party that this may not be the place for him. That man's name is Colonel Thomas Purdie. Jackson answers that the danger is over, that the enemy is routed. As proof, he spurs his horse out ahead. Alone now, in the silence of guns—both cannon and musket—in the silence of battle yells—both ours and theirs —what does he listen for? There's the vast rhyming ring of the Wilderness, barely audible and shrill. And there are the voices of men, the unrouted Yankees, the giving of orders, and the fear-tensed mutterings of the men executing them. Axes, he also hears axes, a sound traveling so well in this acoustical night that they might have been felling the trees that arch blackly over his head. He stands his horse there. Uncharacteristically, for perhaps five seconds in the presence of the enemy, he goes off on a reverie. He remembers standing his horse in a luminous fog on the top of the Massanutton back when he began his Shenandoah campaign. That fog was so bright that it had blinded him and he'd feared that the light he'd stood in then, like the darkness he stands in now, might have concealed the enemy. Either could have, either might. But the light hadn't, that was a fact, and this darkness does. Still unrouted, yes, he admits it now, another fact, and turns his horse to rejoin his men and get on with the bloody job.

Halfway there, a single shot rings out to the south. It is immediately succeeded by more shots, and then by a rolling volley. When Jackson reaches his party the fire, with a cold but irresistible attraction, has moved north, and the men of the Eighteenth North Carolina take it up, shooting at what moves, whatever gives light in the darkness, a horrible thought, at the blues of his eyes. Young Morrison jumps to the ground and orders the men to cease firing. Major John Barry—at last no longer anonymous name—countermands that order with one of his own. "Pour it into them, boys!" he cries. And a kneeling volley erupts across the darkness in a jagged stitching of light, hitting not the Yankees but General Jackson three times—in the upper left arm, in the lower, and in the right hand.

I hear firing, of course I do. We have tightened our grip on Joe Hooker now, and the volley that rips into Jackson's reconnoitering patrol is as clear to my ears as the presentiment that tells me three of those balls struck Jackson. I feel a heat, a sudden surging of heat, and sitting in my tent writing dispatches to the war office I stand, obeying the surge. I feel youthful, aroused, and I think, "Thomas." Frightened by the volley, Little Sorrel, his horse, has bucked off the trail and into the underbrush, and those sudden surges of heat, not unpleasurable, warming my old man's quick, are the branches lashing his face, the low-hanging limb that knocks him flat onto his saddle. His left arm is useless, but with his injured right hand he manages to hold to the reins and stay mounted. Once into the underbrush, Little Sorrel's frenzy continues. It is this frenzy and her wounded rider's pain and senseless starry illumination that bring me to a state of extraordinary alertness. The stinging saplings, snatching vines, and heavy limbs have their go at him. Thorns rake his face, shred that black raincoat he has put on against the night's chill. With his right hand he tries to rein Little Sorrel back in the direction of what instinct tells him is his own lines, but he, like his horse, is disoriented and the dark is full of Southern and Northern voices—and he remembers it was his own men who shot him.

Not knowing where to go or where he would be safely received, he abandons himself for a moment to the crazed thrashing of his horse. It is the one long moment of his life. It passes from panic to resignation, and from despair to a great, rising joy. Finally it bursts on him, this joy, and for an instant he wonders whether he's been hit by a shell. I feel it too but at a much milder remove; it lifts me beyond the meannesses and prejudices of our struggle to a quietly accommodating state of mind. Thomas, it burns clean. He believes he is dying. A life of strenuous petition, doubt, and desire reaches fulfillment then, and he finds his great faith intact. He gladly gives up his wife and daughter, their dream of domesticity; his army and his cause. He gladly gives up on me—and receives his reward. Peace. What anxious possessions we've all been! Peace, pure and unriven, once he leaves us behind. When Major Wilborne finally locates his commander and manages to quiet his horse, Jackson has risen somewhere far above himself and this worthless land we fight for. He will come down. He will reoccupy the body that Wilborne and now fearful others—Kyle, Boswell, Morrison— are laying on the ground. But at the close of that long moment's abandon, what he senses to a certainty is the pettiness of our measurements and misunderstandings; from the height to which he has risen, the abysmal depths to which we have sunk.

Then he comes down.

I return to my tent, pull my stool up to my writing table, and write dispatches while I wait for the messenger to arrive who will tell me that General Jackson has been shot.

IX

Through his window at a distance of perhaps 300 yards he can see Guiney Station, where sixteen days earlier in the rain he met his wife and infant daughter. Lee, fearful of Yankee raids higher up across the Rappahannock, has ordered him transported here for the first stage of his convalescence, freeing Hunter McGuire from the Second Corps Medical Division to accompany the ambulance train. The building he lies in belongs to the Thomas Coleman Chandlers; like the office building at Moss Neck, it stands off from the main house, where among the wounded taken in there cases of erysipelas have been reported. The view, in a succession of lovely spring days, is like a painting he gazes at. The station, with its milling soldiers, incoming and outgoing trains, and cargo wagons, is in constant motion; but despite the motion it is always the same and essentially still. May 5, the day after the day he arrives here, Hooker retreats back across the Rappahannock, taking with him Stoneman's marauding cavalry, and by May 6, a full schedule of trains is running from Richmond up to Guiney, ten miles south of Fredericksburg. Anna and his daughter will be on one of them. They will be but a small part of the increased traffic; food and ammunition must now be brought up to replenish Lee's victorious army. Longstreet's troops will be transferred from North Carolina. Guiney will see them. Somehow he will not. He gazes at the life he has known as at a painting on the wall. Inside the room Dr. McGuire, his medical adviser, Reverend Lacy, his spiritual adviser, and his servant Jim form a team to treat him. For the past three days he understands that these men have barely slept, but periods of sleep and wakefulness, like the comings and goings of soldiers and supplies, also belong in that picture on the wall.

He has been the most self-vigilant of men. Like a monarch wise to the ways of assassins, he has denied himself the pleasures through which assassins customarily strike. He has eaten abstemiously, drunk nothing, attended to every minor ill. What some might call hypochondria, he has known to be the measure of his dedication to his country and his God. He has made of himself a fit instrument to serve.

He wants badly to recover and join Lee for an invasion of the North. Gazing into that picture during those moments when his waking mind is clear, that is all he wants. That that picture moves but somehow doesn't—as though practicing movement, as though shifting the facets on an enormous, stasis-rich diamond—gives him cause to hope that nothing critical will have happened during his absence. Out there he understands that movement charts the course of history and that history is all we are privileged to make of time. But out there he soon grows weak. His breathing labors, there's a pain high in his right side. Out there he has only one arm; but inside, in here, healed and whole, he communes with God.

Reverend Lacy joins him. When it has gone on far longer than it should, Dr. McGuire puts a stop to it so that the general can rest. Jim, a slave with the stamina and single-minded dedication of his master himself, is there to assist with the bandages, the bedclothes, to bring the general items from his trunk—to be his master's now missing second hand. From his months of guarding Jackson's privacy in his tent, Jim wears a loyal and lofty scowl. He obeys only Jackson, not the doctor or the man of God; taken apart from his master he would be thought insufferably proud. But he will not be taken apart. He sleeps on the floor beside the bed, and when Reverend Lacy is there to talk religion and McGuire to put a stop to it, he awaits his master's order to drive either or both of them out—or to absent himself, for he knows the general plans his battles in the absolute secrecy of his soul. Not for a moment would he believe that Jackson has lost his taste for the fight. Too often he has seen the general emerge from prayer in his tent with his face dark and that righteous embattled light shining from his eyes. He knows nothing about any picture on the wall. There is no picture, there's a window and beyond it a pasture not fully cleared of its stumps, then a train station and a depot where so much loading and unloading, shipping and hauling are going on it might look as if nothing were getting done at all.

But inside . . . now Reverend Lacy is there attending Jackson, who speaks with a newfound lucidity and ease. Does the reverend know one of the great errors of our time? That men in their desire to improve their lot and that of their fellows turn away from Christ to study the things of this world. On two counts those men are in error. They are obviously in grave error in respect to their souls, which they risk losing to assure their worldly comfort. And ironically, they are in error as to the very ends they pursue. It has been his observation that a people who have accepted Christ as their savior are a more proficient people in the daily tasks they perform. Would not the Christian cobbler in his humility and his worship of a divine ideal among men produce a better pair of boots than his heathen counterpart? Is there not something inherent in the tenets of Christianity that leads irresistibly to better workmanship in the things of this world? How can a cobbler be a devout Christian and stitch one unvirtuous stitch? He cannot. And does it not stand to reason that a virtuous stitch will be more sightly and durable than an unvirtuous one? Therefore, is it not true that a Christian people are a more proficient people and does not proficiency at last yield true prosperity? Would Reverend Lacy care to remark on that? Yes, the reverend would most emphatically agree, the general has uttered a profound truth. And a useful truth? If adopted and put into practice, a most useful truth. Unless Reverend Lacy mistakes him, that has been the general's point, has it not? Yes, sir. Yes. Since the hour of his wounding Jackson has thought long on his faith, and only at the point of death has he come to understand its beauty and demonstrable value *both* in this world and the next. Perhaps Reverend Lacy could preach a sermon on that. Yes, he will prepare it for the first Sunday General Jackson is back on his feet. No, Jackson wearily shakes his head—sooner. Would he prepare it for next Sunday? Why defer its value from one week to the next?

No reason at all. Flat on his back, the stump at his left shoulder left exposed to the air to heal, his face still bruised and scratched, the bones rising beneath the flesh like the craggy mountains that oversaw his birth, he knows his wishes are commands and that is why he must phrase them with due deference as requests. Perhaps Reverend Lacy could make use of examples from Jackson's own life? Oh, but General Jackson has already become the subject of sermons, the prayers of a nation ... and Reverend Lacy, anxious not to excite the general or cause him distress, does not know whether he should reveal the cloud of apprehension that hangs over the land, that darkens the halls of Congress, the war office, the cities and towns, the house of the common man, the tent of General Lee. Or if he should mention how overnight—it has been more than four nights now—the story of Jackson's amputation has been repeated from pulpit to pulpit as an exemplum of Christian courage and sacrifice. But somehow Jackson knows that. It doesn't interest him. Studying that picture on the wall, he can understand why

190

men out there in the dust and constant motion of no-change must be willing to give up an arm so that future, better-directed generations can keep theirs. But surely he has more to offer than that.

Life, he wants to tell Reverend Lacy, is in every instance a Christian act. About to die, he felt Christ's presence hovering around him; returned to life, he knows that Christ has not left. He is like a powerful dye, reconstituting the very fabric of Jackson's life. This breath is now a Christian breath. This opening and shutting of the eyes. Were he to rise and wash himself in the enamel bowl at the foot of the bed, he would be washing himself in the blood of the lamb. Whatever he ate—the stalest crust of bread, the thinnest broth—would come from the hand of Christ. The donning of his war-blackened uniform—was he not for every morning of his life dressing himself in the immaculate raiment of the saints? He is smiling, and Reverend Lacy will see General Jackson, eyes closed, smiling, but will never know the inexpressible sweetness of Jackson's realization that Christ, in taking on this corruptible flesh, not only sought to save our souls but to bless our lives, to give his divine precedent to the meanest of our acts. Did Christ not walk long hours in the sun, did he not suffer hunger, did he not sleep on rocks—did he not yawn, sneeze, snore, even belch, even defecate? Do not our lives in the meanest particulars but follow in the wake of his? Why should anyone emulate my example when for the virtuous the simple dailiness of Christ's life extends before us like a magnificent turnpike to heaven, each pebble of which is holy?

Jackson opens his eyes. His side hurts, but so did Christ's. He looks through that picturelike window. "If I am to become the subject of sermons," he addresses Reverend Lacy, although never taking his eyes off the struggling world of men, "let it be said that I am a Christian general, and take Christ's counsel before every battle, and seek His guidance and moderating wisdom in the heat of every crisis, and have achieved nothing that is not due to Him. Say that Christ will involve Himself in all our lives, from the meanest private to the most exalted commander. Say that Christ knows no meanness. Say, Reverend Lacy, that all excellence is His!"

"General Jackson! You must rest."

Yes, he must, Reverend Lacy agrees, giving way to Dr. McGuire, who examines General Jackson's stump, which is granulating satisfactorily, then the splint on the fractured right hand. Dr. McGuire is a devout Christian himself, and the expression on his face as he sees to Jackson's wounds shows both a measured grief that they should be so and a humble wonder that they should heal. He has worn that expression for every soldier he has attended. It endears him to his commander, who knows that war forces all men to make the most difficult of accommodations, and who feels an admiration warmed by a deep affection for those who unostentatiously succeed. Dr. McGuire, ten years Jackson's junior, is one of those men. He wants to know how the general feels, and when Jackson mentions again the pain high in his right side, Dr. McGuire inspects the area but can find no contusion or bruise. It passes, Jackson assures him, not caring to upset that equilibrium of grief and gratitude on his young doctor's face, and because this afternoon Dr. McGuire looks especially tired. Yes, Jackson must rest, but so must his doctor, made of the same exhaustible flesh as the rest of us. McGuire consents to the order, then passes a cool cloth over the general's forehead and offers him water. The water, the cloth, the gracious, quiet manner of the man before him—Jackson thinks of the Shenandoah Valley. There in that high, clear air his wounds would heal and his vigor return more quickly, and there—he involves McGuire in his decision; it feels almost forbidden this sharing of a secret—he plans to recuperate. Yes, a splendid idea, McGuire acknowledges the intimacy and smiles, just as soon as the general can be safely moved. Meanwhile, the trains have begun to run again. Surely on the morrow he can expect his wife and daughter. Jackson expresses regret that they must see him in his present state, especially his daughter, whose impressionable nature must be protected from such ... mutilation. He utters the word after searching Dr. McGuire's sad candid eyes. Little Julia will only see her adoring father, McGuire assures him, and leads Reverend Lacy to the door.

Jackson hears the two men walk solemnly through the adjoining room and out into the yard. Jim, who stands off in a corner and sleeps on the floor at night, now moves up to the foot of the bed. "Anything de gin'ral want? Jim close dem curtains so de gin'ral kin sleep?"

"Bring me back Dr. McGuire," Jackson tells him.

"I address the question to you as both a Christian and a man of medicine," Jackson says when the doctor returns. "Jesus performed many miracles. He restored the blind, He healed the lepers, He gave full health to the withered and maimed. A man paralyzed on his bed He told to rise and carry that bed into his own house—and that man did. He raised the living from the dead."

"Yes, there were many miracles."

"I ask you, could any of those poor sufferers cured by Christ—the blind, the lame, the leprous, the withered, and wasted—fall victim to their infirmities again?"

"The same infirmities?"

"Yes, the very same."

"I don't know, sir. I would have to think on it."

"When Jesus healed the leper, the most wretched of men, He told him, 'Be thou clean,' but also, 'see that thou sayest nothing to any man.' Yet the leper spoke it abroad and Jesus, because of the throngs that beseeched Him, could not reenter the city. Could that man's leprosy return?"

"Are you speaking medically, sir?"

"Yes, medically. When Christ cured a disease, did He cure it for the rest of the sufferer's mortal life?"

"I do not know. Perhaps it could return . . ."

"No, sir, it could not," Jackson corrects the younger man with a fond, autocratic forbearance. "Christ walked this earth as a man, and has left traces of his miraculous presence in us all. My hand was wounded and my hand begins to heal— *that* is a trace of Christ. We heal because Christ once wore our flesh. But our flesh is mortal and must of necessity fail. Christ's *touch*, however, his *personal* touch—it is like the infusion of his spirit into a repentant soul. A saved sinner will not fall again. Nor will the man Christ commanded to rise and carry his bed into his own house crawl into it again, unable to walk.

"I see, sir."

"Man must move—until his final hour."

"Will you sleep, sir?"

"I will, but think on it, Dr. McGuire. The cure of Christ is everlasting."

As the light fails at the window, he sleeps. Activity at the station does not stop, and the last flickering reaches of lantern and pine torch give Jim all the visibility he needs to oversee his master. In the early morning, groaning, Jackson wakes his slave. He complains of nausea and intensified pain in his right side. Jim asks for instructions, and for the space of his groan—questioning, almost meditative—Jackson can tell him nothing. Sobered and unsure, Jim admits to himself that he must wake up Dr. McGuire, saying, "Dr. 'Guire gonna havta see 'bout this." No, Jackson intervenes, Dr. McGuire has not slept for three days. With simple assistance the body sometimes heals itself.

His voice quiet, as though cautious, as though in the presence of the enemy, Jackson instructs his slave to wet bandages and apply them to his abdomen. When Jim does, he sees how gaunt and ghostly white the general has become. His belly is a basin, and the bandage sinks into it, rising only partially with his breath. At first Jim changes the bandages when Jackson tells him to; then his master's words struggle and break up, and speech to the slave's mind becomes the halting, ragged advance of a line of infantry, followed at last by the groan. The general's thin face points straight up, the expression gathering to a still finer, more painful point, and Jim has to apply the bandages at his own discretion. He wants badly to summon Dr. McGuire. He has heard them talking about Christ and cures, and he knows the Good Lord will look after General Jackson and Virginia, and when He gets tired of trifling with that Yankee trash will drive it out. But that groan is not the same voice that addressed Dr. McGuire, or even the voice that told him to wet the bandages and lay them on his belly. That groan, if Jim turns his back and looks out the window toward Guiney Station, sounds as if it belongs to a woman. But he has to turn his back. He can't look at the general's craggy, scored face, at the beard and the shoulders, and think woman. But he can't look long at the general either. So he changes the bandages as his master has ordered him to do, then looks away, out of the window to the slow nighttime movement of men and their mule-drawn wagons, yet faster-seeming in the more fitful light. Behind him, like a woman with the miseries—but miseries that will pass—he hears the general groan. Imperceptibly—whether over days or hours, he can't tell—the light changes and the rising sun extinguishes the flickering glow of lanterns and pine torches, bringing Dr. McGuire to Jackson's side.

Jackson wants to know whether Dr. McGuire has slept. Alert now, McGuire surmises Jackson's pain, which betrays no mark, no bruise, originates in the general's right lung.

By midmorning Doctors Breckenridge, Smith, and Tucker have arrived from Richmond, part of the surge north to fill the vacuum left by the retreating Hooker. Resisting that surge, a quiet backwater of the wounded, the Chandler plantation, where an anxious President Davis has sent the best medical minds the capital has to offer. For three days now a superstition has seized the imagination of that most excitable of cities; the press has taken it up, perhaps Davis believes it himself: If Jackson survives, the South is saved; he dies and it is doomed. Perhaps even England and France, withholding their recognition until the South demonstrates its capability to win, have come to the same conclusion. The newly arrived doctors diagnose pleuropneumonia in the right lung, and McGuire, a surgeon, reluctantly agrees. How did it happen? A fall from the litter while the wounded Jackson was being carried back from the front, a blow from a stump or stone? Internal hemorrhaging, the right lung filling up with blood? They debate the etiology of this pain, this labored breathing, this groan. Jim, who until the general revokes his order—or Lincoln frees him—has no choice, seeks to spread the wet bandages across the abdomen again and is stopped by one of the doctors. No, no bandages, they must apply the cups. "Gin'ral, y'all want dese here ban'ges or not?" Through pain now like a slow flameless burning of his most sensitive tissues, Jackson manages to thank his slave for his faithful vigil and care. "So y'all don't want 'em?" In an area the size of an infant's hand the pain in that instant opens and spreads, and it is his master's sudden grimace that drives Jim with his bandages to the far corner of the room. The doctors administer an opiate; when it has taken effect, they will seek to draw blood out of the right lung with hot cupping glasses. Before they start, that tiny burning hand seems to pull back to a distance where Jackson can almost take pleasure in its warmth. "What a blessing!" he moans. He thinks of the words of Paul to the Corinthians: *We are always confident . . . when home in the body . . . when absent from the body . . .* but cannot follow them through.

That afternoon when his wife and daughter step down

from the train, Guiney Station with its unresting motion makers has receded, as it were, to the end of a long lovely shaft of spring weather. He does not see them. Individuals in that cloud of activity out on his horizon have ceased to exist. He no longer hears the trains. He hears the weather, the chiming of the sunlight along the curving blue of the sky. Birds fly about his window—cardinals, their appearance sudden, the impression they leave behind an exultant red—and he hears their long, liquid notes. He also hears a voice, masculine, in a deep whisper telling him to rest. He draws breath with that voice, breathing through the pain. The war, soundless, full of the furious spent bluster of the sinking sun, slips out of sight and mind. When Anna bends down to kiss his forehead, he smiles. He knows the touch of her lips. They belong to Anna. This is Anna, not the Anna of silences and careworn sighs, but the Anna of eventide and song.

"Thomas," she says. "My dear, dear Thomas." Her voice quavers with the uncertainty she cannot hide. Is it he? The face he sees above him belongs to a woman caught questioning the mercies and severities of God's will, and through the face and the voice—the terror in that helpless love—he comes to know himself, the man he is now in his body. They've taken off an arm; his other hand they've bound in bandages and wood; they've disfigured his face with welts and gashes and bruises. Yes—it's the question she fears to ask, the sorrow that underlies her disbelief—they have assaulted his body and his body has given up, its dissolution already begun, irreversible. Why, he realizes, the body dies before we do, well before we do. Given an opportunity to die, the body will take it. The instant it reaches full growth, it lives only to be given that opportunity, and to desert us as though our dreams of long, healthy lives were the rankest of nonsense. Yes, it is not our souls that are prisoners of our bodies, but our bodies we chain like beasts of burden to the halting progress of our souls. Left to itself the flesh would die, and looking up at Anna, who bravely, disbelievingly looks down on him, it is his own flesh he feels sliding off his bones.

"My precious little life," he seeks at his distance to reassure her. "My *esposita*."

"Are you in pain?"

"Of some sort. Now they have given me an opiate."

"Oh, Thomas, they shall cure you soon."

"I believe so. Did you bring Julia?"

"Yes, of course. She is outside with Hetty. Shall I bring her here?"

He is about to nod. In anticipation he has closed his eyes when he is struck by the presentiment that if he saw his body's death through his daughter's eyes, it would mean the death of his soul. His eyes snap open. "No, not now," he whispers to his wife. "I would not have her see me looking like this."

She tells him he must sleep, that she will not leave his side.

He tries. For a few minutes he may succeed. His dream does not startle him, and may in fact be the thought he carries with him into sleep. Lying in his open coffin, he looks up to see the look of his death on the faces of the mourners who pass by. They are all men, and although he recognizes none of them, he believes them to be soldiers from his first brigade. In their faces he sees the struggle accomplished, all their doubts resolved. Then an older man stands looking down at him, and it is his own doubts he sees reflected in that older, familiar face that cause him to sit in his coffin and force the cold lips and stiff tongue into speech.

"What is it, dear? Lie still, you must."

"Read me Second Corinthians, chapter five, verses four through eight," Jackson replies in an urgent hush.

It is Jim, standing back in the corner, who hands her the Bible from the general's trunk. She has not seen him until now. With both their hands on the Bible, she smiles a wan smile of recognition, sympathy, and then takes from him the book her husband has lived by at home and on the march. Its feel and heft, the pliancy of its worn leather cover, recall for her the man to whom she wedded her soul. *This* man, she acknowledges, bravely forcing herself to smile. She reads:

For we that are in this tabernacle do groan, being burdened: not for that we would be unclothed, but clothed upon, that mortality might be swallowed up of life. Now he that hath wrought us for the selfsame thing is God, who also hath given unto us the earnest of the Spirit. Therefore we are always confident, knowing that, whilst we are at home in the body, we are absent from the Lord: (For we walk by faith, not by sight:) We are confident, I say, and willing rather to be absent from the body, and to be present with the Lord.

She closes the book very slowly, as though struck by new meaning in these familiar words, or as though prolonging the moment before she must show her face to her husband again.

"We are confident, we are confident," Jackson mumbles to himself.

She has the impression that the words hover just beyond his reach and that he seeks for something solid to attach them to. Her head is bowed now, her hands clasped in prayer around the worn leather cover. "Anna," she hears, and knows at once that he chooses her.

"Yes, Thomas."

"Are we confident?"

"God will make our earthly pains and losses seem like chaff on the wind," she reassuringly replies.

Jackson summons his strength. "Paul," he says, "writes that we would not be unclothed, but *clothed upon*, that mortality might be swallowed up in life. Can we wear the clothes of the spirit over the clothes of the flesh? Look at me" (and it is the peremptoriness of a forlorn plea she hears, not a command). "Will *this* flesh ever wear the spirit again?"

"Yes, dear. Your wounds will heal," although in that moment she will not look at them. "Now you must rest."

"And my severed arm? I am told my men have buried it."

"God will restore it on that day we rise healed and whole."

"Anna!" His voice sounds both near and distant, her name both whispered and shouted. Horribly, in the very outcry of his whisper, she can hear the gathering forces of his life *and* death, indistinguishable, like opposing armies broken down along a long intermingled line. What is this body? he wants to know. It is contemptible. It is the source of all our vanities and selfish desires. It pains and pleases us only as it inures us to sin. Yet we love it so much that God in His mercy would place His clothes upon ours. He would give our bodies back to us everlastingly! "Why, Anna?"

She shakes her head. "It is His wisdom," she says. "It is His way."

"Do you want your body back?" her husband asks her.

Forgetful of the bruises and scars, she looks him in the face. She remembers the confident measuring vigor of his eyes, now confused and cast adrift.

"Your dress is buttoned to your neck, your sleeves past the wrists," he reminds her. "I see your face and your hands. You can see *only* your hands. I have stared at my hand on occasion until I believed it belonged to another order of nature entirely. Why, Anna, do we want our bodies back?"

"I don't know," she answers sorrowfully, because she would console him, put his mind at rest. "Because they are sign and symbol of our humility," she ventures, "and only humbly should we stand in the eyes of God."

"Making of our humility an eternity?" he asks her.

"No, only until we rise again and God places His clothes upon ours."

"Then you shall be buttoned to the neck and wrists in God's radiance?"

"Yes, dear." She smiles. For one unguarded instant she allows her dreams to speak, a girl whose voice comes back to her like the blown bloom of a rose. "And you will shine forth like the handsome hero who swept my heart away."

His eyes close. He raises his face to the ceiling and she sees, of course, the stark scarred profile of the death's head he will present to God.

"Thomas, please rest now," she pleads with him.

The eyes remain closed, tensed. Not having been present at the great slaughter, how can she know anything of his pain?

"Please believe me," she says.

Presently the eyes relax. "Go, Anna," he says effortlessly, without a quaver. "See to little Julia, rest yourself. You must be tired."

"Believe me, Thomas," she says again, her tone more questioning whisper than command.

"Christ," he answers, "showed us how this life in the flesh must be borne." Then he closes his mouth and eyes, and with a last display of his extraordinary will commits himself to a state of such stillness that she can only admire it in apprehension and not look upon it long.

The next morning the doctors admit to her that they have not been able to relieve the right lung. They are men, except for the young surgeon McGuire, who but two years past in their wealth and prime committed themselves to the dubious fate of the Confederacy and now in the flush of Lee's great victory find themselves powerless to arrest its decline. They cannot disguise from her their concern. They will administer the opiate, apply the cups, but the world out there moving north in the belief that they will save its hero might stop and fall back were it to learn the truth. She asks what she can do.

Keep him quiet, they reply, keep his spirits lifted. She fears she will fail. That afternoon, during a pause in their treatment, she reads Psalms to him, but a fever agitates him now and even his favorite, the fifty-first—*Behold. Thou desirest truth in the inward parts: and in the hidden part Thou make me to know wisdom*—he seems incapable of following. She lays the Bible aside and quietly, as she sponges his forehead with cool water, sings to him from his favorite hymns: *When gathering clouds around I view,/And days are dark, and friends are few,/On Him I lean who not in vain/Experienced every human pain.* When the fever tossings abate, she sits back. She, too, is tired. For some time she has not heard his voice, and the sound she now hears—rasping, unattached—seems to originate within her head. It might be her husband calling back to her through the wastelands of memory. Already he might be dead. Then she snaps awake. How long has she slept?

A voice has said, "The mercy of the Heavenly Father is beyond telling," but peacefully, and Jackson raises to her his bandaged right hand.

But that night the fever and the pain increase, and the doctors administer more opium. Beneath the peace she thought pervaded him lay this terrible, disruptive life, dormant but not dead. Jackson becomes delirious. He seems to enter delirium as he would a dark wood. She has the impression that within the fever of his imagining he contains an entire world, and that world, of course, is at war. His voice is urgent, but toneless and almost musing. Self-addressed, it is a voice that merely escapes to her hearing. "Order A. P. Hill to prepare for action! Pass the infantry to the front! Pendleton? Where is Major Pendleton? I must find out if there is high ground between Chancellorsville and the river!" This is the Wilderness and this is the night of his wounding, she knows. She wonders whether in his delirium he will be shot. She prays—never ceasing to touch the cool cloth to the restless forehead—that he will not; that the future toward which he moves deliriously and which excluded him in the wilderness of fact will include him now. Lee's future, the South's. If her husband does not fall, Hooker might very well be surrounded and annihilated. She understands the great gains and perhaps the incalculable loss of that battle for her country's cause. Does she wish to witness an annihilation now? Is that really what she desires for her husband? She doesn't know. She listens keenly. She is no tireder this evening than she was in the afternoon, but, yes, nearer to collapse. Jackson says, "They are there, there. They will stay to fight." He says this quietly, with quiet satisfaction, as though confirming a suspicion. Then, almost immediately, he utters a long questioning string of sounds, not one of which is a word. Then another, muffled and driven-in. Under her cloth she feels his forehead contract and release, contract and release, as though it, too, were summoning the powers of speech. She senses his entire body strain as she strains to decipher these tautening movements and wordless sounds. Where is he now? Where is her poor heroic Thomas now, duty's disciple and the last man on earth to covet a nation's adoring acclaim? She doesn't know. She thinks Hooker has escaped him, that he's been shot, that he's lying delirious here. Like all of us, she thinks his future is his past, perhaps only one moment of it. Was his in that Wilderness, suddenly shot by his own soldiers and galloped into a crossfire not of blue and gray but simply of boys shooting wildly into the dark?

And hers? When was hers? The day when as a girl of eighteen—only eighteen—she saw him walk through her cousin's door and fail to play the gallant, fail to tell the wittiest jokes, but who impressed her with some correct and elemental understanding that there was such a day, such a fateful moment, and that all that a man could do to meet it with courage and trust in God, he would?

In a relieved, near-rejoicing whisper Jackson then says, "From New Market to the Luray." She recognizes the names and, locating her husband in his beloved Shenandoah Valley, realizes that inside the delirious man lies a man asleep and inside that man, a dream.

The next morning, May 10, Dr. McGuire informs her that they have lost hope and General Jackson must die. Before she can ask why, McGuire tells her. Pneumonia, brought on by a hemorrhaging of the pleural cavity—and that, most probably, by a fall from the litter that carried him back from the front or a hard blow from a tree when his horse raced out of control. But about to prove fatal because General Jackson has driven himself harder than any man should, slept in the saddle, slept on the ground, spent nights praying rather than sleeping in his tent, sucked lemons and munched apples and eaten little else; extended himself to the point where he thought he was large enough to keep the secrets of an entire army unto himself, and then finally gave out, marched that army along a route in a Wilderness few thought possible, drove it with the sheer force of his will through an underbrush as dense as rolled wire, and then, when the lines broke up in the darkness, surpassed his own superhuman limits by reforming them in readiness for a new attack. He spent himself that night. McGuire, himself spent, stops. That balance of grief and gratitude in his face does not tilt, but the whole of him, his surgeon's hard-won acceptance of the strengths and failings of flesh in this world, seems to sink. His voice goes with it. He tells Anna Jackson, "We've had him as our hero for little more than a year. We should not have demanded so much of him so soon. I believe we're all responsible for his condition. I am, the youngest recruit in his Stonewall Brigade is. Even General Lee. God has been just with us, I fear to say."

"Dr. McGuire," Anna replies without resentment, although she will never include herself on McGuire's list, "God is always just. That is the reason my husband prefers the world of God to the world of men."

She herself will tell him. The day has broken mild and cleansed of the smoke and congestion of war. It is a Sabbath. She has often heard her husband express a desire to die on the Lord's day. Being a soldier, he had not expected a period in which to reflect and prepare his soul, although she has heard him express that desire, too. Now he would have it. This she could now give him. But not the power to live.

It is her words, not the cool cloth, she causes to lave over him. "The doctors tell me that before this day closes, you will be with our Savior in heaven."

Exhausted, his pallor pronounced, he seems to have shrunken inside his bandages and wounds. "Is it so? Today?" he asks.

She nods. His voice sounds parched and aged, as though the voice of prayer, the voice of command, had already gone to God. "Today is the Sabbath, Thomas," she says. "You shall be translated on the day of our Lord."

His eyes have opened, but she sees no sight in them. Nothing troubles the lids. "No," he finally utters. "I do not think that I shall die today."

"Do you oppose it if it is God's will?" she asks him.

"I prefer it. But I do not think that I shall die today."

She is gone for perhaps five minutes. In the adjoining room, outside in the yard, there are many men—doctors, reporters, members of her husband's staff. They stand in tired, formless groups, their faces stiff as cured meat. Beyond, on the porch and out of the windows of the Chandler house, disinfected clothes have been hung to dry, and even though it is Sunday more are being boiled in tubs that she can smell if not see. The odor is God-less, astringent, like those well-intentioned men who are ignorant of the beauties of spring, of the lightsome air that arches over this ragged vigil, this ragged war. When she returns to her husband, she takes Dr. McGuire away from these men.

"My Anna tells me I'm to die today," Jackson addresses him. "I did not believe it. Now I have no doubts."

"It is so, sir," McGuire says.

"It is my desire. I have felt my savior fill this room. He is here still. My doubts came from my desire to serve God on this earth, but God's work is the performance of His desire, and my Heavenly Father awaits me in His home. Is Reverend Lacy outside?"

Dr. McGuire leaves to summon Reverend Lacy. Momentarily, Anna stands back from her husband, almost as far as Jim, who no longer stands but sits in his corner of the room, beside the trunk filled with the instruments and memorabilia of his master's holy crusade. She feels unworthy of her husband's presence. Something—that girl, almost certainly, with the voice of a rose—resists this sudden sublimity of her husband's leavetaking, and she is battling that something, chastising that girl for her vain and selfish desires. Her husband no longer belongs to that acquisitive girl. In the instant they beat and shot him and caused him to bleed, her husband already belonged to God. That's what she must understand; that's what that frightened, frivolous girl in her would immediately sense were she to approach the bed. God's presence and authority, His ungainsayable desire. But Anna is afraid.

Instead she watches Reverend Lacy approach her husband. The minister is a fine man who wishes her husband well, but even he is unprepared. She notices it in the forced, futile-sounding words and in the large hands that grip his Bible not in reverence but in disbelief.

Jackson tells him he's not to remain here, but to ride to army headquarters and preach. He's to preach a sermon on the theme they discussed: the dailiness of Christ's life, the *un*meanness of the most negligible and low. He shall not profane the Sabbath by forsaking the cause of the living to comfort a sinner's last hours. Jackson needs no comfort. He dies content.

Reverend Lacy, smiling, grieving now, entering as he is about to leave a state of awe, is to send Major Pendleton, Jackson's chief of staff, in to his commander. Still, she will not go to him. She cannot share his contentment, and because she can't, she reflects bitterly, her husband must lie alone until Sandie Pendleton comes. The slave Jim sits desolate and recalcitrant in his shadow. For other reasons—why aren't they the same reasons, she wonders, what difference between his life and mine?—he will not go to her husband either.

Major Pendleton has come in silently. She looks up and he is there. Her husband has spoken his name. His voice is feeble now, and its failure to command comes as much, she believes, from a disinterest in the things of this world as from a loss of strength. Young Pendleton pretends to be a soldier. He stands stiffly; by glaring sternly at her husband he manages to hold back the tears. He's to express his commander's gratitude to the men of his army and to exhort them not to desist until they have driven the invader from the land. Christians they have been under his command, and so they must remain. Pendleton is to somehow convey that in their general's pride in them, they have contributed greatly to his peace of mind at the moment of his death. But how, Jackson can't say, for his concentration rather than his strength seems once more to have deserted him. He closes his eyes. Major Pendleton remains undecided at her husband's side, the pink gone from his cheeks, the brown curly hair springing off the side of his head, like a boy's leap of affection, she thinks. He *is* the staff officer everybody loves. She closes her eyes. After a moment—long or short, she knows only that the room has become uncomfortably warm—she hears him say, "Yes, sir. God bless you, sir," halt abruptly as though upon command, and then whisper, his voice trembling, "Good-bye, sir," and leave.

Time passes. She's been on her feet all this time. She believes the doctors have come and gone. The sun may be higher, the room warmer, but she can't be sure, for she has what feels like a chamber of coolness inside—a vacancy, as though buttoned to her neck and wrists she stood before the mouth of a cave and didn't perspire. She looks up at her husband, exhausted soldier, dear man. From the miserable wreck she sees on the bed, she thinks back not to his great marches but to a period before the war began when, aided by a manual, he had tried to teach himself to dance and failed. Never the gallant, he was the only man of their acquaintance who could not do the waltz, the cotillion, or even a simple reel. He learned the steps but not the dance. The dance was not the sum of its steps, and he wondered why. He will die now, and never know. She does not grieve. His contentment will be infinitely greater—and it is then that she understands the source of that coolness, so like a spirit-cleansing breeze. That girl has gone. That part of her that would cling to her husband and cajole, has in frustration, in boredom perhaps, abandoned her and left this vacancy whose coolness now offers relief. Their married life has been shattered by separations, but this one standing back from his bed has been the longest. What do we know of the strength of our faith, or of the origin and true end of our devotion? She will not presume to say, but with unquestioning steps she now rejoins her husband. He opens his eyes. "Anna," he says, "ask Jim to come."

And she does, although she doesn't have to. Jim, who would stand guard at the tent so his master could pray, Jim preternaturally sensitive to the urgency and desire in his master's whispered supplications, has heard this one and stands beside Anna now, not at the foot of the bed. With his swollen bandaged hand, Jackson touches Jim's. "You're as Christian as any man," Jackson tells him, "and more loyal than most. With God as my witness, I set you free."

Jim shakes his head stubbornly. "You gonna git outta dat bed and wi' one arm drive dat Yankee trash outta Virginny."

"Yes, the Yankees will be driven out, but you're a free man, Jim."

The head continues to shake. "Ain't studyin' no freedom, Gin'ral," he replies provocatively.

But Jackson can no longer be provoked. He closes his eyes and Jim, a free man, is gone. Then he opens them, and it is like watching a man take steps back into a warm mist, she thinks, the blues are that feverish and pale. "Anna, bring Julia now," he tells her.

She brings Dr. McGuire too, for she knows that her husband would not ask for his daughter unless he felt near the end. When she takes Julia, alert and smiling, from her nurse, she experiences a sharp foreboding that only Julia can now cause her father to regret giving up this life for a greater glory above. For a moment she desperately considers how to deny the man she loves his last look at his daughter. But she knows of no way. With Dr. McGuire at her side, she enters the bedroom and holds Julia out so that Jackson, with his bandaged hand and swollen fingers, can touch his daughter's head. "Sweetheart, my precious little darling," she hears him murmur, and she hears Julia sputter and coo, for it is clear to everyone there that despite the bandages and scars and bruises, she recognizes her father. But only Anna knows that Julia, with her greedy and gleeful capacity for growth, will take the last ounce of life her father possesses and think nothing of it, continue to sputter and coo. She shuts her eyes and prays to God that Julia won't. The sputtering and cooing do not stop; it is Dr. McGuire's touch on her arm that causes her to cease praying and open her eyes, and then with a grief she barely masters to pull back her feeding daughter. Jackson has lowered his arm and shut his eyes, with light panting breaths begun to mutter incoherently. She immediately takes

Julia back out to her nurse. By the time she returns—as quickly as it's been—he is lost to her; in that instant, she fears forever.

He's in the Shenandoah. There is a spring wind blowing north, and a sky full of radiant, racing clouds, and he with an army that will not cease to march does no more than hold his head high in those spirited clouds and allow his men and himself to be blown. They are blown up the Shenandoah, down the Luray, up and about and through the Blue Ridge passes, beside waters that fill their banks, and fields of green grain and corn, and orchards that take the sky's shining as their own. It is a wonderful, light-headed race they run, and then they slow, as though the bones of their bodies, as hollow as birds', had begun to put on the meat of a destination. He hears a voice and understands it to be the voice of those fast-embodying bones. It is gravid, it sounds its weight. "March to McDowell," it tells him. "March there as though this encumbering flesh were a bright cloudy chrysalis you meant to shed. March faster than any man before you." He obeys. "Now to New Market. Do not continue down the valley, where numbers of dull-footed men are waiting, but with the flight left in you march up over the Massanutton, over the mountains, into a radiance you will know at once. There's the Luray, at its head Front Royal. Can you take it? Can you take it without breaking stride?" The voice, measured, gravid, betrays itself in a light, breathy pant. "I know," it confesses, "I gave you this flesh only to ask you to cast it off, but I make this demand in the name of our just and righteous war. Can you take Front Royal?" He takes it. Rushing its streets and hills there is an instant when once more he flies, when the blood surges up through his body as though it were going to blow off his head. As he crosses a burning bridge, that voice races beside him. "Drive them!" it exhorts. "Do not imagine it is only your imagination speaking when I tell you it is possible to move so fast you can

210

regain what I took away from you. Do not imagine I am talking nonsense when I say regain it and I'll give it back. It is not mine to take away; nor mine to give back. It is still there. I only clothed it. Don't stop to question why. Take Winchester." He doesn't stop. He marches at night, up a turnpike, racing, pleading with the starless darkness to strip his bones. Having outraced his army, he is forced to wait. The night is alive with voices, for each of the bullets that whizzes past his ears speaks to him of an insensate speed, of a madness, and he waits for the voice of command, of compassion and lasting promise, to return. When it does it says, "Press on," which he repeats to his men.

Dawn breaks on the brick homes, neat streets, and modest spires of Winchester. It breaks and will not stop breaking. It breaks like a clarion call blown on one unceasing breath, and it comes accompanied by that voice of his body, his blood, saying, "Can you not fly? Can you not drive those people out of that town, out of our land?" He does not know whether he can. Fear that he can't seems for a moment to deprive him of both substance and speed. Then he feels a wind. Its first grazing touches do no more than cool his temples, nudge open a button, dislodge his cap. But he allows it to grow. Somehow it gets inside his shirt and jacket, into his boots where his feet are inflamed. It begins to speak to his memory, this wind, and as he stands in the branching grip of its ascent up his legs, around his chest, he experiences the singular frustration of trying to give a name to something that was *all* he once knew, that was memory's very source. At its height this frustration dizzies him and the dizziness sweeps him up. Then the names no longer matter, for he is out on that wind, which is that long-breaking breath of dawn that is also and finally that voice, saying, "Yes, Thomas, drive them. Drive them into the Potomac, drive them beyond!" He has no choice. It is the wind that drives them, that he, ecstatically, rides. It blows him over a town he believes he once knew, that at the farthest reaches of his affections he might have held dear. Beyond it, like a ground storm—yes, exactly like chaff before a wind—he sees fleeing figures of blue, thousands of them, but behind him, back over the course he has traveled, he sees nothing—the wind has leveled it all. Where else if not from every minute and mile of his life did he think the wind got its flesh-transcending force, its celestial speed? "Look ahead, Thomas, there!" He sees the river, the blue figures floundering in it, the boulders white as the crest of the purest wave, and still. "And there, Thomas!" He sees, out on the horizon, the rich arrogant pinnacles of the all but wind-proof Cities of the North. He laughs. On his laugh he seems to explode.

His eyes are open. He says to the woman standing at his side, clothed to the neck and wrists, and whose features have been effaced by the wind, "Trust General Lee! General Lee will drive the invaders out ... for Julia ..." And then his eyes are closed.

When he opens them again, there are no fleeing men in blue, no Cities of the North, unless the banks of clouds there, on the horizon, suffused with an ever-deepening red, conceal them. There is a shallow flashing river, the boulders lit like the moon in the dying light of day. He sits beside the stream. He waits for the wind—except for those cities and fleeing men all he now remembers—to sweep him up again. But the wind has also died. It is only the water that courses and speaks. What does it say? He strains to make out speech. "Speak, tell me," he patiently pleads, for he no longer commands. Gay and brutish, the water ignores him, until it is night and all the light left in the world belongs to those lunar-pale boulders. Then it speaks, or he does, or both—apart or in unison, it is impossible to tell.

"Let us cross over the river and rest under the shade of the trees," a voice says.

And he does. . . .

* * *

"There was a smile. He never smiled broadly, as you know, sir. But it was a quiet smile, a smile as if he saw a wonderful vision of his Maker, but really very gentle. He was a gentle man, sir. Few people realize that about him. I remember ..."

"Yes, I know, Dr. McGuire."

"Sir?"

"I know about his gentleness. You diagnosed pneumonia?"

"Pleuropneumonia, yes, sir. Except for a pain in his right lung, he suffered no great discomfort. His death came quickly, and at the end was quite peaceful. It was as if he were wearing out before our eyes."

"Do you not find it odd, Dr. McGuire, that a man who defied death again and again in the roar of battle should die so peacefully?"

"With all due respect, General Lee, I no longer find anything 'odd' about war. War assures us of death. It may choose among all possible kinds."

"Do you think General Jackson would have preferred death on the battlefield?"

"He said nothing to make me believe so."

"Many of our officers would have felt cheated to die as General Jackson has. They must hear the cannon and the minié ball."

"He was a deeply religious man."

"I know."

"He died, I feel sure, secure in his faith."

"Yes."

"Although almost his last words, sir, were in reference to you. He said, " 'Trust in General Lee. . . .' ""

"I know that too, Dr. McGuire."

"He seemed to have no doubt that after our great victory

213

at Chancellorsville we would overcome our enemy once and for all."

"No, no doubt."

"His wife and daughter . . ."

"Yes."

"Reverend Lacy."

"Yes."

"His aide Major Pendleton."

"Yes."

"His slave, Jim . . ."

"Yes, they were all there. I know."

"He had the opportunity to take his leave. It was a blessing. I believe all of us felt blessed."

"Yes. Thank you, Dr. McGuire, for coming with such a prompt report on this sad occasion. I shall have to make the news known."

"I grieve for our country."

"For all those who were not there to receive his blessing?"

"For all of us, sir."

"I, too, grieve. You were right, you know, Dr. McGuire."

"Sir?"

"We *are* all responsible. We *did* demand too much of him too soon."

"Sir."

"Will that console us in our grief, or make it doubly hard to bear?"

"I don't know, sir."

"No, neither do I."

X

Although I do now. Were young Dr. McGuire here with me, I would tell him that in demanding too much of Thomas Jackson too soon we spared ourselves the final indignity and ultimate grief of watching him surrender his sword, knowing it would have been my duty to demand that, too, of him—and his to obey.

His death was timely. Only now, sitting at this table where the history of my campaigns will never be written, do I understand how timely, and only now could I measure for him his true worth. If the dead could come back for only an hour, what lessons from them the living might learn. But if Thomas Jackson were to come back, there's much that I could teach him. The purer the desire, the more impure and uncertain the gain—of all truths uttered on this earth, I'd ask him to consider that as the last to give comfort to our souls.

I come here after morning services. My office is located in the basement of the chapel, which was built at my request; close by, beneath the pulpit and choir, are located the mausoleum where my remains and those of my wife and children will rest. By sheer coincidence, it is in *his* town that I serve as president of a college, *his* hilly streets that I walk. The hilliness does not encourage idle conversation; you meet your neighbor on a stroll through town, and you are neither at an advantage nor a disadvantage, but you are almost certainly standing on a slant. When I learned to talk and then to converse, I was standing on Tidewater lowlands surrounded by cousins and unaffected by geographical constraints, our souls, if we had just returned from Sunday service in the Episcopal church, comfortably at rest. The people here are Presbyterian, for whom uphill-downhill exertions carry a special meaning. They have welcomed me and extended every possible accommodation, but either because they hold me in misconceived awe or because they see in me something I look for but can't see in myself, none has come close. I have no real friends. Two days ago my daughter Mildred confronted me. Uncharacteristically, her tone was speculative and plaintive. Characteristically, she is reserved and aloof. She said, "Daddy, you want something. What is it you want?" I replied, "What we all want, daughter, the well-being of our family, peace for our souls," speaking for myself and my neighbors alike. For the United States government, we are citizens of equal impoverished standing in Military District Number One. But we are not alike, and Mildred was not satisfied. And it is just as well. I have too much work to do to trouble my daughters further or to make close friends. I have a college to rescue from disrepair and this never-to-be-written history of my campaigns to write.

And the distaff side of my family to care for. Except for Annie, the war returned them all to me. My sons have also survived; the two youngest cling to sorely reduced ancestral estates on the James, and Custis is a professor of civil engineering at Virginia Military Institute. My daughters live on from one illness to the next—neuralgia and typhoid in the cases of Agnes and Mildred; debilitating dizzy spells that resist diagnosis in the case of Mary. But the effect they cause in the town and among the students who come to the house is of a sentinel-like austerity, as if physical weakness were precisely what they didn't have in common with the rest of the species. We have the Rockbridge Alum Springs not twenty miles away, and it is only there among more accustomed company—or on longer trips to White Sulphur Springs at Greenbriar—that they can give in to their illnesses and in some strange measure enjoy their lives. I offer them my prayers. From her wheelchair my wife Mary spends herself in bitter invective against the radical Republicans and the reconstructed South, the thieves who took and kept her Arlington, and on many occasions when students were present, I have tried to temper her remarks. But these remarks come elegantly of a piece and admit of no debate. The students are confused. Has my own position—expressed to them privately and in welcoming addresses—not been to the effect that nothing is to be gained from not putting the war behind us; that it is time to forget and rebuild? Did I not accept this appointment as president of Washington College because I thought it the most sensible and least controversial way I could serve, in the cause of education? Had the student body not risen from 22 to more than 400? Had the damage that the marauding Yankee General David Hunter inflicted on the porticoed and white-columned buildings not been repaired? Was the faculty not distinguished, and had the endowment not grown? Had I not conducted myself in such a way as to attract distinguished faculty and contributions from wealthy donors? Had I not promoted the cause of the New South at every turn, and before grand juries and congressional committees had I not sought to allay Northern fears that the Old South waited only for the chance to rise again? Had I not asked them to pardon me? Why, then, the correct and confused expressions of these students wanted to know, could I not . . . not control and curb, but instruct and enlist my wife's articulate tongue to our cause? With all due respect, it was true that she had been dispossessed, and obviously true that she had been stricken. Her husband, from whom so much had been expected, was ultimately a failure in her eyes, but of what family in the South could that not be said, and wasn't it time, sir, to go on?

Yes, I could tell him; now I could tell him. My office is

not unadorned. The pine floors are bare, the walls, except for a map of the county—a map I sometimes find myself staring at with blank eyes—are bare, the windows uncurtained. To my knowledge, during the time I have been here not a single student has been bold or curious enough to stoop to look in. There's a secretary and sideboard-turned-bookcase, and a round table with glass topping where I work. I have no amanuensis. I work here alone, and my adornment does not take the form of ghosts—perhaps because there are so many. Or perhaps because I am not the sort of man who invites the confidence of ghosts. But I am adorned. My walls are inner-walled with a presence so dense, so richly compressed, that the noise of the outside world—and we *are* building, we *are* progressing—barely reaches my ears. I can work here. I can write from twenty to thirty letters a day. The parents of all my students receive letters. I write of their son's studies and the development of their moral character. I am in contact with each of our trustees. I plan each budget, I personally study and approve each of these building plans. For work within my inner-walled paper kingdom, I have room. Each student who enters the college comes to this office for an interview, and it is true, we talk of redeeming the time. Some are veterans, and by not dwelling on what we have both endured, by making civil and civilian use of table and chairs, gestures and parting handshakes, we give the impression of moving out ahead. My faculty seeks me here. Reverend Taylor has visited, as has General Francis Smith, the director of Virginia Military Institute, and no one has noticed a thing. Perhaps because no one has come close enough. These walls tell it all. I am not president of this college because I am a skilled engineer called in to correct the list of these buildings and this institution toward oblivion. I am president because I am the living remains of a Lost Cause.

It is palpable being; it is flesh layered so closely on flesh that the last pinprick of space has been taken and shape has been lost to shape. Its smell is of all that is human and animal reduced to something as indissoluble and compacted with age as iron. It is this that they want me to give words. With the same words I write my letters and deliver my commencement addresses, they ask me to close my eyes and then, as if I were no more than a glorified scrivener, to open them and record what is already written there. But it isn't written there in words. After four years of struggle, it might as well be printed in the hieroglyphics of some geologic upheaval. They are patient, deeply deferential: At your convenience, sir, decipher the hieroglyphics, then. And there are times when I understand their reasoning and their desire, and assume that I must. A written record—who will leave it if I don't? During those times I have corresponded with men who served under me in an effort to locate copies of battle reports I believed lost or burned. A few have come back. I study them carefully, converting the language of high-flown commendation or blame into the language of fact, inviting my memory to supply the needed annotations. Nothing happens. My memory does not respond to these skeletal lines of words on a page. My memory responds to flesh. It *is* flesh; it lives crowded behind the smooth expanse of a wall. It has no equivalent in words.

I do not tell them this. It is not the sort of language they expect to hear from the president of their college. But I *could* tell him, tell Thomas Jackson. It was flesh he fought and lived in, and rose out of and longed to get back. It was those Cities of the North, with their underbellies hanging like an unanchored line, that he wanted to drive into. I had to decide between going to Vicksburg to defend the Mississippi or staying in Virginia in hopes of ending the war quickly—and I, too, wanted to drive into the North. An invasion would allow me to provision my army off the enemy for a change; a big battle there in our favor might give the Northern peace party the leverage it needed. He knew the strategy *and* the desire. So I could ask him, Thomas Jackson, to picture me riding along a road I had never been on, toward a farm town that was the hub of many rural roads but a town I knew only as a point on a map. To the steady thudding of artillery where there should be no artillery, soon succeeded by unexplained volleys of musket fire, I am riding up and down a hill; I am riding up and down smaller hills until the last gives me a three-mile vantage on an engagement that should not be under way. If I am accompanied by aides, I am not aware of it. My army is strung out over a twenty-mile stretch of Pennsylvania. I am alone. I could ask him to imagine that anxious, salty residue left on the tongue that comes of not knowing—knowing only that it isn't where and what you meant it to be, mixing with meat juices that can fill the mouth like a flower and that come from knowing only that it is, and that you are riding to it. This was the start of the battle of Gettysburg. But unless you can taste that salt mixing with those meat juices flooding the mouth, all I can tell you of that battle are the names of the places, the citations for gallantry, and the statistics of death.

But I could tell Thomas. He knew the taste. The taste I'm left with—of salt sweetly tinctured with the spores of decay —he would know, too. I was riding to a battle I had not planned for because I had not yet been notified that the enemy had crossed the Potomac to come in our pursuit. General Stuart was to provide reconnaissance on the entire right flank of our advance, and since General Stuart had never failed me and had yet to report, I had my army spread out gathering much-needed provisions. Then I found myself riding blindly into battle. East of Gettysburg there was ground ideally suited for the confrontation I had in mind, and my intention was to attack the enemy as he came up on a forced march in an effort to get between us and those cities of his he had overstocked with supplies. I could catch him extended, fatigued, questioning his worth, and roll up corps after corps. Lincoln had all those troops in the west that he could call back to reinforce his Army of the Potomac, but with his country cut in two, and with my army standing between his capital and Baltimore, Philadelphia, New York, he would have no choice but to sue for an honorable peace.

Yet I am left with this taste. In my thighs I still feel the deep, questioning shudders of Traveller's flanks. Prematurely, a battle is under way, and in my head a thin cloud has begun to form through which General Stuart is partly hidden, partly known to me, and the familiar form of General Longstreet has begun to blur. In the drifting smoke of battle this cloud gives off a stringent, antiseptic odor. It is as though in cleaning my mind I had left behind this smear. To General Stuart, impetuous, high-tempered, depressed by inactivity and made careless by routine, I had given the job that corresponded to his position—the ranking cavalry officer in my army—but not to the man. I had asked him to dutifully ride along and observe the enemy, not engage him. As the battle entered its second and third days I had given General Longstreet, stationed on my right, orders to go aggressively on the attack while everything in his nature begged to invite attack against our entrenched positions atop a ridge. General Stuart reported late and incompletely, and General Longstreet attacked reluctantly and in fitful surges. In that moment of their misuse, who were those men? I saw them behind that hazy antiseptic screen. They were like well-wishers come to the bed of a fever patient. *You* are the man I instructed to smash the Yankee left, and *you* are the man I told to unobtrusively reconnoiter the right of our advance. Why, you aren't those men. How could you be? You are like congeries of men, mere emanations of men, and the men you once were have somehow been squandered or left as part of that smear. J.E.B. Stuart and James Longstreet were lost to me in that moment, lost forever. You know these things from the start; I could tell Thomas Jackson and never utter a word. I rode up to a battle that shouldn't have been, and tasted salt. Then a freshet-rinsing of meat juices filled my mouth. Then the salt returned, pocked by crystallized specks of the men who fell there, barely detectable on the tongue. Stuart and Longstreet did not fall there, but I had a memory of their real taste, the authentic men, and they were among those specks. And tastes do not have words.

I did not fear Grant. I feared what he might be capable of doing, the limits he might be willing to transgress . . . I could tell him this—this, too, he would understand . . . I did not fear the man. I feared the regions in him that answered to no human name. It was said that he drank. There were rumors that before the war reclaimed him, he was cutting wood on a small piece of property he owned near St. Louis and had come to his last tree. Towns thereabouts saw in him the makings of a vagrant. He had not forgotten his West Point training but perhaps he had forgotten the preening and courting of favor that went with it, and he gave the impression of having come up through the ranks. The morning he hit me in the Wilderness, the instant I felt the dull clubbing force of his blow, I thought, A man who goes down to the bottom and starts back up brings the bottom with him. It will give him firm footing—but for anything, anything. A man of that sort might look into the eyes of his adversary and see nothing but sky, water, clouds, meaninglessly suspended flecks. I knew I must have met him as a young man in Mexico, but I could recall no face. We beat back his attack. He hit me five times before noon, five more attacks there in that Wilderness where his artillery counted for nothing, and I thought, He has learned nothing from the past, it contributes nothing to the ground he stands on, he prefers to begin each moment anew. We beat back all his attacks, inflicting heavy casualties. The face that took shape for me out of that same springgreen of second-growth oak and pine was of a monotonous regularity of feature and an inviolate regularity of line. The eyes occupied their sockets like lusterless stones.

How was I to general against such a man? Both his right and left were loosely anchored. The next morning I prepared flanking attacks, but he attacked again at dawn. Longstreet arrived with his corps. As he began to flank Grant's left—in the same Wilderness, the names the same, Brock Road, Plank Road—a volley from his own men brought him down. I thought, We must remember the past, we must believe we can learn from it even if we can't; and even if General James Longstreet had become another and yet another man. We pushed Grant against his flanks and he simply leaned against our center, where we were necessarily thin. The sense of weight was tremendous. I thought then that I understood the man. He would make of his army a natural force. With illimitable resources, he would maintain his army at capacity—a vessel that we might riddle with bullets and whose bloody contents we might send spurting over the ground, but that would always be full. When he released its flow himself, like any natural force, it would move blindly against the point of least resistance. We flanked him, and he pushed against our center. There was a moment when I stood there high on my mount rallying my retreating troops to mend that breach, shouting, "Never! Never!" The air was hot with bullet and exploding shell. My men insisted that I go back. I wanted to explain to them that there was nowhere—except darkness and despair—to go back to, that it was the duty of every man to mend that breach, contain that force. They mended the breach; my lines held. The fighting had been so intense that by dusk their muskets were too hot for my soldiers to hold. That night the Wilderness burned. The orange light brightened and dimmed, brightened and dimmed as the flames reached new areas of combustion, the wounded left lying there—theirs and ours—in the most fierce and intimate of embraces. I consulted the past and concluded that if history was willing to repeat itself one last time, in the morning Grant would be gone.

In the morning my pickets reported that he was—back across the Rapidan, I allowed myself to hope. Then I realized that, unlike armies led by recognizable men, natural forces did not retreat; they grew until they found a way around every impediment. Grant had swung out to his left and begun a march toward Spotsylvania that would take him flowing on toward Richmond. It was the simplest of maneuvers. For him a slide and one-step ahead. Mirroring his movements, I slid and stepped with him. We had performed a simple two-step, although that was not how it was. We were not dancing. That was only how it might appear on a map or sound in words. Just as I reached Spotsylvania Courthouse and drew up my lines he hit me hard, and something of that deep bottom he hit me with, something of the gravity-rich earth and the chemical conversions going on there—the conversion of plant and animal remains over the millennia to fuel and stone—got into my arms and legs as I sought to defend myself and allowed me to check his flow. Two days of pounding me there, and he was gone again.

I never knew soon enough that he was going. My strategy was to catch him on the march and hit him before he had an opportunity to draw up his forces before me, but there was so much of him, so many of him, that he could abandon a position and still man the crossroads and throw down a line that would at first glance lead me to believe he had not gone at all. By the second glance, he would have stolen a march on me. I needed Stuart to ride dashing circles around the enemy and apprise me of his movements—the sort of thing Stuart did best. But Stuart had not been able to wait. I had lost him. General Stuart had felt the need to reclaim his nature and near a hamlet called Yellow Tavern had charged into enemy fire. He lay dead now in Richmond.

So, faster than my encumbered opponent, I was always catching up. *He* would understand. Speed that always asks for more, that feeds on itself and never has enough—of all the men who have ever marched armies, he would understand. Grant had slid to his left and stepped forward on a long diagonal, and I raced him again, this time to the ford of the North Anna at Hanover Junction. He engaged me there briefly, then slid and stepped off again. Richmond, of course, was the prize we were circling. If I were thrown back on our works there and Grant undertook a siege, he could starve us out. At Old Cold Harbor he concentrated his force once again, and I thought, It will come here, he will want to push me back here; one step-and-slide more, and he will be in the James. I made my dispositions. On our right there was a hill where I stationed artillery. That afternoon it rained heavily. My men dug their trenches in mud. The mud might have saved us. Before dawn Yankee artillery laid down a barrage that woke every sleeper in Richmond and shook every complacent soul, and then across muddy slashed ground, crosshatched with ditches, the enemy made his general assault. They came up and down the entire front, and they came again and again. By eight o'clock my First Corps alone had withstood fourteen attacks. Every man I had was on the line, so that a breakthrough at any point might have been disastrous, but my lines held and the Yankee bodies began to pile up in the mud. Grant had these men to give; natural forces create pressures that are painful to bear and dangerous in and unto themselves. He gave these men and relieved the pressure. By eleven o'clock he had stopped. From that elevated ground to our right I could see that he still had abundant reserves left, but as a force he had accomplished at least one of his objectives: He had not blown himself up. The mud now crawled with his wounded soldiers. Years from now wars would be fought in just this way, I quite understood; the open country of maneuver would be reduced to bloody squares of mud, where the dead would lie ten to twenty deep. Grant learned from the future, not the past.

The next day the Yankee wounded moaned for water. I waited for Grant to request a suspension of hostilities so that he could bring his wounded out. I waited for two days. Did he think he would be admitting defeat? Finally the request came, but by then the mud had taken the wounded under and their replacements had flowed in, bringing his force to capacity again. For that freshly seeded mud, abominably rich to the nose, a soughing of dying whispers to the ear, a slippery, quilted swaling to the eye, what words?

Then Grant and his Army of the Potomac disappeared. For five days I didn't know whether he was north or south of the James, and I wired General Beauregard in Petersburg for news. How could all those men, all that ordnance, those interminable trains of supplies, just disappear? While I was studying that mud and reading its half-transformed shapes into the future, had I been taken off guard? I assume I had dropped into a daze—just as *he*, sitting on a log with a biscuit between his teeth, had gone into a daze—and when I finally woke out of it, I woke with a craving for speed.

But did I wake out of it? Yes, Grant had crossed the James and was now marching to join Butler in his siege of Petersburg, and I stumbled after him, slipping into our works there before he could attack, perhaps only because he wanted me there before him, in the closest of close quarters, the trenches a stone's throw apart. But it may be that I never woke up, or that when I did after that fearful battle, at the conclusion of those sprinting marches, there was less of me to wake up to. It felt like a dream, the mud I seemed to carry with me as I marched my army on to Petersburg. I exhorted myself to snap out of it, reminding myself that the roads were dry. In Petersburg we would be pinned down for the rest of the year. Alarming reports would reach me from Tennessee, then Georgia, then South Carolina—wherever Sherman marched his men. Sheridan was employing the same scorched-earth tactics in the Shenandoah. More of my men would die that winter from hunger than they would from Grant's sharpshooters' balls or from his intermittent charges. I was ready to abandon Richmond to its fate—which had so often squandered its stamina in political wrangles that left my army unprovisioned and undermanned. There were abundant supplies waiting for us in Danville, one hundred miles to our south. General Johnston could march north out of South Carolina to meet me there. Together we might maneuver in open ground, smash Sherman, turn and smash Grant. The relief of escaping Petersburg and taking one breath without Grant in my face would be worth it—it might even work miracles! Yes, I woke that day in Old Cold Harbor with a craving for speed.

Or did I wake? I would have to ask *him*. I would have to ask Thomas Jackson to tell me: As we pulled out of our trenches at Petersburg, 30,000 strong, and began our march south, as the open ground, however decimated and stripped of supplies, caused our spirits to soar, as trains of rations moved north out of Danville to meet us, as those rations remained, miragelike, just one more town head—in Amelia Springs, in Farmville, at Appomattox—as the men began to fall by the wayside and an army of 30,000 became an army of 8,000, as 8,000 men lived on air, tried raggedly to march on air, while a Yankee army, heavy with their suppers, overtook them, as 8,000 men, weightless now, came to a trembling halt at Appomattox, surrounded by the full weight of Grant and his men, as the leader of those beleaguered men rode to surrender his sword, which he wore but didn't surrender, and whose men, but wraiths of themselves, were past the point of surrendering, as the moment arrived and I stood in the house of one Wilmer McLean, who had owned the farm on which we fought the first real battle of the war at Manassas, and had moved south looking for peace—a haven for his family, a world remote from the one about to assemble here—as that world assembled and I stood before the man, the little speed I had managed for myself come to a halt in this place, on this particular day of this particular year, I should have to ask him, ask *you*, General Thomas J. Jackson, who battled your flesh every day of your life and, disincarnate, led your men—"Was I asleep or awake?"

And without malice or hint of disrespect, you should answer: "Neither asleep nor awake. You had simply gotten old, old man."

I must confess something to you, Thomas. There in the Wilderness, after Grant had first hit me and withdrawn, then hit me again and we had burned the forest so that no one should mistake the inferno we had created for ourselves, I thought of you. You had wanted light to continue your attack. Light, of course, would have changed everything—your reconnoitering mission alone in the dark, the tragic mistake Major John Barry and his Eighteenth North Carolina made. I watched the Wilderness burn that night, thinking how well General Grant and I understood each other. Remove the extraordinary man, and this senseless destruction was war. Then when he made his first lurching move on me, I thought of you again. If you had been dragging along behind you an army the size of Grant's, if you had been less extraordinary and almost comically encumbered with your might, you might have moved that way. That bearish roll of his across the peninsula, even that ponderous disappearing act—they did you no credit, no justice, but they kept you alive for me. Then he stepped up onto McLean's front porch and I stood up in McLean's parlor to receive him. Before he appeared at the door, I felt the man's vitality fill the room. I recognized it at once. It was the same vitality that raised forts and then allowed them to crumble; that cut deep, improvident rivers in the land and then watched them shelve in. It was the vitality of powerful eruption succeeded by waste, and in some manner I had fought it all my life. So I knew what to expect. He was your height, his beard fuller than yours. I stood before him in full formal dress while he, like you, preferred the mud-spattered boots and leggings of his marches. His expression was solemn, but not stern. Nor was it clean. Bits of all that it had looked on seemed to have stuck to it, which could only mean that however horrible the sight, he would be will-

228

ing to look on it again and again. He extended his hand. No, it was not unexpected—the surge, that dark current coursing into my arm—and I thought of you, Thomas. No, I said. He wanted to talk of Mexico. In his own earnest, graceless way, he wanted to do me a reverence—he had never forgotten what an impression I'd made riding up from General Scott's camp—and I said no. Before he released my hand, just perceptibly he bowed his head. The war ended here for me. I stood apart, my hands now lowered, tremors rushing to fill the vacancy at my knees. It was the onset of rheumatism. I could ask for his hand again—this spendthrift of men and bludgeon master of the war was not an inconsiderate man— but I said no, "No, General Grant. No. I have come to surrender an army. Will you accept it?"

That is not the kind of language the trustees of this college who made me their president want to hear. They answer: "Whatever language you choose to employ, General Lee. Only you can write the history of your campaigns. The other letters can wait. Those parents whose sons are in your charge can wait. If the rheumatism that has now spread to your hands is too painful, we would be honored to hold the pen. . . ."

Thomas.

This morning I interviewed a delinquent student in this office. He had missed chapel and cut classes for three successive days, for which I reprimanded him by pointing out that somebody had gone to some effort and expense to maintain him here. I interviewed all delinquent students. Of the very small minority of men fortunate enough to attend a college in these days of want, there was a tiny minority who gave the regrettable impression of disdaining that good fortune, those efforts, and that expense. I always spoke quietly, unaccusingly. I could usually count on the student to accuse himself, perhaps even to picture himself and those of his tiny unregenerate kin in a hell of their own making. This student gave his name as James Dalton. He had a long face and large

229

fatigued eyes that hung in it like pools. He did not appear sick, however. He looked at me as if he saw far beyond my words, and when I concluded my remarks he said, "I fought beside you, General Lee."

This was not the first student who had volunteered such information. The tone in which he said it, however, I had not heard before. It seemed incredulous and complicitous at the same time.

I said, "Yes, Mr. Dalton. In which regiment was that?"

He said, "I fought beside Stonewall Jackson, General Lee. I was in the Fifth Regiment of the Stonewall Brigade."

"The Fighting Fifth," I mused involuntarily.

"Yes, sir."

"When no Yankees were available, you fought among yourselves."

"We were there to fight, General Lee. While we were looking for the enemy, we practiced on ourselves. When General Jackson died I fought beside you, sir." He lowered his voice, although there was no reason to. We were alone. "I fought beside you to the end."

So many people—townspeople, faculty members, members of the press, the occasional student—invited me to reminisce about the war that I had developed a sort of practiced recoil that put an end to the matter. I recoiled off the table then, back onto the high back and armrests of my leather chair. Mr. Dalton did not move. Then he bent forward and placed his large, sinewy hands palm down on the glass tabletop, and I found myself sitting back up in the chair, my right forearm on the table, the hand half closed around the shoots of pain.

"Yes . . . yes . . ." I said. Something was forcing words out of me that I had not prepared. "I am sorry . . . I don't remember you, Mr. Dalton."

"You surrendered me at Appomattox. I can't say I belonged to any regiment by then . . ."

"So many had lost their regiments," I allowed. "We seemed so many but in fact we were very few."

"I would have fought beside you until there were only the two of us, General Lee. But I was relieved when we surrendered—I don't deny that. Every day since then, that relief has been running out."

I was not being dull. There was something sadly arresting about this young man's voice and eyes, the hands he held palm down against the glass, as though to turn them over now would be to expose more of himself than he could bear. I repeated, "Running out?"

"Sir, could I ask you a question?"

I must have given some motion of assent, otherwise he would not have continued. But I recall assenting to nothing.

"Have there been times when you wished we had fought until there were just the two of us, and then until there was none?" he asked.

This time the recoil was not practiced. I was back in my chair. The question I had heard before, but not in that presuming and very private tone, which seemed to envision what it asked—the two of us, as it were, fighting off the same lifeblood.

"Mr. Dalton," I said, "we are here to talk about your absences."

He took the rebuke. At last the large watery eyes fell away from mine. He looked at his hands, which he lifted off the glass and cupped away from me, exhaustion in his face now, some last, lingering doubt that in better days would have been amazement. I quite understood that gripped around a musket, a bayonet, a throat, the hands had killed Yankees. He would never have lasted the entire time without killing Yankees. He put the hands in his lap.

"Yes, sir," he quietly acquiesced.

"You talk of soldiering. A student cannot attend only the classes he chooses, just as a soldier cannot fight only the battles that suit him. We do not have the time or the luxury for that."

"No, sir."

"You absences from morning services are particularly worrisome."

He nodded, then audibly drew breath in an effort to rise out of his slump. He rose perhaps halfway. I waited until I saw that, unassisted, he could do himself no further good.

"You have no explanation to offer?" I said.

"Only that my relief ran out," he mumbled.

"Speak plainly, sir," I said.

I had caused him to sit up. What passed through his eyes was not so much anger as irritation, frustration. The eyes tensed against their downward flow. "It is not clear to me, sir," he said plainly.

"You have remained in town these past three days?"

"Yes, sir. In my room."

"Were you studying? Preparing an examination?"

"No, sir. I can't really say that."

"Thinking? Considering your future?"

"I mostly slept."

"But you were not ill?"

"No . . . I had no illness."

"Well, Mr. Dalton, the time has come to think. What do you propose to do?"

He waited until my dissatisfaction with him was palpable in the room. Then, rousing himself, he straightened up and extended his arms out over the table. The hands were palm down again on the glass, but they gave the impression of being dug in there now, the heels of the hands. The shoulders were stiff, on guard.

"I propose to ask you that question again, General Lee," he said.

"Do not do so, Mr. Dalton," I said.

"It is not the question you think it is, sir," he replied. "I do not refer to our war against the North, to the nation we never were, or to the Lost Cause. . . ."

"I must warn you, Mr. Dalton, that you are jeopardizing your standing here as a student. If I decide that you should be expelled, there is no board of appeal."

"Sir. My question is only if it has happened to you, if since the war ended there have been periods, periods of three days, for instance, when the position you occupy in this college meant nothing to you, when ..."

"It *is* the question, Mr. Dalton."

He showed the courage to finish, and I understood that no coward could have survived that war, not in my army "... when it was a fight you needed, when it was a war somewhere you had to have?"

I thought of my father. I thought of my father about to go off to fight in the French Revolution—a war, any war—until the man for whom this college was named and whom I could imagine sitting behind a table such as this persuaded him not to. I was absent only for a moment. Not long enough to have relinquished my power or my privilege. I replied, "If it does you any good, Mr. Dalton, the answer is yes. Nevertheless, another day of absences this term and I must ask you to surrender your place to someone ... to someone more motivated. Is that understood?"

"Yes, sir."

"I am sorry."

"Sir."

That was all. He had gotten the answer to his question, and he was the first to stand. That weariness in his face had not become purposeful, it had simply hardened, and I felt certain that before the term was out we would lose him. His handshake was proper, neither obsequious nor too warm. I knew that I could turn the hand over and read in the palm another history of our wars, but I checked the impulse and watched him go out the door. For the rest of that morning my walls were extraordinarily active. But this interview had lasted longer than I'd expected and I had letters to write, business to transact. That afternoon, as was my custom, I went out riding on Traveller. This afternoon. Now.

Do you understand, Thomas, that this cannot go on? I do not refer to the rheumatism, which at any rate is less aggravating on horseback. Or to the discomfort around the heart, which the doctors describe as an inflammation of the heart sac, but for which they clearly do not yet have the right name. It grieves me to see my wife dispossessed and my daughters overly solicitous of me and unwed. But not that.

The beauty of these hills, you know only too well. In the afternoon light they lose every sharp angle, every hard line, and take on a nubile fullness of form. If it is the beginning of spring, as it is now, they are covered in a light-green fuzz. The forsythia has flowered, the redbud, and the dogwood, that most ornamental of trees, with the peculiar definition of its petals and the peculiar layered arrangement of its limbs, grows plentiful here, and wild. I ride away from the town and the Blue Ridge. West of the college there's a gorge I must descend and a stream I must ford, and then upland pastures alternate with patches of wood, primroses with spring beauties, until the horizon where the Appalachians succeed themselves, range after sun-softened range. I ride toward those distant mountains, across pastures that seem to lift me, like a heave of the sea, toward a clearer perspective. Many of the farm buildings here were burned to the ground by Hunter's triumphant and vindictive soldiers, and I count on the upsurge of these pastures to raise my sight and my spirits. But you know this land. I've been told by scattered farmers that Major Jackson used to ride this way. It was as Major Jackson that they knew you then. Apparently when the classroom became too confining, there was a plot up here you used to till. . . . Damn them, Thomas! I do not wait for a burned barn or a charred chimney or a field gone to seed. Frequently it comes on me when the valley is at its loveliest and the way is clear all the way to the mountains. I put the spur to Traveller and ride the two of us to a high lather, the smell of my old man's sweat a long time in reaching my nose. But eventually it comes, a thin aging taint rises on the breeze that is nothing other than the smell of my battle blood risen, and then there are any number of scenes to choose from. They're all there—Manassas, Fredericksburg, the north bank of the Chickahominy, Chancellorsville where you fell.

You see that it can't go on. I intend to take a trip soon. I want to visit the graves of my father and my dear daughter Annie. While I have any strength left me, I want to set their gravestones upright, which, like everything else in this South of ours, will surely have been knocked awry. There is no way to avoid it—this trip will take me across the most devastated area of our country. At every stop of the train, people will cheer me. They have already done so. The people here in Lexington are less demonstrative, or more accustomed, but beyond these hills they wait for me standing in the ruins of their cities, or standing on the ruins of their farms, and cheer *me*—another ruin. The women bring me endless dishes of food, their babies to touch. I am forced to rent hotel lobbies to hold receptions in; the line of men waiting to shake my hand will extend for blocks. It is not false modesty—you know it's not—if I tell you that I do not understand it, that I wish it weren't so. On the return, I shall have to pass through our entire state. They will demand it of me. This Virginia we loved, Thomas, without quite understanding why—it is better that you never saw what was done to it. Those plantations along the James. The cities—Norfolk, Petersburg, the capital, Richmond, which I abandoned to its fate and where they worship me the most. The Yankees burned almost the whole of Richmond. They gutted its industry, its waterfront; the finest of its homes, they reduced to shoulder-high rubble. The capitol they left to stand over this waste, a monument to the politicians whose boast and bombast assured us of this end. You lay there in state. For that day of mourning, the best of Virginia's men and women passed before your casket in lines exceeding any of mine. Then the politicians returned.

My doctors actually prescribe this trip for my health, and the college insists that I take the time. But I know the state of my health better than my doctors, monitor it with each charge I make up these sloping hills, and I know that it can't go on.

Although it's not my inflamed heart sac I'm talking about, or my rheumatic joints.

You know what it is. Poor James Dalton does, in full possession of his unsatisfiable youth. My father knew. Perhaps even General, now President, Ulysses S. Grant knows what it is. We may be legion, but for shame we do not say.

Thomas, I have visited your grave. Your marker is simple, broad-shouldered, contained. A graveled path has been laid around it so that your admirers might mourn your passing from each point on the circle. I have visited your house; it was not sacked as others were. It is being preserved for you, although not sufficiently aired. As a strange sort of tribute, your garden in back has been allowed to grow wild. I have visited the First Presbyterian Church—it was a favor your pastor, Dr. White, extended. He assured me that it was your pew I sat in and your hymnal I opened to your favorite hymn, "Come, humble sinner, in whose breast a thousand thoughts revolve." General Smith has admitted me to the classroom where you taught your classes in natural philosophy. Others have volunteered information: "When he ate here, this is where he sat; he preferred this chair when I cut his hair. Over there, in the shade of that oak, was his favorite bench." I have taken what little was left of you in each of these places, and I have not gone back. Not six months after the war ended, I saw Anna, your wife. That soon, no one in the state enjoyed the pink of health. She seemed grim and quiet, as though at the start of a long campaign. She brought with her the manuscript of a book written by your former chief of staff, Major Dabney. Would I read it, offer suggestions, make corrections, express an opinion on how much credit it did you as a soldier? I could not recoil from her, Thomas. The hand that held that manuscript out to me had held that cool cloth to your forehead. For a moment before I took those pages not back to my present office that will serve as an anteroom to my mausoleum, but to another enclosure, another retreat, we held them together. They were wrapped in brown paper and tied with white twine. I said, "Dear Anna, I wish this weren't necessary," and she understood exactly what I meant. At the moment, it was all she had.

And it wasn't enough. I read them, offered a few corrections, professed them to be moving and sad, then I said no more. You are gone, Thomas. Anna will become one of those dedicated and indomitable women our reconstructed South will be known by, but she won't get you back. This is the sad-seeming and crushing futility of words. She will write a book herself, your officers who survived will step forward with pen in hand, an unknown and barely lettered man will emerge from the ranks to offer his view of the truth—but who could ever convey that sense we had every minute of our warring lives of firing out to the very limit of our desire, as though tethered there, before snapping back? That tether extended from Virginia and the cause we fought for to the most secret of our needs—needs, states of being, body and mind, inaccessible to words. I could say the most secret of those needs was *not* to snap back to duty and homeland but with meteor speed to snap free toward the apotheosis of release, perhaps of extinction. I *can* say it, and that tether tension is no more than a flagging drag. I could continue: Perhaps you in the concentrated force of your desire snapped all the way to the lap of God. I could even agree with Anna Jackson that you, Thomas, with the keenness of your vision and your implacable will, are the man we need to snap back and live among us, to reinfuse this land with a mission that classes in the applied sciences and civil engineering could never accomplish. I *do* say it, and not just to please your wife. It takes most of the strength I have left. But it won't happen.

There was no tether, only a manner of speaking. You won't come back in the pages of a book. Later, perhaps, when men and women are content to re-create in words what they can no longer aspire to in the flesh, something might be managed, but it won't be your battle blood or mine that rises, and this land, I fear, won't be worth the lifting of your sword to save.

It's gone on too long already, Thomas.

They retreat before me into patches of wood that mock my memory of that Wilderness we trampled and burned. Yellow jasmine grows up the trunks of trees. The air here is damp and fecund, and the sweetness so young it's barely detectable. There are no tongues of flame, no low stone walls behind which the enemy can crouch and fire.

Behind me the Blue Ridge rises in the afternoon light with that astonishing equableness of detail. Puffs of white are spotted over the lower reaches that, in spite of my failing vision, I quite understand are apple and cherry trees. My hearing is poor, but enough remains to tell me that that tuneful jabber all around me is the warbling of spring birds. I quite understand. But, this time, what if it's not? What if this time that birdsong is the onset of a wild rebel yell? And what if this time, among the apple and cherry trees, there are puffs of white that belong to exploding shell? You see, Thomas, how long it's gone on? The past instructs us to stay alert, and the past is a great master. What's to keep that downhill ride, back to college and town, from one day being a ride to you don't know what—only that the salt of your anxiety mixes with the meat juice of your desire and you are riding to it? It's been going on and on. I come to this point every afternoon, I watch the enemy pass over the next hill, into the next wood, I gaze at the mountains on the horizon, as unapproachable as mountains painted in words. I steady Traveller, for some time now steadier than I. I turn.

We turn.

When I was eighteen I left Clayboro, Georgia, to go to college. By then I'd become reconciled to the decision my mother had made. Things had not returned to normal—quite simply because there had been no "normal" for things to return to—but my mother had re-joined her bridge-playing, tea-sipping friends and on Sundays had retreated back behind her veil. I walked through town by myself and ended up at Willard Ewell's drugstore, where Willard wouldn't squirt cherry in my Cokes anymore, for apparently I'd outgrown that, but where we had begun to talk. Like so many others in town, Willard had missed his guess. I was no athlete. In a town where of the various ways a man might prove himself, certainly one was the ability to sell anything at any price, I was no salesman. I showed no interest in becoming a druggist. But I had grown—in fact, I'd inherited some-thing of my father's fine proportions—and on the day I left for col-lege, Willard stood to my shoulder, no more.

*He told me how pleased he'd been by my choice of colleges. Just to have been admitted to that school was an honor in itself. Then he asked me if I knew that the South's two greatest warriors were enshrined in that same town where I was going to study (like many Southern men of his generation, he occupied himself during football off-seasons by re-reading books on the Civil War). Obviously there was a good chance that one was—the school's name, Washington and Lee, told me that. The other? (For many men of my post-*Gone with the Wind *genera-tion, the Civil War had become technicolor froth.)*

But Willard Ewell, with his Buddha's browless face and his wise slit of an eye, shook his head. "One's never enough," he said. "It's a lesson history teaches us again and again."

I said I didn't understand.

He replied that after four years up there where they lived and worked and were buried, maybe I would. What did I know about history?

I said I was thinking of majoring in it.

He stood beside me, a short, stumpy-legged man, the flesh around his neck bull-thick yet loose at the same time. Then he placed a hand on my shoulder. He placed it there encouragingly, as a coach might, and he placed it there consolingly, as if the game he were coaching me for was, after all the fanfare, of no consequence whatsoever. He said a lot that afternoon, including the famous and I had always thought slightly ridiculous name of the other. But what he finally said, or what he said that stuck, was: "We don't satisfy ourselves. There's not enough to any one of us. Maybe the first thing a college education should teach you is where to look for the rest."

I traveled north to school and kept traveling north, coming to a halt in a basement apartment that looked up on Sheridan Square in that largest of the Cities of the North. On breaks from my work I would sit out on a bench in the park, close to a statue that showed General Sheridan, the scourge of the Shenandoah, leaning cockily on his sword. He had, I decided, a boy's unconscionable face, full of nut-round protuberances. While working I would look up through my two barred windows to see the feet of New York pass by. There were the jazzy running shoes and the stylish wing tips and the breezy summer sandals and the flattened black pumps out of which red ankles grew. The secret to feet, I decided, was that they all wanted to fly.

Then my mother called me to say that the pin-strokes that had been enough to put Willard Ewell into a nursing home had at last been followed by the stroke that had put him into a coma. If I wanted to see him alive, she urged me to come home now.

It had not been "home" for more than twenty years. I was a common breed of Southerner for whom invasions of the North had been rewarded with moderate success. Following the success had come severe trials; following the trials, strange recrudescences of Southern-ness. My sister, Evie, had had the upbringing that suited her and then had married a high-salaried factotum of Atlanta's grand new Peachtree Plaza Hotel. Following his speculator's star into Alabama and Florida, my brother, Johnny, had made and lost two modest fortunes buying up land where shopping plazas, condominiums, or expressway roundabouts either would or wouldn't be built. My mother had never left Clayboro, Georgia. He was, she said, the sweet-est man. He was smiling the sweetest smile. If for nothing else, I would want to come home to see Willard Ewell's smile.

I would not have called it a sweet smile, but then I had been places, seen and done things my mother had not. The head nurse, who had sus-pended visiting-hour regulations to take us to his bed, said that in all the time he'd been there he had never given them a minute's worth of trou-ble. She called him an angel, and she, too, directed me to his smile.

I did not think it looked angelic. Rather, I thought his paralysis had caught him in a moment of keen and finally triumphant understanding that looked beyond the angels and the centaurs and all the other legend-ary beings we peopled our boyish minds with, and had fixed the smile there, made it hard. It was a hard and not very comforting intelligence I saw expressed on my stepfather's lips. There was about it something finely wry and exclusive. The rest of him—the deep slanted forehead, the browless eyes, the frail temples and the small overgrown ears, the neck, swollen like a toad's or a football lineman's—was the Willard Ewell I remembered, grown anciently old. He did not move. The sheet rose slightly with his breath, and a clear liquid inched along an intrave-nous tube into his arm, but his hands lay white and still like small as-sortments of bones at the back of caves.

For some reason the picture that flashed before my mind then was not of Willard Ewell as I first knew him, squirting cherry syrup into my frosty Coke and prophesying for me a grand future, but of my father—that collection of carefree muscles, tight sandy curls, and small mouth opened wide to take everything in that I called a father. The next picture was of the two of them with their heads bent in close over the drugstore counter, and that was the picture that took and stayed. I had withdrawn *with my Coke to the end of the counter, or I had already begun my backward-stepping, reminiscent journey through the town.*

That evening both Evie and Johnny arrived at my mother's house. Evie brought her husband, Bo Stewart, with her, but Johnny, who had divorced the wife the family approved of only to marry a woman the family was deliberately slow to get to know, came alone. No children were present. Willard Ewell had been in the nursing home so long now that his impending death, and Mother's second widowhood, would have nothing of that brutal and almost tracelessly clean reversal of fates that came in the wake of my father's death, and I got the impression that Evie and Johnny were there to see me. We sat in Mother's parlor on wing chairs before tables scrupulously polished and arranged with small objects—china animals and enameled boxes—that even as children we had known were too fragile to touch. A thinning odor of lavender and rose water hung in the air. I deflected every question onto Willard Ewell. His patience, his humility, his equableness, his steadfastness, his longevity, wondering in so many words what all that hid. Evie's husband Bo Stewart had a face of the newly prospering South. It was the face of a boy with his lineaments and his lineage lost, and his mouth stuffed full. Bo Stewart said that my stepfather was the kind of fellow you didn't see anymore unless you strayed into little towns like this one and needed to get a prescription filled, and wasn't it a shame. Evie played golf, so the pouches in her face were already tanned, even wind-cured; she didn't need the makeup, which made of the natural coloring something darkly ostentatious. She said that I had always been Willard's favorite and the shame for her—which hinted at a penance I would have to perform—was that I had arrived too late to tell him how much I really thought of him. My mother's reading of Willard's smile indicated that she knew of no such lack in her second husband's life. Perhaps he had not missed me as much as Evie thought; or perhaps he had found a way to include his disappointment in that friendly stoic wall he showed to the world, making of his lack his strength. Mother said that she didn't know how many times she had offered Willard a penny for his thoughts and been told to keep her

penny, that it was worth a lot more than anything he could offer in
its place. He kept things to himself; it was what she thought of as his
. . . and here a surprised look came over her face, surprise that left
her on an instant's alert but still allowed her to savor a private
satisfaction—why, it was his gallantry, she said.

Her privacy aside, I understood that my mother was thinking of
her first husband, my father, in that instant, and was surprised be-
cause she had found a word to describe a quality that until then she
had not realized her two husbands had had in common. Their gal-
lantry. One was gallant in what he spared her, the other in what he
showered at her feet. Mother was looking at Johnny now, and Johnny,
with his hazel eyes, round cheekbones, small guileless nose, and very
unlazy mouth, was a taller, rangier version of my father. He lounged
in his chair the way my father lounged in his pew at church, the way
he lounged at every stop around town. Had Harry Brazelton ever
planted his feet and sat up straight, everybody's life might have been
different. Johnny lounged around three states and sold a dreamy,
musical view of the future that could win the confidence and assuage
the conscience of anyone with money to invest. How was Johnny to
understand Willard Ewell, hunkered over his microscope or his type-
writer, measuring powders or counting out pills?

"He tried to smack some sense into me. He said, 'Put half your
winnings in your pocket and play with what's left.' Half your win-
nings plus . . . what else?"

"What?" I said.

"You know," Johnny said.

"I do?"

"Sure you do. Think. What would Willard tell you to hang on
to till the bitter end?"

"Your first nickle?" I said.

Johnny threw back his head and laughed. It was precisely the sort
of irreverence that everybody forgave him. "You better believe your
first nickle! If I know Willard, he's got his hid around here some-
where. Mother, you know what I'd do?"

Powerless, Mother smiled and shook her head.

243

"I'd turn this house upside down until I found Willard's first nickle. Then while we still had a chance, I'd go out and spend it for him."

Two fathers had failed. Perhaps I could teach this youngest Brazelton some semblance of decorum. In mock despair, Mother looked appealingly to me. Then Evie and Bo Stewart did. Johnny, I saw, had set the whole thing up just to see what I would do with it.

I did this:

"It will be at the back of a drawer somewhere. We'll have to go through a lot of his stuff to get to it. You'll learn some things about Willard you wish you hadn't. A lot of it will be a deadly bore. The only one who'll be able to make any sense of it will be Willard himself, who's lying there in the nursing home with that very exclusive smile on his face. Then once we do find it, it will be tied up in a small box. There'll be a string with a knot in it that once again you'll have to put yourself in Willard's place to figure out how to untie. Sooner or later, one of us will. But then someone's going to have to open that box. You know what's going to come rushing out when you do? All the old air and trapped minutes since Willard tied down that lid. Every treasure's got its dragon. You'll hear the hiss. Even when you don't, I'm not sure I'd touch that nickle. Money like that'll burn a hole in your pocket before you can get it to the drugstore counter and order your first cherry Coke. . . ."

Just like Father, Johnny smiled and smiled, then told the hard truth. "Brother, you've been away too long. It's a lot homelier than all that. Willard kept all his valuable coins in an old brown sock—am I right, Mother? And he kept that sock with all the others balled up in his sock drawer. Sometimes he'd open that drawer in a hurry and the sock with the coins in it would thump against the wood. I've heard it—and so have you."

I had. It was just one more of the leaden, lusterless sounds I'd held against him during my boyhood.

"The way I figure it," Johnny went on, not entirely sitting up straight but getting far enough up on his elbows to give the impression that he was making a serious effort, "in your line of work you can more or less live where you want to. There's nothing to keep you from staying up there with the Yankees in New York City or from trying out the Left Bank in Paris or some cave in the Himalayas if that's where the guru you're looking for is holed up. But now that we've got you down here with us, it'd be a damned shame if you got away without taking another look at Willard's coin sock. Want me to get it for you?"

It made such a distinct thump against the wood because it was a nylon sock and slid easily against the bottom of the drawer. It was knotted once, high in the part that covered Willard Ewell's white shin. The brown had long since been washed dull, or the sock had long since been turned inside out.

"It's not necessary," I said.

"Make you a friendly bet"—but the voice was not friendly, it was edged with a con man's cunning—"bet you I can find that sock before you find your box with the dragon in it."

"No bet," I said.

"Mother," Johnny said.

"Think about it, son."

"Think about what?"

"Staying here where you belong!" Evie broke in, exasperated with such a willful and wanton circling of a point. Her husband, living testimony, at the top of his game, packing the pounds that might have kept a company of Lee's veterans going a day past Appomattox, showed the good sense to keep his mouth shut.

That night I dreamed of Stonewall Jackson in the Wilderness. I watched him form his lines for the attack against Howard's corps, and I was either one of his aides or his slave, Jim, for I followed close behind him as he guided his horse through dense second-growth hardwood. Sun-spotted, the small trees shook as we approached them and took on the shapes of men. I did not turn my head—preferring to keep my eyes on my leader's back—but I was given to understand that once we passed them, those men would become small trees again. There were these sudden localized shakings of light, and then there was a world of close-rooted shadow. I wanted to ride up to my general and warn him—You've got no army, you've got men electrified into being by your presence, but the second you pass they're

245

turncoats, men who make common cause with the *Wilderness* again —but I didn't. I knew to obey his judgment. For as long as I could remember, his will had prevailed.

Suddenly I did turn in my saddle, seized by an insuperable curiosity and dread. Behind me, trampling the green, masses of men formed a chinkless wall of flesh. I saw no aides, no slave Jim.

Then Jim appeared beside us, holding the reins of a black stallion, the saddle and bridle gleaming like gifts that had never been used. Jackson said, The *Wilderness* waits for no man. Jim looked at me dubiously, shaking his head. You Harry Brazelton's boy?

I said that I had had two fathers. I named Willard Ewell.

You Harry Brazelton's boy. De Gin'ral say for you to get on up 'ere.

I rode beside Jackson now. He had the profile of a granite-faced New Englander. The beard was lustrous and black, but the mouth it hid was as delicate as an infant's. He didn't speak. I thought, We're riding north, we're invading the North. I can already feel the chill. But he took me through briars and vines that miraculously did not snatch at us to the edge of a clearing where the men of Howard's corps were lying about. When he stepped his horse out into the open, I made bold to stop him. General Jackson! I whispered. He turned on me then. I was expecting his wrath, but he showed me a smile so blissful and unperturbed I could only conclude that he had sat beside his Maker—just as I was sitting beside him—and taken the light of his salvation into his eyes. You are a writer, he addressed me with due deference and gentle regard. Writers should not be despised. Just as you have need of me, I have need of you. Will you write a letter to my wife? Will you observe closely what I am about to show you, and will you listen carefully to what I am about to say, and then will you make it into something beautiful for her to remember me by?

We were equals, we faced each other. I was even superiorly mounted. I set my condition. Will you love slaughter a little less?

The smile offered sympathy, the light in his eyes consoled. This is war, he said in a terribly tender voice, as though he were addressing his wife himself. But I saw no rising of his battle blood.

246

He continued. This Wilderness was my body, my benighted mind, my soul steeped in sin. It was teeming with life.

Listen.

With the first firing of the skirmishers, I heard the onset of the attack. Then I heard the bugles signaling the general advance. The chorus of rebel yells that immediately followed sounded like the mad warbling of thousands of jungle birds.

Now observe.

The men of Howard's corps were leaping about in their clearing like boys who had heard from every quarter the whooing of ghosts. They turned this way and that, pulling on boots and scrambling for their arms. To the east and south, shallow trenches had been dug; there was a half-hearted abatis.

Now listen.

I heard not the crashing of soldiers through the Wilderness but first and unmistakably the lighter-footed and many-gaited stamped-ing of animals. Then, rising above the sounds of the onrushing sol-diers, I heard the animals' cries: the startled bark of the fox, the squeal of the rabbit, the bleating death groan of the deer.

Now observe.

Yankee officers were urgently trying to get their half-booted and half-dressed men into ranks. But some had already begun to flee, and others seemed deprived of their senses and moved like St. Vitus's dancers from one formation to another. Orders were being shouted— I could see the officers' mouths working furiously—but I heard noth-ing for I'd been told only to observe.

Now listen.

At the heart of a deep-blooded roar, I heard with a preternatural closeness the snap of a twig and the scraping of stiff young leaves. I then heard, or perhaps only felt passing up out of the ground, a faint flurry of hoofbeats. It was as though a child's heart were racing.

Now observe.

A deer—it was a doe—had broken cover and darted in frantic zigs and zags across the clearing we stood at the edge of. As she moved

247

among them, the Yankee soldiers went suddenly still. The doe was a herald, I understood. In her panic she visited them all, and to a man the Yankees' mouths fell open and their hands released whatever they'd hoped to save from the Southern onslaught—their weapons, their keepsakes, food and clothing, a hand of cards showing three kings. Stricken and dispossessed, they now watched as the animal life of the Wilderness stampeded across their clearing, erupting out of the forest with an unnerving scrupulousness and speed. The men were not touched, not a boot tip nor a hair on their heads. They were multitudinously raced among, the ground alive with rodents and snakes, the air streaming with birds. The middle ground belonged to the Wilderness's beasts. Then at the tree line, emerging out of the shaking spring leaf, a new species appeared—another sort of beast.

Now write (and the voice, though deferential still, was the voice of command).

My sweetheart, my esposita, my dove. That Wilderness was my body. In marching my men through a forest so dense that no one had thought an attack from that quarter possible, I was harrowing my sinful self and driving out in a panic all that lived a life of blind instinct, that lived forever in search of sensual surfeit and sin. The Yankee soldier stood astonished, transfixed before the extraordinary spectacle of the animal life of the Wilderness overrunning his camp, and never knew, poor boy, what it all meant. But I knew, and until this moment have kept close counsel: Those terrified rabbits, foxes, rodents and coons, serpents, and even the meek-faced deer all belonged to me, they were my bestial inhabitants, and only after I had driven them out of myself could I appear to give him, that still-astonished Yankee, his death. How did I feel? Purged, trembling, cleansed, new-born—I felt at the moment, and thus my long-kept secret, as free of sin as my savior Jesus Christ. Had I died then . . . but I did not. I led my attack and, disencumbered of all worldly weight, danced it through to a moment in the darkness when I shone so my men did not know who I was. But they saw me and they shot me, and my body came back. . . .

This is a letter that can never be written, never be sent.